The Yemeni Effect

She Outfoxes the Jihadists

by

Garth Tuxford

I hope you enjoy my tale.

MY BOOKS: PAPERBACK AND KINDLE.
ALL AVAILABLE FROM AMAZON
Garth Tuxford

CHECK OUT MY WEBSITE FOR MORE DETAILS.
https://www.garthtuxford-author.com/

MY NOVELS
The Yemeni Effect
Regby Dornik - A Chilling Warning
Regby Dornik – The Fury of Inanna (sequel)
The Lion Hunter

CHILDREN'S BOOKS
Marti the Magnificent with Oscar and Riley
Clive the Caterpillar with Oscar and Riley
Lily, (The White Chihuahua)

POETRY
Poetry Like No Other

CUISINE
Memaw's Recipes
International Quizine

PETS
Your Dog, Ultimate Guide
Helpful Hints for Your Kitty

DEDICATION

Judy and I married in 2014; we had previously been married and widowed and now both of us, in our 70s, have embarked on a very exciting and fun new life.

Between us, we have a bunch of children, a bigger bunch of grandchildren, and are now at number six on the great grandchildren list at the last count with another one arriving in December 2021.

I would like to say a big thank you to Judy, who has put up with me and read every word I have written more times than I can remember. We had fun with the spelling because I am English and she is American and I always like to say that the Americans love throwing letters out of words.

Thank you for your love and your encouragement — you were the driving force that got me to the end of this action-packed and exciting tale.

I have also written three other novels, several children's books, and a book of 100 poems. Judy was there prodding me and constantly encouraging me to continue writing and to be the best that I could. Without her, I would not have succeeded.

Contents

The Yemeni Effect

The British Secret Service, MI6, and other Security Forces Internationally including the SAS (Special Air Service) face the threat of widespread terrorism.

This is a story about the efforts and successes of a young English agent who thought that the Royal Navy was the only organisation she had joined, but went on to face huge odds as she became one of the agency's most successful MI6 Agents.

To get there, she went through an intense and vigorous training programme that took place in some of the world's most inhospitable areas of terrain, which were under the leadership of sadistic, evil, hard-line terrorists, where she endured many intimidating situations.

She is a born leader and showed the most incredible courage and fortitude, not only to survive, but in succeeding to close an entire organisation hell-bent on trying to end western civilisation.

I: About Jennifer Talbot

In memory of Jennifer Talbot, my dear cousin, who passed away far too soon several years ago.

Jenny was born in Coventry, but while she was still young, her parents moved to Clevedon in Somerset, about thirteen miles from Bristol. Clevedon is set on the Bristol Channel, and most of the year the coast of Wales can be seen clearly on the other side.

Clevedon is a pretty little town set amongst seven hills with a population of just over twenty thousand people. The seven hills are Church Hill, Wain's Hill (which has the remains of an Iron Age hill fort), Dial Hill, Strawberry Hill, Castle Hill, Hangstone Hill, and Court Hill.

In many ways it is just like a village. About a quarter of the residents are retired and a number of them have lived there nearly all their lives. There are many beautiful, picturesque walks. Visiting this Victorian town makes you feel as if you have taken a step back in time. Jutting out from its pebbled beach is the Grade-I listed pier, one hundred and fifty years old.

It is relaxing to take a long stroll along the promenade. At one end of the promenade is the Marine Lake opened in 1929, a safe place for children to swim, and nestled against Wains Hill and Church Hill. Poets walk winds its way across these two hills, which are named after famous poets such as Tennyson and Coleridge who visited Clevedon.

This small town is the home to the Curzon Cinema, which is the oldest purpose-built cinema still in working order in the world.

There are many other breath-taking views and sites to see in Clevedon that instead of penning my yarn about Jenny, I could fill a book just writing about Clevedon alone.

Jenny loved to read my books, and as a tribute, I have decided to write a book using her name as the main character.

The story is complete fiction and does not represent her in any way, shape, or form but she would have giggled at the thought, and I believe she would have enjoyed this sailor's yarn.

II: HMS *Dornik*

The name of the Royal Navy ship, HMS *Dornik* is also fictitious and is named after the main character in a previous novel.

The only ship with a similar name was a Minesweeper called HMS *Dornock* in operation during the Second World War.

HMS *Dornik* is a Destroyer used mainly for patrolling various hot spots around the world, and is the only full surveillance ship ever built and manned by many secret agents. Its radar and sonar capabilities are top secret, and apart from its specially trained operators, no one else on board knew much about it. It also has weapons systems of incredible capabilities not seen on any other warship anywhere in the world, which are also top secret.

Length	500 feet.
Beam	50 feet.
Propulsion	Gas turbines
Speed	40 knots???
Range	4,000 miles
Complement	450
Weaponry	Unspecified

HMS *Dornik* – The Senior Team

Lieutenant Jennifer Talbot	Jenny
Captain James John Crowe	Jim
Commander Michael Cheetham	Mike

Lt Commander Robin Hills	Robin
Chief Radio Supervisor William Overton	Bill
Provost Marshal Neil Bennet	Wiggy
Lieutenant Annette Saunders	Captain's PA

24 Hour Clock

The 24-hour clock, popularly referred to as military time, is the convention of timekeeping in which the day runs from midnight to midnight and is divided into 24 hours.

0000	12.00 midnight		12.00 noon
0100	1.00 am	13.00	1.00 pm
0200	2.00 am	14.00	2.00 pm
0300	3.00 am	15.00	3.00 pm
0400	4.00 am	16.00	4.00 pm
0500	5.00 am	17.00	5.00 pm
0600	6.00 am	18.00	6.00 pm
0700	7.00 am	19.00	7.00 pm
0800	8.00 am	20.00	8.00 pm
0900	9.00 am	21.00	9.00 pm
1000	10.00 am	22.00	10.00 pm
1100	11.00 am	23.00	11.00 pm

Preface

Jennifer Talbot was twenty-three years old and had been in the Royal Navy for just over four years. She stood five feet four inches tall in her bare feet and was a keep-fit fanatic. She was known by several names: Jennifer, used by her family, and Jenny, by her friends. Most of her Royal Navy colleagues also called her Jenny or Jen.

However, since this is now, perhaps I should fill in the gap from when she was nineteen. During those four years, her life altered very dramatically.

As a nineteen-year-old, she had no plan for her future and on a whim decided to join the Royal Navy, encouraged by her older cousin who was already in the Royal Navy. One day she went to her nearest recruiting office, which was in Bristol. After her initial interview and acceptance, she found herself on the train to Plymouth and then onto Torpoint and HMS *Raleigh* to begin her ten weeks of basic training.

She worked hard during her basic training and had caught the attention of various people. Perhaps it is a good time at this point to offer no further explanation and delve straight into the life of this complex but highly effective young lady. She had no idea what was in store for her.

Chapter I. Basic Training

I was not an easy person to get along with and did not suffer fools gladly. On several occasions, I had found myself in hot water because of my attitude towards both my peers and my seniors.

During my basic training at HMS *Raleigh*, I liked to keep to myself and had been tagged by my Chief as cold and not a team player.

I had gotten into a couple of fights with other girls who had called me an ignorant, miserable cow. One was left with a bloody nose and the other had to go to the sick bay for a sprained wrist. The two girls involved had tried to intimidate me and I was not about to be bullied by anyone.

Because of this altercation, I had been sent for by my Divisional Officer who let me do the talking, although I was not much of a talker. He tried to coax from me what the problem was with my relationship with others.

I thought that I would be punished because that was the way the world was, but my DO said that he understood my situation and told me to try to control my temper and complete my basic training without any further incidents.

He also told me that he had something in mind for me, but refused to elaborate until my training was complete. I initially thought it was a ruse to keep me out of trouble. Little did I know.

I spent much of my spare time in the gym and the swimming pool and enjoyed weight training – and, of all things, was interested in boxing. I also liked to run, sometimes on my own and at other times with other enthusiastic runners.

A favourite place to run was from HMS *Raleigh* and down to the small village of St John and back again. The picturesque Church of St John was built back in the year 1150, and it was worth the run just to take in the view from this ancient village with a population of fewer than four hundred people.

The Physical Trainer who helped me with my workouts was also a boxing coach. He was intrigued because he had never had a girl in his squad.

I was quick to learn, and he wanted to try me out in the ring but had to seek advice because he had never been faced with this sort of dilemma. Was it even legal to put a girl in the ring with a boy?

I was enthusiastic in my boxing training and spent a great deal of time on the bags, and my trainer even had several sessions with me on the pads. He was still worried about putting me in the ring with a real opponent.

Finally, after several weeks of asking, I was given the permission that I needed to enter the ring to box a male opponent.

I worked hard on my fitness and boxing training and the Physical Trainer, or 'Clubs' as they are known, told me that he had arranged for my first bout that coming Saturday.

"Well, Clubs, we have made it!" I said and beamed at him.

It was the first time he had seen me look happy; in fact, it was the first time he had really seen me smile.

"Yes, we have," he replied.

"And you look incredibly happy about it. It is the weekend so there won't be too many spectators," he said.

"I don't mind, at least I will be able to judge if I am up to this task."

Clubs replied, "I think you are going to surprise everybody; I have a great feeling about it. I am so impressed with your work ethic and your enthusiasm that I believe you will probably surprise yourself."

I just grinned broadly.

"Dare I say it before the match, you are the best boxing starter I have ever trained."

I just gave a wry smile and nodded.

Well, when Saturday evening arrived, my trainer could not believe his eyes. The gymnasium was full of spectators, and when he got close to the ring, he could also see many officers, which included the Captain, the Training Commander, the Education (Schoolie) Commander, and all the Divisional Officers.

From my dressing room at the end of the gym, I could hear the cacophony of people talking and poked my head out. I was astounded that so many people were there to see me box. For the first time, I was starting to feel nervous. So, I should! It was a big occasion.

"Tonight is going to be a big debut for you, but I have no doubt about the outcome," he said as he grinned at me. "There are going to be several Club swingers (Clubs) out there as officials, referee, timekeepers, and corners, so from now on you can call me Gerry."

"I know it is a bit late, but you haven't told me who I am boxing against."

"You have probably seen him in the gym a few times; his name is Terry (Slammer) Woods," replied Gerry. "Stocky, powerful-looking lad who is strong and fearsome, but he is a fighter and not a boxer. Stick to what I have taught you, stay back and box him, and under no circumstances try to mix it with him. Do not get in close unless you have him on the back foot and he is moving away from you, then use your skill to pick him off. He is tough, but you can beat him."

I was not frightened, but nevertheless, my legs were shaking. For me, this was the big unknown. I had never been in the ring for a competitive bout, and I did not know what to anticipate.

Woods had never lost a fight, and his reputation preceded him. He was strong, heavy, and always tried to take the fight early. He had not trained as much as he should have, and maybe he thought this was going to be a pushover. I was hoping he was heavier than he usually was and that his fists were not as fast. I remembered what Gerry had told me: "Don't fight him, box him."

It was too late to have second thoughts, as suddenly I was being escorted to the ring amid huge applause and loud cheering. I could also hear the Woods supporters.

"Come on, Slammer, don't get beaten by a girl."

Woods was already climbing into the ring, but the usual cheeky grin was not there. He looked somewhat subdued as he was probably pondering punching a girl.

I heard his coach tell him, "She is just another opponent, treat her like all the rest and put her down."

The next few minutes went by very quickly and I barely remembered climbing into the ring, or the announcement of the bout, or even the referee's instructions.

I suddenly became aware when I saw Gerry smiling with his thumbs up and then the bell rang.

I came out of my trance in a hurry as Woods was grimacing and moving across the ring towards me. He was coming fast and I easily sidestepped him, but he came after me again very quickly and took me off guard. He swung a huge right hand, and I felt the wind on my cheek as I deftly sidestepped. He tried another fast approach; it was very apparent that he thought that he could end this quickly. He missed again and this time I managed to get a glove on him with a glancing blow to his right temple.

I had survived the initial storm and was still on my feet; his fight was not going to plan. As my confidence started to grow, I managed to move in quickly with several lefts and rights and then back away from his heavy counter punches. He was trying to make this a one-punch fight and searching for the killer blow. I was too wily for him and respect for me was etched on his face. I was hitting him too easily but there was little power in my blows and he probably began to think that I did not really have a good punch.

He moved in quickly, feinted with the left hand, and threw a powerhouse with the right. I avoided him easily, but caught him with a stunning right hand as he went by. He was completely off balance and struggled to keep his feet — great timing; the bell rang for the end of round one.

Gerry was in my corner and was nodding gently. "Good job, JT, good job."

I suddenly became aware of the crowd who were all chanting, "Je-nny, Je-nny, Je-nny, Je-nny." It continued for about twenty seconds.

Before the bell rang for the start of round two, I glanced across the ring at my opponent. His coach was shouting in his ear and he was nodding his head and scowling heavily.

Ding, ding round two.

The hurricane came across the ring almost before my second had removed the stool. This man meant business and it did not bode well. I had my back to the corner post, and he tried to hit me with everything he had. I covered up and I heard Gerry shout at me, "Get out of the corner and box him."

I slipped to one side and then quickly back the other way and suddenly, I found myself in the centre of the ring facing my opponent and ready to box.

Straight away, it seemed as if a huge weight had been lifted and I started to feel confident. I was faster than my opponent and much lighter on my feet and he was warier of me knowing that I did have a good punch after all. For the rest of the round, I boxed him expertly and he barely managed to lay a glove on me.

Ding, round two was over.

Gerry was smiling as I went back to my corner.

"Now we are getting on with business," he said. "The final round is coming up and you are ahead on points, so keep out of trouble and do exactly what you have just done and a win is surely yours. Do not let him get close."

The third round began as the second, with Woods almost running across the ring, but this time I was ready for him, and moved very quickly to my left and hit him with a solid left hook. He was stunned and I moved in closer and hit him with a flurry of rights and lefts. He pushed me away roughly; now he was starting to lose all his confidence and looked quite weary.

Hesitance was visible on his face, so I followed up with several more rights and lefts and then quickly moved out of his way. I remembered what Gerry had said and I easily bounced out of range. Woods knew now that he could not win on points as he was too far behind. His only chance was a knockout, and he threw every punch as if it were his last.

The end of the round was approaching fast, and he made one final brutal assault, trying to hit me with a barrage of blows on both sides. I covered up for a few seconds, and then as he tried to change sides, I hit him with a thudding right hand to his temple. He went down and sprawled across the ring, looking completely dazed.

The final bell rang just as he tried to scramble to his feet. It was too late, and the bout was over.

The crowd set up their roaring of *Je-nny, Je-nny* again, until the bell rang for the referee to announce the result of the bout.

The referee stepped into the centre of the ring and had both boxers held by the wrists, one either side of him.

"The winner," he announced, "is Jenny Talbot," and raised my hand in the air.

Despite being beaten by a young woman, Woods was gracious in defeat and nodded his head while he smilingly said, "Well done, great job."

After this first victory, Gerry kept me under his wing and took me on to several more victories during my basic training.

I was also an excellent swimmer and liked nothing more than to swim at least twenty lengths every morning — swimming up and down the pool to start my day. All this and my boxing training plus my regular Physical Training classes and weight circuits culminated in maintaining a great level of fitness.

Cross country was another area I excelled at, and loved the outward-bound aspect of the training, spending several days on Bodmin Moor, map reading, camping, and leading a team of trainees covering many miles to complete a vigorous regimen.

Of course, all my successes had not gone unnoticed by the Physical Training Officer who was already earmarking me, although I did not know it at the time, as a potential future Physical Trainer. I was also being scrutinised by my Divisional Officer who was also making plans for me.

During the last few days of my basic training, I was invited to go for a meeting with my Divisional Officer. There was nothing unusual about having a meeting because all trainees had to undergo a final interview. However, this was going to be an interview that would affect me for the rest of my naval career and would also have a huge impact on the rest of my life.

When I arrived for my appointment, I was taken aback to see so many officers in the room. Among them were my Divisional Officer, Physical Training Officer, Training Commander, the Commander of HMS *Raleigh*, and a Lt. Commander who I did not recognise.

They invited me to sit down.

The Commander addressed me first and began to speak very seriously.

"Young lady," he began. "The abilities you have shown during your training here have alerted us to the huge potential that we believe you have for an incredibly special job and position within the Royal Navy. I am not at liberty to explain exactly what that is at this juncture, but believe it is something beyond your wildest dreams. If you accept this challenge, it may well be a few years before you know precisely what that role is, but I can assure you that you will be a huge asset to the Royal Navy and your country."

He paused for a moment and then continued. "These other gentlemen here, who I am sure you recognise, will, over the course of the next hour or so, plan out your immediate future should you accept this huge responsibility."

The Commander stood up, smiled at me, and said, "I know that this may all sound clandestine; believe me, it is."

He remained standing for a few minutes and then continued. "Without giving you too many details at this point, we are going to make you an exceptional offer, which you may not understand right now, but you will after you have completed further training. I am leaving now but I am sure I will get to know your answer very soon."

I stood up quickly as he approached me, reached over, and shook my hand, and with a broad smile said, "Choose wisely, young lady, and I am sure our paths will cross again in the future."

The other officers all stood up as the Commander left the room.

My Divisional Officer now moved into the Commander's vacated seat and said, "Jennifer Talbot, you need to try to take in as much as you can over the next few minutes as each of these officers explains what is in your immediate future. Let me introduce all of these gentlemen to you."

Of course, I knew all but one of them, and he was soon introduced as Lt Cdr Johnson, the Senior Diving Officer in charge of all Royal Navy diving.

Lt Cdr Johnson remained seated and was the first to speak.

"Considering your overall fitness and your excellent swimming abilities, I would like to invite you to carry out a Diving Course at the Royal Navy Diving Centre based at Horsea in Portsmouth. I will personally be monitoring your activities and we will have some informal chats as you progress through the course. If you do well, then by week three, we will also include the Diving Supervisor Section; it will mean extending your stay there for a further three days and is precisely the same course that the Diving Officers do."

He handed me a single sheet of paper.

"Here, read these notes that explain the details of what to expect."

COURSE AIM

To train the student, who has satisfactorily completed a selection test, to dive to a maximum depth of 30 m using self-contained compressed air breathing apparatus.

SYLLABUS OUTLINE

Two weeks of basic diving training in a manmade lake followed by two weeks of open water diving, training in simple underwater tasks, and diving to a maximum depth of 30 m.

ENTRY STANDARDS

Minimum age to start course: 18. Must pass Diving Professional Fitness Test (DPFT), 1.5 mile (2.4 km) run in 10:30 min, 4 heaves (chin-ups), 8 dips, and 30 sit-ups.

REMARKS

The course is a Pass/Fail criterion with both Written and Practical assessments.

I quickly read through the notes he had given me and knew immediately that the physical attributes of the course were well within my grasp. I smiled to myself because I enjoyed watching diving programmes on the television and had even managed to get some old footage of Jacques Cousteau. For a couple of years, I had been viewing his old documentaries and knew quite a lot about his history. Cousteau had been a French naval officer, explorer, conservationist, filmmaker, innovator, scientist, photographer, author, and researcher.

When I finished reading, I handed the paper back to Lt Cdr Johnson and nodded, saying, "Thank you, Sir, I am looking forward to it."

He smiled at me and replied, "That is just as well, because your four-week course starts a week on Monday. My office will get the details to you by the end of the day."

Lt Cdr Johnson then stood up and said, "Gentlemen, that is all from me, I have another appointment; Jenny, I will see you soon." And with that, he grabbed his briefcase and left the room.

I subsequently found out that Lt Cdr Dave Johnson started his career as a Physical Training Instructor and then became a commissioned officer and changed his career to become a Diving Officer a few years later.

My Divisional Officer now began speaking again. "I would like to introduce you to Commander Shone; he is the Training Commander or better known as the 'Schoolie' Commander."

"Hello, Jenny. I should have been the last one to speak to you today, but my daughter is getting married this afternoon and my wife insists that I be there, so I am jumping the queue, so to speak," he said with a broad smile.

"I am responsible for all of our education needs here and am also a language specialist. For the foreseeable future you are going to be based in the Portsmouth area, so I will be liaising with the team over there to get in touch with you after you have been there for a couple of days."

I looked at him quizzically and said, "I did French and Spanish at school to General Certificate of Education level if that is any good?"

His face cracked into a broad grin and he said, "Yes, I think we already know that. I believe you have a friend from Paris who you are still in touch with after your exchange visit a few years ago."

My cheeks coloured slightly, wondering how they knew about my French friend René. He also briefly mentioned my own close family.

"Father, Engineer; Mother, Housewife; Older Brother, Sergeant Royal Airforce; Older Sister, Store Manager. No red flags showing in any of your family or friends and associates. Sorry Jenny, we had to do many security checks given the position that you are going to be offered. We did not intend to embarrass you in any way," he said as he smiled benevolently.

I regained my composure as Commander Shone continued.

"We need to get both your French and Spanish reading and speaking skills to a much higher level so that you are easily able to converse in both languages. You will also learn the basics of Arabic and Korean."

I was unsure of what sort of response to make so I just nodded and said, "Yes, okay."

Commander Shone continued, "This might start to become a little bit onerous, taking language lessons while continuing with your fitness training. You will need to keep your fitness to the highest level and improve your diving skills. There is a diving centre in both of the locations of your language schools that we have used for previous operatives, so they will know what you need to be doing."

I nodded and asked, "Where will I go for my fitness training?"

"You seem to be very motivated, so I am sure you can work out your own fitness regimen," he replied. "Let us just say that it will be advantageous to improve your skills but also for us to assess your capabilities under some pressure."

I exhaled gently and just nodded.

"On the bright side, once your specialist training is complete, we will need to send you for a couple of working holidays in both Spain and France, where the language schools are located, to improve your language skills. Mixing and talking with locals makes your learning quicker and more productive, plus you will make new friends, colleagues, and acquaintances. It is not all hard work and some of it will be great fun.

"However, we do not want to jump too far ahead, so just concentrate on each day as it comes. You will have continued support throughout your training. After all, if you accept these challenges, then the government will be investing a great deal of money, time, and resources in your success, which will ultimately be a success for all of us. Do you have any questions so far?"

"No, Sir, not right now, but I am sure I will have many questions once I have time to reflect on what will be expected of me."

"That is good, we will expect many questions and input from you once your training starts. This project is a new one for us all, so we are all in the same boat, if you will excuse the pun. Jenny, use all of the skills you already have and improve on them, embrace new ones, and approach everything with an open mind and enthusiasm."

"Yes, Sir, I will, and I will give it my all," I replied.

"Thank you, Jenny, we will talk again very soon. Before I go, I will tell you that all the people in this room and those who have already left have a huge amount of faith in you. On some days you may feel that this is all too much."

He paused for a moment to let it sink in.

"We are all in this together."

With that, he stood up, nodded to those officers remaining, and made his departure.

The final part of my interview today was with the Physical Training Officer with whom I was already reasonably well acquainted. I had met him on several occasions when I had been training at the gym on my own and with Gerry in preparation for my numerous boxing matches. He was a big man and I found out that he had played in the front row in the Navy Rugby Squad.

Lieutenant Commander Lloyd had been responsible for getting me permission to compete in my first boxing match. Apparently, not before or since my matches, had a female been allowed to take part in an amateur boxing bout with a male competitor. All in all, I had been allowed to participate in five matches, and won them all before the plug was pulled.

"Well, Jenny, it looks as if you have a full itinerary for the next few months. By the time you have finished your diving course, it will be the middle of December," he said.

"Not the time of year I would have enjoyed doing my diving course. Still, you are much younger and probably far more resilient than me. I do not like the cold. We are going to make sure that you will get about three weeks leave for Christmas and you will Join HMS *Temeraire*, the Royal Navy School of Physical Training, on the sixth of January for a six-month Physical Training course."

He gave me a few moments to take it all in and then said, "Do you have any questions?"

"No, Sir, but I do hope that someone is going to write my itinerary down for me."

"Do not worry about that, your Divisional Officer will arrange all the details for you, and you will be in no doubt when and where you will need to be. I am sure I will see you at the gym before now and the end of next week."

"Yes, you will, Sir," I replied.

With that, Lt Cdr Bob Lloyd smiled at me, nodded at my Divisional Officer, and left the room.

"Well, Jenny, it has been a busy couple of hours for you," said my Divisional Officer.

"Yes, it has, Sir," I replied.

"How do you feel about all the things that have been proposed?"

Before waiting for me to reply he continued, "Do you wish to think it over for a couple of days or are you able to answer now?"

"No, Sir, I mean yes, Sir, if this is the right thing to say, yes, I'm in."

My Divisional Officer gave a perceptible sigh of relief and continued, "Jenny, you are about to begin an adventure greater than anything you might ever imagine. I can tell you a little about it but not in any great detail – that will all come later. Let me just say that you will be part of an elite group of people responsible for national security."

He paused to let his words sink in.

"One more thing, Jenny, not a word to anyone about this, not even your family. It might compromise your career and could also put your life at risk."

***

The next eight months flew by, I loved the diving course, which was followed by the Diving Supervisors course. I had always enjoyed scuba diving, but this was a much bigger step beyond that.

In no time at all, early in the new year, I found myself walking through the hallowed doors of HMS *Temeraire*. What an incredible experience. I improved my skill in the sports that I loved, and learned many other sports that I never dreamed of playing. It was a complete joy learning coaching skills, refereeing skills, all about physio and anatomy, and so much more. I made many good friends during my time there. There was so much to learn, and the six months just flew by. Soon, I was on my way to France.

Chapter 2. Becoming a Linguist

I spent nearly a year at a language school in Montreux, which is a stunning setting for a French language course. I enjoyed this gorgeous place, which is located on the banks of Lake Geneva, at the foot of the Alps. The Swiss town enjoys an almost Mediterranean climate. From the palm-lined quays, to the intense blues of the lake, and the listed vineyards of Lavaux interspersed with picturesque villages, everything here contributes to the beauty of the town and surrounding area.

Since the sixties, Montreux had hosted the annual Montreux Jazz Festival where many exceptionally talented and well-known rock, blues, and jazz musicians entertained the locals and the numerous visitors there.

I had been fortunate enough to enjoy the festival during my time in this captivating city.

So, it had not been all hard work and I managed to fully take advantage of Montreux, the vineyards, and the mountains that overlook Lake Geneva. Instead of finding a gym, I kept myself fit with long hard walks among the foothills of the Alps and long hard swims in the lake.

All the local people spoke French and did not like to speak English unless they had to, so my French speaking became natural to me and I enjoyed the conversations that I had with everyone I encountered, although there were one or two embarrassing moments with my grammar early on.

***

I had been in Montreux for nearly a year but all too soon it was time to move to my Spanish language lessons in Gibraltar.

Information about Gibraltar had come from numerous instructors during my time in basic training. I was a British base on the southern tip of Spain. They all seemed sad that the Royal Navy Base there had closed and said it had been a great place to live and visit. Every ship in the fleet had at some time visited there at least once. I was looking forward to spending about nine months there for my Spanish language education. My accommodation was at the Caleta Palace Hotel on the Mediterranean side of Gibraltar.

I had a week before my scheduled Spanish lessons began and decided not to fly directly to Gibraltar. Instead, I booked a flight to Malaga and hired a car to drive down through Costa del Sol and on down the coast to Gibraltar.

It was only a twenty-minute drive from Malaga down to the coast at Benalmadena and I decided I would follow the coast from Benalmadena down to Gibraltar. It had been drizzling as I left the airport, and I was a little disappointed, but as the Mediterranean came into view, I could see the bright sunshine twinkling out on the pellucid waters.

The main highway would get me to Gibraltar far quicker, but I decided I would prefer to drive along the coast. Having spent several holidays in this part of Spain, I had fond memories of being here. But I'd never been across the border into Gibraltar, because for some political reasons, the Spanish had closed the border. It was now open again.

I decided to stop at Riviera Del Sol to see if there were any changes. I also remembered a small coffee shop where they had a great choice of cakes and pastries. I was not disappointed, and it did not seem any different from when I was younger. Perhaps it was busier, as I did not remember there being so many tourists.

In just a few minutes, I was back on the coast road and turned right. I felt quite nostalgic having had some memorable holidays there with my family.

I then took a leisurely drive down along the coast, passing several well-known resort towns. I was close to Marbella and it was getting even busier as I drove west. Then, coming up ahead, was the iconic concrete stone arch stretching across the road with the name 'Marbella' cut into it.

Onwards without stopping to Estepona. I was in no hurry and was enjoying my leisurely drive, but then decided to stop for lunch at Casares anyway, a little picturesque village away from the coast and just under ten miles from Estepona.

When I was just a young girl, Mum and Dad had taken me and my siblings to Casares on several occasions. It was stunning, to say the least, with a population of a little over three thousand. Virtually every building is pure white and as you top the rise going into Casares, you will see the battlements of an aged Arab castle with the houses all nudging its battlements.

It has also managed to retain its appeal because few tourists go there and have come to Spain for the sunshine and the beach. I remembered a quaint little restaurant high up away from the road on the way into Casares and as I approached the village, I could see the short drive that was leading up to it.

The inside had not changed, and it was full of character with its Andalusian style of old southern Spain.

I could not resist ordering the local Paella and I was not disappointed.

Before leaving Casares, I took a drive down into the main part of the village and its ancient square. Nothing had changed – it was lost in a time warp as I drove nostalgically into Plaza de España, the main square. The four-spout Carlos III fountain has brought fresh water to this village square since 1785 and sits right in the centre.

I wanted to spend more time here, but I knew I should get on the road to Gibraltar.

On arrival, I thought it seemed odd, but to get into Gibraltar, the main road leads straight across the airport runway.

With still a week before my Spanish classes began, I thought it would give me an opportunity to explore Gibraltar thoroughly. Fortunately for me, the hotel room was booked from today.

✵✵✵

Gibraltar was an exceedingly small town, but it had been so much fun wandering around all the small, quaint shops in the narrow back streets all built alongside the huge rock that jutted up into the skyline at the entrance from the Atlantic Ocean to the Mediterranean. It was also a great area for me to maintain my fitness levels by taking on the arduous Up the Rock challenge. An uphill run all the way up to the top at over thirteen hundred feet.

I lost count of the times I did it while I was there.

The first time I ran up the Rock, it had taken me about twenty-seven minutes and had been quite a challenge. I tried to find out what the record was and was amazed at how long it had stood.

There is a small shop and coffee bar at about halfway up for weary walkers to stop and have a break and get refreshments. So, one evening I decided to just take a walk and enjoy the stunning views and whatever else there was to see. I went into the shop to get a cold drink and asked the lady if she knew what the running record was for the Rock.

She smiled and said, "Of course, I do," and then handed me a leaflet with a photo of a young Royal Navy Officer.

It said beneath his photo: *The current Rock Race record was set back in 1986 by Sub Lieutenant Chris Robison, who ran the Rock in an incredible time of seventeen minutes and twenty-nine seconds; it is estimated that more than forty thousand people have run the race since then, but no one else has come close to that time.*

Then below that, there were several more photos of him in shorts and sports shirt at various stages of the race with no one else in sight.

I felt a little daunted, having completed the challenge in nearly ten minutes slower than the fastest time. I persevered and my efforts paid off and before leaving Gibraltar, I managed to get my time down to just a little over twenty minutes.

The Caleta Palace Hotel had a swimming pool, but I preferred to swim from one side of Catalan Bay and back. There was no record to beat here, but I still managed to improve my own time quite considerably. I loved the feel of the swelling tide rather than the monotony of the still water of a hotel pool.

Chapter 3. MI6 Security

When my time in Gibraltar was over, I was booked on a flight back to Heathrow Airport where I would be met by a driver, so I would have to look out for a placard with my name on it when I passed through customs.

The flight from Gibraltar to London is under three hours and I took that time to try to relax because I had no idea what was coming next.

I knew that my training was now approaching a crucial part of what I imagined my job was all about. This was the final hurdle, and once this part was complete, I would become part of a very specialist and covert team of operators. I was aware that this last section was probably one of the most important aspects, but all the other segments combined would make me a fully rounded operative.

I was feeling extremely nervous about this unknown part of my training. To date, I had not been fully briefed on what I was going to become, but I reasoned that this was something incredibly special and felt privileged to have been selected.

After passing through immigration and customs at Heathrow Airport, I pushed my way into the bustling Arrivals lounge. I had almost given up hope of finding the driver when I finally saw a placard with my name on it.

I asked him if he was my driver; he smiled and said, "Yes, I guess you can call me that. I'm Dave Wilson, just call me Dave; I believe I have the honour of being your trainer for a while."

"I am so sorry," I replied. "I was told that a driver would meet me."

"Well, that's just about right, I did meet you and I can drive," he said and grinned.

I felt a little embarrassed, but he quickly put me at ease.

"I am told that you will be staying at the Union Jack Club in Waterloo, so we will get you there and settled in, and you'd better be ready for a busy number of weeks ahead of you."

Dave expertly negotiated the busy London traffic and we arrived at the Union Jack Club in under an hour.

"Be ready early tomorrow morning, I will pick you up at seven o'clock. By the way, there was actually a driver supposed to pick you up at the airport, but I thought it would be better if we met first before we rush into a busy week starting tomorrow."

"Thanks, I feel better now," I replied.

***

The next morning Dave was already in the lobby when I exited the lift down from my room at the Union Jack Club. Although not usually a nervous person, I had to admit that for some reason, I was feeling quite on edge and had not slept particularly well.

He greeted me with a smile and said cheerfully, "Good morning, Jenny. You have a busy timetable ahead of you today, are you ready for it?"

I smiled back at him and replied, trying to be jocular, "Of course, 'Into the valley of death rode the six hundred'."

He grinned back and opened the car door for me to get in.

"It will be a long day, but you will do fine, just be your natural self. The next few weeks are a steep learning curve process, but the first day is always the worst," he said trying to put me at ease.

"I will be with you for a lot of your training, but you will also spend time with several other operatives who are experts in their field."

I had thought that he was going to take me to MI6 Headquarters, but I realised that we were driving alongside the River Thames towards Chelsea.

He saw me look at my surroundings with a quizzical look and said, "We are going to our discreet office just off the Kings Road; security at headquarters is very tight and they do not just let anyone in until they are fully vetted."

I smiled sheepishly and replied, "Of course, I didn't think about that."

"We will be there in a few minutes and today will be spent answering questions and talking to our head of new recruits: Personnel Director, Miss Morgan. She is a retired schoolteacher and is known by everyone as Miss Morgan. I don't think she has a first name," he said with a grin.

"Just to let you know, she has no sense of humour and appears quite severe, but by the end of today you might even warm to her."

Dave pulled the car into a very tight opening between two buildings at the far end of Kings Road almost at the northern end of Putney Bridge. Behind the old red brick building was a small car park that was just about big enough to accommodate six small cars.

I got out of the car and followed Dave to a dirty, drab-looking building on the side of the carpark away from Kings Road. There was an unseen camera in the small window looking out into the carpark. Dave stood there for a few seconds and the door opened to let us in. We had to climb two flights of stairs that were lit only by a low wattage bulb in the high ceiling above the stairs.

At the top of the stairs, there was a solitary dark, green painted door, which had not seen a lick of paint for many a year. Dave pulled a card from his pocket and pushed it against the lock of the door and, as if by magic, the door opened.

Dave was waiting to see the look of total surprise on my face as I took in the surroundings in front of me.

I found myself standing in an extremely tastefully furnished office with a thick fitted expensive carpet that looked about a foot deep, and a very solid mahogany desk, which was huge and had a polished shine to it. Everything about the room reeked of quality, and sitting behind the desk was a grey-haired old lady wearing spectacles and looking for all intents and purposes like an old schoolmarm.

She stood up and firmly shook my hand and I could see that the rest of her dress and demeanour confirmed my suspicion that she was indeed a Head Mistress. She had a greyish brown tweed skirt and a plain white shirt with a green cardigan to complete the ensemble.

"Good morning, Miss Talbot, I have the pleasure of taking care of you for a few days."

She glanced over my shoulder and barked at Dave, "You can go now, David, thank you, I will take over from here."

With that, Dave grinned sheepishly, turned on his heel, and left the room.

I looked around the room again and saw a door leading off it to the right of her. Miss Morgan saw me looking at it and said, "Yes, it is the training room with a desk, and you will be spending quite a lot of time in that room for the immediate future."

She told me to go and get a chair and to put it in front of her desk.

I sat there for several minutes before she spoke.

"Do you drink coffee?" she asked.

"Yes, please," I responded.

She spoke into the phone and within a few moments, a man appeared with a tray and two coffees. He put one in front of me and one in front of Miss Morgan.

She sat in silence drinking her coffee and I did the same.

She took me by surprise as she suddenly announced, "Miss Talbot, for the next forty-five minutes I will be asking you some personal questions about yourself and then you will spend however long it takes you to fill out a questionnaire in the training room."

I was not sure she required an answer so just nodded in acquiescence.

"State your full name."

"Jennifer Talbot."

"Who are your siblings and are they older or younger than you?"

"Graham Gordon Talbot, older brother, and Jane Talbot, older sister."

"Are your parents still alive and do they live together?"

"Yes, to both questions."

"What do your siblings do?"

"My brother is a Sergeant in the Royal Air Force and my sister is a Shop Manager at a local fabric and wool shop."

"What are your parents' occupations?"

"Dad is an aircraft engineer and Mum is a housewife."

"Is he a Commercial aircraft engineer or Military aircraft engineer?"

"Commercial."

"Has your mother ever worked anywhere else other than being a housewife?"

"Before she was married, she helped in the family grocery store."

"Miss Talbot, if you wish to say a few more things in connection with the questions I ask then please feel free to expand on your answers."

"Sorry, Miss Morgan, I thought you just wanted straight answers,"

"Perhaps I will rearrange my questions slightly to get the best out of you," added Miss Morgan.

"Miss Talbot, tell me about your brother."

"Yes, Graham is ten years older than me, he is married and has two young children: a boy, and a girl. He is a Sergeant Technical Electrician. He is also a very keen photographer and he used to develop his own photographs. However, now that the world has gone digital, he no longer needs to do that."

"How about your sister Jane?"

"Jane has been married for seven years but she and her husband Robert never had any children. She enjoys working at the wool shop and has been there since she left school and knows nearly everyone in the town where she lives."

"And her husband Robert, what do you know about him?"

"I know truly little about him; he is very withdrawn and does not socialise with anyone. Whenever he does talk, it is mostly about communism and how they have a much better system than the west. I do not think he belongs to any group; they appear to be his own strange views."

"What are Jennifer Talbot's interests?"

I almost detected a smile beneath that stern countenance.

"As a child, I often felt lonely; my brother and sister were so much older than me and I felt almost like an only child. My father seemed cold and hard at times and he had some old-fashioned ideas. Jennifer was what I was to be called, and he would not allow it to be shortened. Jenny or Jen was forbidden, and he would scold anyone who used those shortened versions.

"He hated men on television who belittled themselves and believed that men had a status to maintain. My mum was gentle and kind and it was good to be with her, but Dad ruled the roost and when he was at home, even Mum seemed in awe of him.

"We had an exceptionally large garden and I used to spend hours outside. I would climb trees and hide from imaginary friends. Many times, I felt like a prisoner and longed for the time when I was grown up and could go and do my things without scrutiny or scorn.

"After I had finished school, I envied my brother and wanted to leave home and go and join something, anything I suppose. I lived only a few miles from Bristol and one day the school arranged a train trip to Bristol. About ten of us were on this day trip and we left the train at Temple Meads Station. As we left the station and spilled out onto the busy main road, we saw a noisy group of people on the other side of the road. When we finally got across the road, we saw a big sign saying Royal Navy Recruiting Office. I was given a fistful of leaflets and took them home with me. The rest, I believe, is history. I was captivated by what I read and knew this was what I wanted to do. Mum was sympathetic but Dad said an emphatic no!

"I let it go for a few weeks and then I faced him again, and after a long argument, I told him that I would be happier if he let me go willingly, but if it came to it, I was old enough to join without his permission. Six months later, I joined and started my training at Her Majesty's Ship *Raleigh* in Cornwall."

Miss Morgan did not say anything for several minutes and then said, "Well, are you happy?"

"Yes, I am," I answered her honestly.

For the rest of the morning, the formal questions stopped, and the interrogation turned into a far less rigid affair. It became more of a friendly conversation, with her gently coercing answers out of me. I knew she was probing, but I had nothing to hide and felt far more relaxed as time went by.

We stopped at lunchtime for about forty-five minutes. Miss Morgan asked me to run down the steps and open the door and bring our lunch upstairs. I smiled at the spectacle of a pizza delivery boy bringing lunch to the door. He had no idea what was going on in that office and how different it was upstairs. Miss Morgan and I sat in complete silence and ate our pizza, which we washed down with cold tap water.

"Miss Talbot, for the rest of the afternoon you will complete the questionnaire that is waiting for you on the desk in the training room. Please answer all the questions as fully and honestly as you can. If you find a question that you are unable to answer, just leave it blank. When you have completed the questionnaire, you are free to go back to your hotel. Do you have any questions?"

"Only one, Miss Morgan, how do I get back to the hotel?"

For the first time, she smiled gently and said, "Oh dear, I nearly forgot."

With that, she handed me a set of car keys and said, "There is a pale blue Fiat 500 parked in the car park below; it is yours for the duration of your stay with us."

"Thank you, Miss Morgan."

I walked through the door into the Training Room. On the left side of the room were two windows with blinds; the other three walls were completely covered with bookshelves, which in turn were filled with books. In the middle of the room was a conference table, eight-foot long and four-foot wide with eight chairs around it. On the end, away from and facing the door was a writing pad and a set of question papers, and to the side on small white cloth stood a jug of water and a glass.

I walked to the window and gently pulled back the blinds. I could see the brand-new Fiat 500 in the far corner of the small car park. I smiled to myself and sat down and started to read the questionnaire.

There were five sheets of A4 papers filled with questions. I wanted to share a few of the questions from the first page, some of them seemed completely ridiculous.

The Handwritten Questionnaire.

This handwritten questionnaire asks for a lot of information you have already supplied on the security forms, such as: name, age, education, marital status, and children (if any).

- Describe the relationship with your mother.
- Describe the relationship with your father.
- Describe your parents' relationship with each other.
- Have you ever had psychological counselling? (when/how long, etc.)
- Have any relatives ever had psychological counselling?
- Have you ever attempted suicide?
- Have you ever had a substance abuse problem?
- Do you drink? If so, how many drinks per week? Per day?
- When was the first time you drank alcohol?
- Have you ever had interpersonal issues at work? (e.g., work relationships)
- Have you ever had disciplinary issues at school/military?
- Have you ever been convicted of a misdemeanour/felony?
- Have you ever been questioned by the police/authorities?

- Do you have any relatives that were in trouble with police/authorities?
- Have you ever taken something that was not yours?
- Have you ever committed computer abuse? (Hacking, Scamming, Illegal Credit Card use.)
- Have you ever been the victim of a violent crime?
- Have you ever had a relationship with a married man/woman?
- Have you ever had a relationship or friendship with a foreign national?
- Have you ever had a media friend from anywhere outside the UK? (Fb, Twitter, etc.)

(End of page 1 of 5) For security reasons only page one is viewable.

Some of the questions I was asked made me wonder if anyone had ever completed this form truthfully.
Several of the questions I could not answer because I honestly did not know.

By the time I completed the questionnaire, it was nearly five o'clock and I realised I was now going to have to negotiate a car that was new to me through a busy London rush hour. I knew I could do it, but nevertheless, it was a little daunting. After all, I had survived the day with Miss Morgan.

I walked into Miss Morgan's room. She was on the phone and nodded as I whispered, "Good evening."

I was pleased when I closed the door behind me and almost ran across to the car. I sat in the driver's seat and adjusted it and the mirrors to my satisfaction. Then I took a deep breath and closed my eyes for a few moments. I had survived my first day; it had been quite stressful.

By the time I reached my hotel room, I felt exhausted. I knew that the best way to relax was to have a workout. I changed into my sportswear and made my way down to the fitness centre. I was pleased to see that it was well organised and had a full range of training equipment, including freestanding weights.

Although I was tired, I still managed to get in a good workout and after half an hour felt fully invigorated. I used the sauna for about ten minutes and then went through into the swimming pool. There were only a couple of other people in the pool, so I was able to complete twenty lengths before deciding I had done enough for the day. I was so pleased that this facility was available in order for me to be able to train daily.

To date, I had not been informed how long I was to stay with MI6.

Just after I unlocked the door to my room, my mobile phone rang – it was Dave Wilson.

"Hi, Jenny, sorry to call so late in the day but we have run into a small snag with your security pass. Do not worry; it is not something you have done but rather something that someone else has not done. We must rely on different agencies such as the police, doctors, Royal Navy Provost Marshall, and so on. There are about twenty of them in total and two of them have not responded even though they have had these requests for over a month now."

"So, what happens now, Dave?" I responded.

"We just wait," he replied. "The absentee responders have been approached with an urgent message to contact the agency immediately. The request for confidential information does not come in an envelope with MI6 printed on it, but from our legal team. Often people tend to mistake it with general mail even though it has 'Please Reply Urgently' emblazoned across the top of the envelope."

"Is there anything I can do to speed things up?" I asked him.

"Even I am not privy to who they are, so we just wait," he answered.

"That's OK," I responded.

I was a little disappointed, as I thought that tomorrow would be the beginning of my training. All the other stuff was just getting me ready for whatever the Royal Navy had in store for me. I had been working hard at so many different skills for nearly three years now, and I felt a little bit deflated. Looking out of my bedroom window did not help; it was a cold and damp November night, and, outside, the London streets were dark and grey.

Dave noticed from the tone in my voice that I was feeling a little disappointed. His response was light and cheery, and my spirits lifted immediately.

"Why don't I come to the hotel in the morning to pick you up and we will go and visit a few valuable people to know?"

"That would be great, but I do have a car now; I could come and meet you somewhere."

"I know, it was me that chose it, picked it up, and drove it to the car park."

Before I had time to thank him, he said, "Leave the car at the hotel, I will be over there around seven-thirty in the morning and I will give you a tour of London to remember."

I smiled and replied, "That sounds good. I'll be ready."

Chapter 4. Learning the Ropes

I was happy at the thought of spending the day with him. Believe me when I tell you I did not have any designs on him, but he was polite, easy to talk to, and put me completely at ease. He was just over six feet tall, with a full head of dark hair, and when he smiled, his whole face and forehead showed that he was smiling. He was in his early forties and happily married, with two gorgeous little daughters, which I found out about later in the day.

At exactly seven-thirty in the morning, there was a call from the hotel lobby to let me know that he was there. He was prompt, and so I immediately made my way to the lift and down to the ground floor.

We exchanged greetings and I climbed into the car.

He said, "Earlier on this morning, I spoke to an old friend of mine who is part of the Metropolitan Police in the Criminal Investigation Department (CID) at Scotland Yard and he works closely with The Security Service, also known as MI5, which is short for Military Intelligence, Section 5. It is the United Kingdom's domestic counterintelligence and security agency and is part of its intelligence machinery alongside the Secret Intelligence Service commonly known as MI6, Government Communications Headquarters (GCHQ) and Defence Intelligence."

"Gosh, that is quite a mouthful," I uttered.

"Yes, it is; I have been practicing that all morning," he said and grinned.

"In a nutshell, that is the make-up of our Intelligence agencies; there are other smaller splinter groups, and all combined they are the British Intelligence Service. Depending on the intel, CID will decide which of the other agencies needs to be involved in a particular crime – some or all of them."

He went on, "What I was starting to tell you but got carried away with explaining how all the agencies are intertwined, was that we are going to spend some time with my friend and colleague who is a Chief Inspector at Scotland Yard. He is an interesting man and could keep you entertained with stories for weeks if he had the time."

Dave had been talking for most of the journey, and I was so intrigued with everything he had to tell me and wanted to absorb as much as I could from all he had to say. I knew that I must learn quickly and comprehensively. I wanted to take notes, but Dave advised me not to.

"It would not be good for anyone to get hold of any of the information you are privy to over the coming weeks. You need to learn how to glean information but also to keep it in your head and not written down. Always keep this phrase to the forefront of your brain, 'Keep Our Secrets Secret'. That does not just mean national secrets, but also processes we use to investigate crimes or potential crimes."

Dave parked the car, and a few minutes later, we were walking into Scotland Yard. Dave produced his identity card, and we were ushered along some passageways into the office of the Chief Inspector. I almost gawked when I saw him. My mind was jumping furiously. Where had I seen this man before? I regained my composure when Dave introduced me to him.

"Aled, this is my new colleague from the Royal Navy who will be spending several months with us to learn all the tricks of our nefarious trade," Dave said.

I did not wish to sound rude, but I blurted out, "Do I know you?"

He looked at me for a few seconds and then answered. "No, I don't think so; I rarely get out to meet new people, unless, of course, they are criminals or terrorists," he said with a chuckle.

I shook hands with him. He had a firm handshake as he greeted me by name and was still smiling when I let go.

"OK, young lady, I will tell you the truth. A lot of people have mistaken me for my brother; apparently we look very much alike."

His face crinkled into a large smile.

"I was forewarned of our meeting by my brother, Lt Cdr Bob Lloyd. He is my older twin. I cannot understand why people think we are alike because I am younger and much better looking!" He guffawed loudly as he shared this.

Suddenly the penny dropped.

"Sorry, I didn't mean to gawk, but you are very much alike. Of course, the Physical Training Officer from HMS *Raleigh*."

"It is fortunate that we do look alike. We have done a few operations together and being twins has played into our hands – on numerous occasions. Some bad, bad people are now locked away because of our collaboration with each other. When we have more time, I will tell you about a few of our exploits together.

"When we work together, he is also known as Chief Inspector Lloyd. However, there was one occasion where we busted a drugs cartel working inside Devonport Royal Navy Dockyard and I had the privilege of wearing his uniform as a Lieutenant Commander. The Security Services will stop at nothing to get their quarry."

I smiled at this gentle giant of a man and said, "I will ever take anything for granted again."

Aled spoke again but this time he addressed Dave.

"I know it is simple stuff, but it is a good place to start. We are having a line-up in about forty minutes. It would be good for Jenny to see some of the easy stuff. We have three felons who broke into a Cabinet Minister's house and were caught on camera, but they thought they were wise enough to keep their faces away from the camera. Fortunately, the neighbour's wife from next door saw them from behind bushes in her garden and is going to see if she can pick them out of the line-up."

Excitedly I asked, "Is this just a robbery or is it something more sinister?"

"Jenny, we are not entirely sure. The perpetrators do not appear to have a record and are therefore not known to the police. However, their lawyers are very upmarket, which makes us wonder why a few small-time thieves would have such a powerful and expensive team batting for them. We need to find out!"

A little while later, Dave, Aled, and I were quietly escorted into the room with cameras and a one-way mirror.

"Jenny, watch everything you see and scrutinise them and try to remember even the smallest detail. If you see something that sparks your interest, tell us after the viewing. Then we can analyse the video afterward. Every pair of eyes can make a difference."

The lady who was there to view the line-up was extremely nervous. She said that she felt as if it were her that was the criminal, although the police did all they possibly could to make her feel relaxed.

The sergeant who brought her in told her that all three suspected criminals would come out in a different line-up and that all the line-ups would be six different people. Apart from the suspects themselves, all the other members of the line-ups were just random people who they had asked off the street to help them out. I was told they were given a free cup of coffee and a doughnut.

I smiled to myself and thought: big spenders.

The first six came in and I noticed that they were all a similar height, and all were white. The lady was extremely nervous, and she was visibly shaking. The Sergeant told her to relax and take her time. After several minutes she apologised and said that she did not recognise anyone from the line-up.

They then brought in the next six and she was physically shocked almost immediately before all six were in place. She pointed at the man carrying placard number two.

"That is one of them," she said with no hesitation.

With the third group, it took her a little longer but she eventually pointed and said number five. The Sergeant asked her if she was sure and why had she hesitated. She pointed at number three and said, "I initially thought that it might be him; he looks similar, but no, I am positive that it was number five."

When the line had disappeared, the Sergeant remarked to the lady that it had not been as bad as she had feared. She just smiled and shook her head and answered, "No."

We left the viewing room and went back to Aled's office.

Aled said to me, "There you are, Jenny; you have finally started."

I just nodded my head and said, "Thank you."

I had enjoyed the experience of the line-up, having seen a few of them in films on television, but it was vastly different seeing it happen for real. There had been palpable fear on the lady's face who had to identify those villains. The police had been very gentle with her and tried to put her at ease, but it had been an extremely harrowing experience and one that she would probably relive again and again for a long time.

Aled turned to Dave and said, "I do not know what your plans are for the rest of the day, but we have sources that tell us that many high-profile churches in London are the subject of terrorist activity and we believe they are being targeted by a local Islamic group who are looking for soft targets to try to ingratiate themselves with known terrorist groups in and around Afghanistan. Terrorist groups are using Afghanistan and Pakistan as their bases and recruitment centres to support and organise their fighters. Most of them are under the umbrella of the Taliban."

He looked at us and continued.

"If you have time, it might be a great experience for Jenny to look at this type of situation and to see that it is going on right in the heart of London just a few miles away. Even closer to home, there are whispers that they are targeting Westminster Abbey, which is extremely close to the seat of government."

He stopped to allow me to let it all sink in.

"We have agents from Scotland Yard, MI5, and MI6 involved with this one. It may be nothing, but we cannot leave anything to chance. While we are there, Jenny, just carefully watch everything and remember what you see, Even the slightest thing might be paramount to the investigation."

I was looking forward to this afternoon for several reasons. Perhaps for me, it was not only the task, but more the fact that Aled had just informed us that we were going to St Paul's Cathedral first. I knew it was about the second or third largest cathedral in the country, but more than anything else, I had never been there before. I should have been thinking about why we were going, rather than a selfish whim of wishing to see St Paul's.

Aled broke my train of thought and asked, "Jenny, do you like Chinese food?"

"Yes, I do," I replied.

He continued, "We need to be at St Paul's at two-thirty and so we have just under two hours to kill. I suggest we go to a small discreet Chinese restaurant off to the side of Chinatown for lunch."

Dave and I just nodded our agreement.

"Dave, you leave your car here and we will all go in mine."

Aled knew all the back streets in London and, in no time at all, we were parking outside the Golden Lion in Dean Street. He locked the car and we crossed Shaftesbury Avenue and slipped between two buildings. Within just a few minutes we were in Chinatown. It was like going through a portal into a completely different world.

The streets were all decorated with Chinese symbols, dragons, and lanterns and even the street signs were in both English and Chinese. There were stone lions, art sculptures, and Chinese gates. Even the telephone boxes had the tops decorated with symbols. It was fascinating to walk around this bustling area with so many visitors but also many, many Chinese people all with friendly, smiling faces. We walked down to the Wardour Street end of Chinatown and I was impressed by the largest Chinese gate in the country, completed just a few years ago and built in traditional Qing dynasty style.

Aled was watching me completely enthralled by all I could see.

"Jenny, do not be fooled by appearances; we have a regular group of our people down here looking for all sorts of nefarious activities. Most of it is insignificant, but the Chinese are Provosts of espionage and deep undercover activity who continually pass stuff back to China. Most of it is done via the dark web. They have more photos of London back in Beijing than we do here."

"I imagine in future I will see most things in a totally different light," I interjected.

Aled went on, "They are also experts at importing and dealing drugs, as well as being involved in car theft, and human trafficking. So, this pleasant façade that you see catering to the tourists does not make them a lot of money, but what goes on behind the scenes does. We know what they do, and they know that we know, so it is a game of cat and mouse with one side trying to outsmart the other. They are good, but so are we."

"If that is the case, why isn't Chinatown closed down," I asked.

"Well, let us put it this way, it is easier to monitor them when they are all in one place than it would be if they were spread all over London. There is a link to all other groups of Chinatowns and communities in the country and they are all connected on a secure private internet network. However, it is not as private as they think. So, you see it is imperative that we keep them where they all are so that we can carefully follow all their activities. We have a large team of operatives working twenty-four hours a day monitoring everything that they do."

I replied to his disquisition of Chinatown. "It is quite difficult to associate this apparent genteel activity with the villainous goings-on that you depict."

Aled grunted and went on, "That is how they have become the most powerful and dangerous country in the world. Do not ever underestimate their subterfuge and cunning."

After we entered the restaurant, I sat for several minutes reflecting on the things that he had said; there was no doubt that there was complete accuracy in his summation of the Chinese. The problem was trying to marry the thought that these seemingly innocuous restaurateurs had anything to do with the Chinese activities seen almost daily in the National news outlets.

We finished our lunch, and I was deep in thought as we made our way back to the car. Aled chatted to Dave and me as we wove our way through the West London streets to St Paul's Cathedral. He pointed out several places where he had previously been involved with the activities of keeping London and Great Britain free of terrorists.

Suddenly we rounded a corner, and there in front of me, was the biggest building I had ever seen; St Paul's was huge.

Dave said quietly to me, "From the second you get out of the car, try to take in as much information as you can. This is the sort of occasion that you can take notes and I encourage you to do so. You can use the memo on your phone initially, but I urge you to transcribe them into a notebook later today when you go back to your hotel—"

I interrupted him and offered, "Is it safe to transcribe them onto paper?"

"Well," he replied, "there are several reasons why. Probably one of the most important is that your phone could be hacked, and people can read your notes. They can also delete what you have written, or even steal your phone, and it might be vitally crucial in an investigation if you are called to testify or even share information with the department."

"I see," I said, nodding.

"As soon as you have transcribed the notes from your phone, ensure that they are exactly as you had recorded them and then delete them off your phone. It is also easier to read from notes. Imagine you are giving evidence and your phone shuts down or, even worse, rings while you are testifying. Also, make sure that your notes are clear and concise and keep your notebook safe."

"Is there any particular size of notebook that is best to use?" I asked him.

"There is nothing officially recommended, but I suggest something that can be easily carried in your pocket. Here is mine, which also has a coded lock on the front. I will give you details later today when we are finished of where you can acquire one like this if you like?"

I said immediately, "Yes, that would be good, thank you."

"From now on, try to document everything you can as we walk around the Cathedral; it might be vital," Aled told me.

"I will, Aled," I responded.

Aled parked his car close to the Cathedral and placed his official permit on the inside of his windscreen. I smiled at the thought of him just taking his wife to the theatre and making use of his pass. Maybe he would or maybe not; I decided it was inappropriate to ask.

We climbed the steps leading to the front door of the Cathedral, passing between the huge Corinthian columns and to the massive double doors of the main entrance. I thought to myself that a well-placed explosive device to take out the huge columns could do inestimable damage. I noticed that there were plenty of security cameras, but I could also see areas that were not covered by camera views.

As soon as we entered the Cathedral, I was completely dumbfounded. It was bigger than I could have ever imagined, with a plethora of statues and structures. There were so many side rooms and chapels that it would be impossible to try to count them. I was wondering how a place like this could be thoroughly searched to unearth any criminal activity.

I did the best I could and wrote a long list of observations. I was later advised that I was not looking for the obvious, but anything that looked as if it did not belong or looked out of place. From the moment we entered, Aled had been whisked away by the security teams that were looking for anything that seemed amiss.

I spent all my time taking notes, and was sorry at the end of the day that I had not seen what a tourist saw. I made a promise to myself that when I had the time, I would come and be just a visitor. I later discovered that as part of the security services, I would be privileged free entry into most venues. Authorities always welcomed agents to come along as a guest because it was often a valuable opportunity to be advised of any security lapses when they left, or a phone call later with constructive advice. A win / win situation.

I had so much to learn.

Later that evening when Dave was taking me back to the Union Jack Club (UJC), we discussed the day.

"Did you take lots of notes?" he enquired.

"Yes," I replied with a laugh. "Probably too many."

"It is a valuable skill, and you will soon learn what you need to jot down and things that you do not," he added. "Did you see anything unusual or out of the ordinary today?" he quipped.

"I don't think so, but maybe," I answered.

"Don't leave it too long to decide, just in case St Paul's gets blown up while you prevaricate."

It was the first time that he had spoken to me harshly, so I stayed quiet for the rest of the journey.

We arrived at the UJC and he let me out of the car.

"We are going to Westminster Abbey tomorrow; I will be here to fetch you at eight-thirty in the morning. I think Aled has four more churches that we are going to check out after that."

He smiled broadly and said, "Goodnight, Jenny, I will see you tomorrow morning ready for another action-packed day."

"Goodnight, Dave, and thank you for today."

With a nod of his head, he drove away.

The Fitness Centre was packed, and I decided that I would settle for a leisurely swim. Strangely enough, two people were exiting the water, leaving it empty. I thought I would take advantage of the empty pool and opted for a quick circuit across its width. The idea was to sprint across the pool as quickly as I could and pull myself out at the other side, down for twenty press-ups and back into the pool, and sprint back over to the other side. Get out of the pool and down on the side for twenty sit-ups. Sprint back across, get out and do twenty burpees, sprint back across the pool, get out and do twenty squats. One circuit completed. I did two more complete repetitions of all the above.

By the time I had finished, I was breathing heavily and walked gently around the pool and quickly recovered. I followed this activity with a twenty-length swim alternating between freestyle and breaststroke, completing the last length with the butterfly stroke. This is a stroke that I always found difficult, so it was an excellent way to finish my workout.

I was not feeling very hungry after eating a substantial lunch in Chinatown, so remembering that they provided a very plentiful dessert table in the restaurant, I strolled down there and got myself an apple and a banana. I poured myself a cup of hot chocolate and returned to my room.

I wanted to do some research about St Paul's Cathedral and its history, so switched on my laptop and was trying to find out if there had ever been any attacks on St Paul's.

I read for a couple of hours and the time flew by as I became enthralled with all the information I uncovered. The following are just a few extracts that I managed to find and thought they were worth knowing.

Suffragette bombing and Arson Campaign.
A bomb is discovered at St. Paul's Cathedral, London on 10 May 1913. A bomb is also discovered in the waiting room at Liverpool Street Station, London, made from iron nuts and bolts intended to maximise damage to property and cause serious injury to anyone in proximity.

Man killed in London Bridge terror attack named…

news.sky.com/story/man-killed-in-london-bridge…

Dec 01, 2019 · A list of other potential targets included the names and addresses of the Dean of St Paul's Cathedral in London, then London mayor Mr. Johnson, two rabbis, and the American Embassy in London.

Woman jailed for plotting to bomb St Paul's Cathedral

A woman who had plotted a suicide bomb attack on London's St Paul's Cathedral at Easter 2020 in support of Islamic State was jailed for life on Friday and told she must serve at least 14 years behind bars.

Safiyya Shaikh, 37, had planned to set off a bomb at the popular tourist attraction, to kill herself and visitors to the famous cathedral, and another bomb at the hotel where they would have stayed before the attack, prosecutors said.

However, the husband-and-wife extremists she had contacted online to obtain the bombs and whom she believed shared her view of violent jihad were undercover officers.

After scanning the internet for information, I was feeling very tired and realised it was getting late and I needed to sleep. I lay there for ages thinking about the things that I had done today. I was far from being an agent, but was feeling excited about the future. Then I remembered the almost sharp words from Dave and came down to earth with a jolt. What if he was right and what I had seen was important, even vital in their investigations.

I cogitated for some time and wondered about what exactly I had seen. I was pretty sure it was nothing. My mind was full of conflictions and it took a long time to fall asleep.

✳✳✳

The following morning, and feeling well rested, I went to the restaurant and ate a hearty breakfast. I wondered what the day was going to bring and how much longer I would have to wait for my security clearance.

Dave appeared right on time as usual and we chatted on the way to Westminster Abbey. Because he had a security pass, he just parked his car in the Houses of Parliament carpark about one hundred yards from the Abbey. He made no mention of our conversation last night about what I might have seen.

Aled was standing outside by the front of the Abbey and broke off his conversation and came over to us.

"Good to see you here bright and early; we have another busy day today. We are going to be here for a few hours and then on to possibly another four churches, which are a lot smaller than here or St Paul's. Dave, if you and Jenny would like to take care of yourselves for a little while, I have a few people to meet and the dreaded press have also got hold of something, so I need to go and fob them off. I sometimes think that the world would be a lot safer without the press. They are forever trying to score points over each other. Gone are the days when the press would just report the news. They have now got to compete and provide the biggest and most dramatic story that they possibly can. The freedom of the press has gone too far; they are a clear and present danger to democracy and the truth."

I was a little on edge as we approached the entrance to Westminster Abbey. This was the main and north entrance to the Abbey. The design and structure were stunning, but I barely had eyes for its beauty. I wanted to look and see if there were any black marks etched on the doors.

Dave went inside but I hung back and spent many long minutes scrutinising every inch of the doors. My heart had been beating fast, but when it was obvious there was nothing there to see, my heart rhythm returned to normal. I followed Dave inside.

"I thought I had lost you," he said.

"No, I was enthralled with the architecture outside the Abbey," I lied.

"Oh, I just remembered, I had a phone call a little while ago."

He stopped talking and I said, "Phone call, what phone call, what about?"

"Nothing much, you have to come to the office tomorrow," he replied.

I just grinned at him and said, "What are you saying, are all my enquiries in now?"

"Yes, they are, and you are now on your way to becoming an agent."

I felt as if a huge weight had been taken off my shoulders. I was also aware that this was just the beginning. I would enjoy the rest of today out in the field.

We wandered around the Abbey and we could see agents working in different areas, writing notes, and taking photographs. At this point, I was not aware that there was another main entrance to Westminster Abbey. I had never been here before.

"Is that another entrance over there?" I asked Dave.

"Yes, it is and, in my mind, the most stunning of the two entrances."

I turned on my heel and almost ran back to the entrance where I had entered. Dave said something to me, but I was already moving too quickly away from him to respond.

I ran out into the fresh air and round the side of the Abbey, running for all I was worth to the other entrance. Dave was right. It was a beautiful sight to see: two towers and one of them with an ornate gold leaf clock. Even though the Abbey was currently closed to the public, there was still a large crowd of sightseers milling around, talking, pointing, and some taking photos. I moved my way past them until I reached the doors.

They were not as large as the doors to St Paul's Cathedral. I stood in front of them and immediately started to scrutinise all along the bottom but could not see anything unusual. I looked at the door posts on either side, but still nothing. Slowly I started to scan up the door and suddenly my heart started beating extremely fast. At the level of my eyes, I could clearly see two black marks. They were exceedingly small, but without a doubt, they were there.

I needed to go and find Dave and tell him immediately. I found him talking with some of the other agents and he was deep in conversation, so I waited quietly until they had finished talking. After what seemed an age, but was only about fifteen minutes, he finished his conversation and strolled over to join me.

"What was the hurry just now when you rushed off outside as if you were being chased?"

He could see that I still looked serious and added, "Is something wrong?"

"I don't know, maybe, but your words to me last night about prevaricating got to me, and I was worried about it all night."

He opened his mouth to say something, but I raised my hand and said, "Dave, I know I am very new at this and you have very experienced people here, but I think I may have seen something."

He smiled benevolently and said, "Tell all?"

I took a big deep breath and launched into what I had seen at St Paul's Cathedral yesterday and what I had discovered today.

"It may have been nothing, and the black marks were not in the same position on the doors, but I thought someone ought to know."

Dave replied, "Look, it is better to say something and be wrong, than to say nothing and be right. You would have to live with those consequences for the rest of your life."

Now I was feeling somewhat contrite.

Dave added, "I will deal with it immediately; if it is nothing, you will hear nothing, if the intel is valid, you will be told."

"Thank you," I muttered.

***

The following day I was finally going to the MI6 offices at 85 Albert Embankment in Vauxhall, South London. Dave advised me that it would be a new beginning and not to worry about anything. He said that I would probably spend most of the day with Human Resources where they would go over all the question-and-answer papers that I had completed and all the research into my history to date.

Dave collected me from the UJC at eight-thirty to take me to headquarters. He brought my security pass and I put it in my pocket. I had retained a copy of my Background Investigation questions and my notes appertaining to it and brought them with me.

My Background Investigation

All the following had already been done many weeks in advance of me being invited to come to MI6.

The initial part of checking my application was a polygraph test. You feel as if you are guilty of something before you even sit down. There were a few tense moments but, in the end, all was good. They told me that I had passed the polygraph test. Of course, I knew I would because I had not done anything wrong, but it still gives you an odd feeling.

The next part of the background investigation is where investigators pore over the applicant's security forms and personally verify the authenticity of the information provided.

This investigation also comes after the polygraph and psychological examination. I had already filled out so many forms and answered hundreds of questions that I am not sure which one was the actual psychological exam. Friends, relatives, former colleagues, neighbours; apparently everyone is fair game. As it should be for an investigation at this level.

I had alerted nearly everybody on my forms that an investigator might be coming around so that nobody would think I did anything wrong or was in trouble. I subsequently got feedback from all those people when investigators visited them.

My neighbours were interviewed for approximately twenty minutes apiece; it is not like I was hiding outside the windows and listening. The most common questions were: -

How long have you known her?

What is your relationship with her?
How often do you see her?
Is she happily married or in a relationship?
Any issues that you know of?
Does she gamble?
Do drugs?
Have a drinking problem?
Any strange behaviour?
Would you consider her trustworthy?
Does she know any foreign nationals?
Who?
How often does she see them?
Of the five neighbouring houses in our cul-de-sac, the local investigator stopped by four of them for a chat. Interviews with former managers and colleagues lasted a bit longer. I am told that the interviews were usually at least an hour.

I had not realised that that the investigation into my life was going to be so thorough. I was investigated as if I were a potential terrorist and Dave wanted me to know that the full extent of the investigation might seem troubling. After all, in the last fifty years, there had been several high-profile cases of senior agents from all branches caught as double agents or selling highly classified information and secrets. Getting into one of the agencies was becoming more and more difficult.

Dave also handed me a sheet of paper to read as we were heading for the offices at MI6.

I thanked him for everything he had done for me in the last few days, and I hoped that I had not been too much trouble.

He just nodded and smiled and then added, "You will make a great agent, but you will have to work at it."

I then read the paper he handed me.

ACTIONS THAT AMOUNT TO ACTS OF TERRORISM

These are several actions that can be considered as acts of terrorism if they are carried out to advance religious, ideological, racial, or political means. They include:

Acts of serious violence against another person, people, or property.

Acts that endanger another person's life.

Acts that are carried out with the intent of causing significant interference or serious disruption to electronic systems.

Behaviours that seriously risk the health and safety of the public or any number of people or group within society.

The law does not require a person to have carried out one of the acts above for them to be convicted of a terrorist offence. Instead, a person can be convicted if they are found guilty of planning, assisting with, or even gathering information on how to carry out one of the acts.

Deputy Training Overseer.
Dave Wilson

We arrived at MI6 and walked into the foyer and there in front of me was a door with details emblazoned on it.

Human Resources MI6 HQ

A small sign underneath announced:
Enter at Your Peril

I knocked loudly on the big heavy wooden door and a cheery voice shouted, "Come in."

I was standing in a large well-lit office with about half a dozen desks that had someone behind each one. Most of them had their heads down and were talking on a phone.

A middle-aged lady, who I imagined was the one who said come in said, "Good morning, can I help you?"

"Yes, I am joining today and was told to be here by 9 a.m."

She said, "Alright, just give me a moment and I will find out where you need to be today."

She came back within just a few seconds and said, "I think you are due to spend the day with Jack Rawcliffe. He has been around a long time and you will be pleased to hear that he is Royal Navy retired; not that anyone ever retires in this line of work."

I thanked her and she said that he would be along to greet me in a few minutes.

"Jack joined us as a Warrant Officer, was out in the field for many years, ended up as a Commander and is now head of Human Resources for the whole agency. He still enjoys being called Commander." She smiled.

"Thank you, I will remember that when I meet him."

A few minutes later an older gent with a full head of grey hair and a welcoming smile walked into the room, walked up to me, and greeted me with, "Good morning, Clubs."

"Good morning, Commander," I responded, and his smile became even bigger.

"Come with me, young lady, let us get you started on your new career."

***

I spent the next two days with Commander Rawcliffe, and we went through all the forms that I filled out and all the results from family, neighbours, employers, employees, friends, and colleagues. There had also been a deep search carried out by Law Enforcement. They even had reports back from my time in Switzerland and Gibraltar. Nothing was sacred – even my French pen pal René had been investigated. My internet and my mobile phone records had all been checked out. This included all my media accounts and even Skype. I had been under the scope.

Included in the files were reports from both of the language schools and a report from my time spent at HMS Raleigh and also a personal note from Commander Shone.

The following is a quick overview of Commander Micky Shone's notes on the day that he had interviewed Jenny Talbot.

I have always had a huge involvement with espionage and undercover exercises, however, this young lady looks very promising. Most people think of me of being just a 'Schoolie'. I often think back over the years since I had been recruited into this little-known government department who were a related and an integral part of the MI6.

There is so much about the Secret Intelligence Service (SIS), commonly known as MI6, (Military Intelligence, Section 6), which is the foreign intelligence service of the United Kingdom, tasked mainly with the covert overseas collection and analysis of human intelligence in support of the United Kingdom's national security that she needs to learn about.

Reflecting on my own career, I am happy where I am today, but feel for this young lady who is only at the beginning of a huge life-changing experience. I remember the fear and the confusion I went through as a new young operative.

I have a strong feeling that she is going to be a one in a million operative who already has many more skills at this stage of her training than I had when I started. Yes, she is going to be good.

After reading the numerous notes and reports, I took a big deep breath and felt elated and also humbled by Commander Shone's personal thoughts

Commander Rawcliffe said, "You look a little drained, are you OK?"

"Yes, just a little shocked to realise how much I had been scrutinised; I realise that all of it is necessary, but it is unnerving."

He smiled and said, "If it helps any, we all had to go through this scrutiny. I was much older than you when I joined but I do not regret a single day. I could have retired some time ago, but nobody is pushing, and I am not in a hurry." He smiled broadly.

***

The next few weeks flew by and every day was filled with some sort of activity. Much of it was out in the field investigating reports of terrorist activity. A lot of it was from disgruntled neighbours, or domestic violence, or disenfranchised people who either from grief or anger or other emotion saw terrorists at every turn. Unfortunately, each case had to be investigated and thousands of man-hours were spent getting to the bottom of each case.

Despite all of that, I enjoyed honing my new skills and became sharper at discerning truth from fiction. It was now approaching Christmas, and I was going to be given some time off before jetting off to join my first posting HMS Dornik.

The day before heading off home for a well-earned break, I was told that there was an important meeting to be held in the conference room and everyone had to attend. There were whispers that an agent was receiving a commendation. Unlike any other branch, medals are not given because it would endanger the life of the recipient and their colleagues if outsiders got to know what the medal was for. Apparently, they received a commendation and after holding it and reading it, the commendation would be returned to the secure vaults where all agents' confidential details were kept. It made sense.

Any agent who had a uniform was invited to wear them. I was no exception and had been warned to keep it ready for use at any time. I had been allocated a small locker adjacent to the lady's room on day one and my Royal Navy Petty Officer's uniform was hanging in there.

There was an hour to go, and I was told to go and get myself ready. I was walking down the passageway towards the locker room when I saw a man walking towards me in civilian clothes who I did not instantly recognise. I looked up as he approached and said to me, "Hello, Jenny, how is your training going?"

It had been a couple of years since I had last seen him before leaving HMS *Raleigh*. It was none other than Commander Micky Shone. I was a bit taken aback as I had not expected to see him here. Although I do not know why; he was, after all, a member of the security service and had been responsible for me being here.

"Hello, Sir," I gushed. "It is good to see you, and yes, I am enjoying every minute of it."

He added, "Sorry I am unable to stop and chat, but I have a meeting to attend, good luck, Jenny."

"Thank you, Sir, perhaps we will meet again soon," I added.

He chuckled. "I'm sure we will, Jenny, I'm sure we will."

I put on my uniform and checked myself in the mirror. It had been a while since I had put it on, and I was worried in case it did not fit properly. It was perfect and fitted me better than I remembered.

There was a knock at the door. Dave was standing there in a very smart army uniform. It was strange because he had never discussed his background. All I knew was that he was married and had two young daughters. I glanced up at his lapels and saw that he was a Colonel.

Smiling at him I said, "Good morning, Sir. A Colonel, huh? You never mentioned that while I was training with you."

He replied in a jocular manner and said, "I didn't want my lofty position to interfere with our relationship."

I recovered my composure and said to him, "What is this meeting about?"

He replied, "Oh, nothing important really, we have these from time to time just to update us on the world in general."

I just nodded.

"Sometimes it could be a special alert and very occasionally it is a commendation."

By the time we arrived at the conference room, it was packed. I was surprised as the front row seats all had names on them, and Dave and I were shown to the middle of the front row. They were clearly marked Wilson and Talbot.

We waited for about five minutes and suddenly the room went incredibly quiet. Miss Morgan appeared on the stage and walked up to the microphone.

"Good morning, colleagues, it is good to see so many of you here today." She looked out at everybody in the audience, smiled, and continued, "I hope the world is safe today with so many of you off the streets and just maybe it's safer without you villains out there causing mayhem."

Loud laughter reverberated around the room.

"Well, I come with important news. After more than forty years with the agency, I have decided it is time to put on my slippers and take a well-earned retirement."

There was the sound of clapping and well wishes from around the room which continued for several minutes. Commander Rawcliffe appeared on the stage with Miss Morgan and presented her with the proverbial gold watch and no less than a Rolex Oyster and a cheque; although the amount was not mentioned.

When the cheering died down, Commander Rawcliffe continued.

"It is not too often and perhaps not often enough that we have the opportunity to thank one of our own for exceptional work in the field, which probably saved hundreds of lives. As you are all aware, there have been ongoing investigations here in London with regards to an Islamic terrorist organisation who had planned a vigorous and deadly campaign aimed at the very heart of our Christian Establishment. This one agent alone with attention to detail and hawk-like eyes alerted us to this almost certain calamity."

"I would like to invite Commander, no I apologise, Captain Micky Shone to come up onto the stage and present this well-deserved commendation."

For the next few minutes, there was a lot of chattering around the Conference room with all those gathered looking to see who it might be.

Captain Micky Shone, in uniform, stepped onto the stage to uproarious cheering and clapping. He was a popular figure amongst those of the agency and he knew many of them personally. He waited for the noise to abate before starting to speak.

"I have spent the last few years as the Training Commander at HMS *Raleigh* down in the West Country and it has been a fulfilling post, to say the least. However, there is so much activity these days in the agency that I am trying to shuffle between my Royal Navy duties and those of this agency. So, in their wisdom, our leaders have promoted me so that I do not have to work quite so hard at being a sailor. As the Captain of HMS *Raleigh*, I am needed more for ceremonial occasions and as a figurehead, which frees up a lot of time for me to continue my work here.

"However, today was not to talk about me, but to give this commendation to one of our agents that Commander Rawcliffe alluded to. So, without further ado, please come up on the stage and be recognised, Jennifer Talbot."

I had never been so shocked in my life and the blood just drained from my face. The incident at St Paul's Cathedral and Westminster Abbey were all but forgotten.

Dave helped me up and then came up on the stage and stood behind me. The rest of the audience were generous with their clapping and words of congratulations. Captain Shone stood with a huge grin, hugged me, and whispered his congratulations, and then handed me the commendation.

Thank goodness I was not expected to speak. I was still overwhelmed and dumbfounded.

I punched Dave on the arm and said to him, "You knew all about this and never said a word, thank you."

Dave responded and said, "You have done well, and I am exceedingly proud of you but remember it is a big bad world out there so when you leave us here, go out and do great good."

I went back into the Human Resources office to collect my instructions for joining HMS *Dornik*. Commander Rawcliffe also enlightened me on how my information had culminated in a successful operation that included the capture of several terrorists who would be going away for a long time.

The dark marks that I had spotted on the doors were, in fact, yellow, fluorescent marks that could only be seen completely with an ultraviolet light. When the ultraviolet light was brought into play, the team had found marks at seven out of eight churches that had been earmarked as potential targets. They later found more illuminated marks near the security systems in each of these churches and at all the homes of the senior clergy for those churches.

"You did a good job, Jenny," he stated.

I thanked him for his kindness and said, "Doubtless we will see each other again soon. Oh, I nearly forgot, what would you like me to do with my car?"

He replied, "Why don't you keep it for the time being, use it to drive home and on vacation, and when it is time for you to go and join the ship, take it to Royal Airforce Lyneham and we will collect it from there."

I was thrilled, I had thoroughly enjoyed having this little car.

After all the things I had done since leaving home, it seemed a complete anti-climax being back there after such a long time and although it was good to see my family, I was itching to be going to join HMS *Dornik*.

✲✲✲

I had only been home a couple of days when I received instructions for my flight out to Diego Garcia. Ten in the morning from Royal Airforce Lyneham on the sixth of January. I was excited.

Christmas came and went, and it was soon the sixth of January. It was a three-hour drive to Lyneham and so I had to leave home at six in the morning. Dad did not speak, and Mum and Jane were in tears. I felt a little emotional as I hugged them goodbye and then climbed into my borrowed Fiat and drove away.

It was a great feeling — four years of hard work and now finally I was on my way to start doing what I had been training for. Little did I know but there was one more big surprise coming when I joined the ship.

Chapter 5. HMS *Dornik*

Nearly four years later and now Petty Officer Jennifer Talbot – I – was sitting onboard a Royal Airforce plane heading for Diego Garcia, a remote tropical island in the Indian Ocean, which is a secretive, strategically vital US military base. On occasions, Royal Navy ships and Military aircraft also perform operations from the island, mostly in conjunction with United States personnel.

The base has served as a launchpad for United States military operations in the Middle East and as a refuelling point for Air Force patrols headed to the South China Sea.

It had been a tough four years and my education in honing my special skills as a covert operator had been extensive. As I half dozed in my seat, I reflected on what had been accomplished in that time.

My time had certainly not been wasted, and finally all that work and effort was about to pay off as I was on a journey to join Her Majesty's Ship *Dornik*. It was the most sophisticated, secretive surveillance ship in the world and all its crew had been handpicked and trained to perform specialist activities, although not all were secret agents.

In the last three and a half years, I had become a Diver, a Physical Training Instructor, and a linguist in French and Spanish, with a smattering of other languages including Arabic and Korean.

The pilot informed us that we would be flying to Royal Air Force Akrotiri in Cyprus for a refuelling stop and to pick up supplies for Diego Garcia and then finally on to the destination at Royal Australian Air Force base Richmond, Sydney, Australia.

I had my eyes closed, and smiled to myself, wondering if I had been classified as supplies for Diego Garcia. The first leg of the flight to Cyprus was about four and a half hours and I drifted in and out of sleep for the best part of the flight. I was feeling nervous about joining HMS

Dornik and did not feel like eating, although I did manage some cheese and biscuits and a cup of coffee.

As we approached Cyprus, I could see the Troodos Mountain Range with Mount Olympus, the highest point, reaching up nearly six and a half thousand feet above sea level. It was an impressive sight. We were flying in from the west and so it was late afternoon as we came down to land. The sun was shining through the plane's windows where I was sitting, and I had to shade my eyes to take in the incredible view outside. Then, in just a few minutes, the plane was on the runway. Because of the two-hour time difference, it was now just after four-thirty.

The doors opened and a warm Mediterranean air wafted through the cabin. It was so pleasant after the freezing cold of England when we took off just a few hours ago. The captain announced that we would be in Cyprus for about an hour and a half during which time we could disembark if we wished to, but we were not to leave the base. The plane would take off at six-thirty sharp and we should all be back in our seats by six o'clock local time.

It was nice to get off and stretch my legs. In the two seats next to mine was an RAF Sergeant and Flight Sergeant who were on their way to Australia. They were relocating from the Royal Air Force to the Royal Australian Air Force and the three of us went off together to explore the base. In the main building, we found a coffee shop with an outdoor patio, where we placed our order and went and sat outside.

It was, of course, winter here as well, but the temperatures were so much warmer than England at this time of year. The temperature showing on the large clock thermometer was showing sixty-nine degrees Fahrenheit and far better than the thirty degrees when we took off.

My two companions told me that their wives and children had already relocated and were living just outside Sydney in RAAF Quarters. They had both served for more than twenty years and transferring gave them at least another fifteen years and quite a considerable pay increase on their salary in the RAF. The older one of the two laughed and said he was not moving for the money but the warmer weather.

By the time we had chatted over coffee, it was time to return to the aircraft. It was about five minutes to six as we settled back in our seats and already the sun had almost disappeared. The light went quickly at that time of year.

The captain's voice came over the loudspeaker informing us that he was doing final checks and we would be ready for take-off on time. He announced that the flight time would be ten hours and forty-one minutes and, including four hours' time difference, we would be arriving at just after nine tomorrow morning in Diego Garcia. He then wished us a pleasant flight.

At about seven-thirty, dinner was provided and I was incredibly surprised that we were offered a glass of wine. Wine on a Services flight – not bad! Soon after dinner, I settled down for the long flight. It did not take long to drop off to sleep.

***

I must have slept well, because on waking I could see the sun shining brightly ahead of us through the window. Just the thought of getting closer to Diego Garcia made me feel extremely nervous. This was going to be my first ship, not only as a Physical Trainer but also as a government agent. I took a big deep breath to calm my nerves. Right now, I felt more nervous than when I stepped into the boxing ring to face Slammer Woods all those years ago. Why was I so nervous considering it was what I had been trained to do?

The hostess came round with coffee and I soon started to feel better. We still had just over two hours before we started to descend to Diego Garcia. I had read all about the island and I knew from photographs that it was like a large lagoon with land wrapped around it.

Breakfast came and I managed to eat some egg on toast. By the time breakfast had been cleared away, we started to descend. It had been quite cloudy up to now and I could not see the ocean below. Then suddenly, we broke through the bank of cloud to reveal a beautiful sunny day and below, the warm waters of the Indian Ocean glinting in the bright sunlight.

The plane dropped lower and lower and it looked as if we were just skimming the calm mirror-like surface. I heard the wheels go down and I still could not see Diego Garcia. Then it swiftly appeared, and it looked as if the plane was going to drop into the water. The island came up extremely fast, and seconds after reaching the shore, we touched down on the firm runway of Diego Garcia right at the appointed time.

As I left the plane, the captain and all the hostesses wished me 'bon voyage'. Apparently, I was the only passenger leaving the plane, although stores were being dropped off. The rest of the passengers were Australia bound.

It was unlike any other airport: there was no arrivals lounge, no immigration, and no customs. A United States land rover screeched to a halt alongside me and a young man in US Naval uniform jumped out, saluted me, and then pushed my two suitcases into the rear of the vehicle.

I grinned like a Cheshire cat; I had never been saluted before, ever, by anyone. *Oh well, I guess that is what he has been instructed to do.* We drove off the runway and close to what looked like some terminal buildings. As we rounded the corner, I could see a helicopter sitting in a white painted circle with its rotor blades turning. Blazoned on the side of it was DOR I.

I smiled at the young American sailor and said, "Is that my ride?"

"It is, ma'am," he replied.

I got out of the vehicle and the driver retrieved my cases and took them to a Royal Navy airman who pushed them into the door of the helicopter. The driver of the land rover saluted once more and entered his vehicle and drove away.

The noise of the helicopter was too loud for conversation, so he just pointed the way to the front of it and gesticulated for me to get in. The pilot chopped me off a quick salute and mouthed, "Hello, Jenny."

I felt important; I had received three salutes in under ten minutes – it must be my special day.

The helicopter took off and headed out to sea but within about ten minutes he was coming into land on a ship. It looked big and impressive, and my knees started to tremble. There were no markings on the ship, no numbers, nothing to indicate where it was from or who it belonged to.

This was my new home; this was the mighty 'Dornik'. As I stepped out of the helicopter, the airman pulled my cases out of the back and handed them to me. He ran off to the front of the helicopter and pulled off the DOR 1 sign, so, like the ship, it had no identification marks visible. Talk about secrecy.

I was taken straight to the Bridge to meet the Captain, Commander, and the Officer of the Watch. The Captain gave orders to the Officer of the Watch to secure the doors to the Bridge and deny access to anyone who tried to come in.

"Sorry about that, but for now I just wanted to keep you away from prying eyes and ears."

I looked at the three officers who were all looking at me in a most peculiar way.

The Captain spoke again.

"Welcome aboard, Lieutenant Talbot, we have been looking forward to meeting you."

I just stood completely still for a few seconds, dumbfounded.

"I think you have made a mistake, Sir; I don't know who you were expecting, but I am Petty Officer Physical Trainer Jennifer Talbot."

The Captain and Commander both guffawed loudly and the Commander quickly added, "Jenny, you were promoted the day you left MI6, but for the sake of secrecy, it was kept a secret, even from you. We cannot afford for everyone to know who you are, and we needed someone who was completely new to this ship and not known to the ship's company. Apart from those present and the pilot of the chopper, (Helicopter) and my Personal Assistant who is also a lieutenant, nobody else knows who you are, just yet."

My head was reeling, and I was struggling to take it all in. I felt like I was mumbling incoherently.

"Jenny, let's adjourn to my private dining room where we can have a leisurely lunch and fully brief you on your forthcoming project."

I was soon introduced to the Captain's Personal Assistant, Lieutenant Annette Saunders. I smiled at her and she greeted me with, "Hi, Jenny."

As soon as we were seated, the Captain said, "I think proper introductions are called for. This is Commander Mike Cheetham, you have already met Annette and I am Captain James John Crowe. That is Sir in public, but Jim when we are in the Wardroom.

"Having just told you that you are now a Lieutenant, and of course you are, but we have an ongoing investigation that we have been unable to solve.

"Let me quickly explain to you how this ship works. All the officers onboard are fully trained agents. The Chiefs and Petty Officers are partially trained and many of them will find themselves drafted somewhere to be fully trained after this trip and will be sent to do many of the things that you did. After this training, they may find themselves back here or at another Naval attachment or they may be utilised in whatever way the agency deems fit."

A buzzer sounded and the Captain excused himself, saying that he was required on the Bridge.

"Mike, please carry on with the briefing for Jenny."

Mike continued where the Captain had left off.

"The lower deck ratings are only trained on the unique equipment that we have onboard and are sworn to secrecy. For example, we do not use numbers for the names of our special radar, sonar, or communications systems; they all have male names. You will learn these very quickly.

"There are three different types of radar: Andrew, Bob, and Charlie; three different sonar: Daniel, Ezekiel, and Festus. We also have an incredibly special missile capability known as 'Ferris' and a clever piece of equipment it is. All will be revealed to you in due course."

He paused for me to take it all in and then continued.

"Communications are a different category because we use different approaches depending on the recipient and the secrecy of the message. A brief explanation of their use and purpose is that shortwave radio provides unique and extraordinary access to worldwide communications. With a relatively simple antenna, it is possible to listen to international broadcasts, ships at sea, transatlantic airliners, military stations, and even international spies! It also has an image projector to send pictures. This is just called Williams and the other one is called Code Williams for sending morse code. However, even our morse code is a unique code and it changes every month."

"Mike, how much of the operating of this equipment will I be involved with?" I asked.

"Probably very little, because most of the time we use it to disseminate all the intel that comes in. However, knowing the names of all the different pieces of equipment is important. It helps for us to be able to decide on what action to take from how the intel is received."

"I see," I replied. "So how do I fit into this scheme of things?"

"For the time being, you are going to revert to an LPT (Leading Physical Trainer), and we are placing you down below with the rest of the ship's company. We have an incredibly special task for you starting very soon, but first, we need to get you integrated. Tomorrow you will be introduced to the Diving Team, which you will take over and become the Diving Supervisor. You are going to be an extremely busy lady, believe me."

I smiled and just nodded my head.

"The Captain is currently on the Bridge talking to the Stores Chief and the Provost Marshall. They have been told that one of your suitcases seems to be missing and is probably on its way to Australia. You will be fitted out with a completely new kit apart from your PT uniform, which I understand you have with you?"

"Yes, that is right," I replied.

"The Provost Marshall is a fully trained agent, who holds the rank of Lieutenant Commander and he will take you down below and introduce you to your new cabin mate and settle you in. Once you have taken over the Diving Team and done a few press-ups etc with the crew, you will quickly become just the Clubswinger, and a darn good one from all your reports."

"Thanks, Mike, and I will be on my best behaviour tomorrow, Sir, I promise."

"I know you will, Jenny, I know you will. Now let us go and introduce you to the Provost Marshall."

As the Provost Marshall and I went down the ladder to the lower deck, we passed several lads in the passageways who gawked as we went by; one of them even gave a little whistle.

"All right, boys, calm down, this is your new Clubswinger so be careful, or you might get more than you bargained for. She is the only lady boxing champion in the Royal Navy; never lost a bout."

Several of the lads stopped and welcomed me onboard. I smiled at them and said, "Thanks!"

One mouthy young lad piped up, "It's easy when you are fighting another girl, but a man would be quite a different thing."

"Be careful what you say, Jones, she did a good job on the Royal Navy Youth Boxing Champion, called Slammer Woods. Put him down pretty good from all accounts."

Jones did not utter another word.

As we continued along the passageway, I said to the Provost Marshall, "Thank you, Sir, you know a lot about me."

"I do, Jenny, it's part of the job." He grinned.

"By the way, my name is Neil Bennet, Wiggy when we are on our own or up in the Wardroom, just Sir when we are in public."

I was looking around me as I went with him down the main passageway. We passed the NAAFI Canteen (Navy Army and Air Force Institutes). An onboard store that sells most things that a sailor might need from soap, cigarettes, chocolate, etc; basically, a small general store. We passed the Regulating Office where he informed me that three of his RPO's (Regulating Petty Officers) worked from. Then as we turned a small corner in the passageway, there was a Fire and Safety area with hoses, axes, a first aid kit, oxygen masks and air bottles, and several other items for use in the event of an emergency.

A few yards further down he stopped and banged on a door. The door opened and a girl of about my age was standing there.

"Hello, Sir, what can I do for you?"

"Hello, Sophie, this is Jenny Talbot, she is going to be your new cabin mate."

Sophie opened the door wide and said, "Come into my home; it has been boring for the last two months since Danielle left. "Sorry, let me introduce myself. Sophia Lynch, known as Sophie, Soph, or as one of my friends calls me So and So. I cut hair, manicure nails, do make-up, and then apparently, I have a Navy job, which is maintaining the safety equipment that I can leave lying around in the passageway outside the door. I must be the only person on board that can leave their stuff cluttering up the passageway," she said with a grin.

"Perhaps I can help you with the tidying up some time," I responded, smiling. "I am the Ship's new Physical Trainer and soon to be the ship's Diving Supervisor."

"In that case, Jenny, we will be working with each other because I also maintain the Diving Equipment and look after the Diving Store."

With a cheeky smile, she said, "OK, Sir, you can go now, I'll look after Jenny."

"I know you will, Sophie, thank you."

He turned around and went back to his office.

"Let me show you around our palace."

The cabin was almost split in two in the bunk area, with the two beds separated cleverly by two kit lockers standing side by side, one facing each way towards the bunks. At either end of the lockers was a taller wardrobe for hanging coats, which were large enough to accommodate a couple of cases. At the bottom end of the beds was a comfortable sitting area with two easy chairs and a television and a Compact Disc player unit incorporated into a single piece of furniture. There was another room to the right of the television leading onto a reasonable shower and bathroom. This was surprisingly also quite roomy.

"Not bad, not bad at all," I commented.

Sophie looked around and said, "By the way, where is all your kit?"

"Well, some of it is probably in Australia by now," I lied convincingly.

"The rest of it should be here in a few minutes; the Airman said he would bring it down from the chopper as soon as he was told where I was being berthed; his words not mine." I smiled.

I spent the next hour telling Sophie a bit about my life in the Royal Navy to date. That meant omitting a great deal of it, but I had been briefed and I knew what to say. Talking about my family was a lot easier because none of it had to be fabricated.

During the time that we were chatting, the airman came down with my cases and a few minutes later the Stores Chief also came with replacements for the kit that I did not have.

"Oh, how lucky to lose your case, now you get new stuff to wear," Sophie said.

"I was fortunate that none of it was irreplaceable," I added.

"Does everyone on board have big cabins like this, Sophie?" I asked.

"Not at all. Danielle was here before me and she was already a Petty Officer. They did not have enough space for another girl, so I was given this cabin to share with her. Nearly all of the Senior rates and Officers have cabins like this one."

"Where did Danielle go?" I asked her.

"I think she went off to London for more training, but I don't know for sure."

Sophie then left me to sort out my kit and have a shower, and by the time I had finished, it was time to go down to the Dining Room for dinner. The Dining Room was just one deck down and only a few yards further to the rear of the ship. By the time we got down there, it was well packed. Many of the ship's company wandered past where Sophie and I were seated. Some stopped to greet me with, "Welcome aboard, Clubs, we could do with some training and some games." Similar comments came from many of the crew.

I found myself relaxing a little bit. There were one or two dissenters with comments like, "Oh no, not a woman Clubswinger."

I just smiled at their jibes.

Sophie pointed out several of the Ship's divers; the whole team comprised of five men and three ladies.

"Including you, Jenny, there will be nine divers in all plus the Diving Officer, Lieutenant Dave Wilkins. He is tall, blonde, and good looking but sadly he is leaving."

I was taking over his job as the Diving officer because he had been appointed back to Britannia Royal Navy College at Dartmouth in Devon. He had been promoted and was going there as an Instructor. I heard from Commander Mike Cheetham later that he would be surreptitiously looking for more agents as well. Everyone from the Agency seemed to have more than one job to do.

After supper, we went back to our cabin and I put away the rest of the kit that I would need in my locker, and the stuff I did not need I left in my case and shoved it in the bottom of my wardrobe.

After my long flight from England, plus the time difference, I was feeling very tired and decided to go to bed early. Sophie said that she was going up top for a breath of fresh air. Sometime during the night, I heard the ship's engines start to hum and then realised that we were moving.

***

I dozed back off, but early in the morning, the Captain's voice came over the Tannoy (Ship's Broadcast).

"Good morning, this is the Captain speaking. We are heading northwest at top speed to intercept two Iranian warships who are chasing and threatening a Portuguese tanker called *Alvares Cabral*. It will take about twenty-four hours for us to reach the tanker, and we have signalled them to make their heading southeast at top speed. We believe that the Iranian warships are quite small, with a top speed of about thirty knots. We have calculated that it will take the Iranians about twenty-two hours to reach them."

(Pedro Álvares Cabral was a Portuguese nobleman, military commander, navigator, and explorer regarded as the European discoverer of Brazil. The Portuguese also always name one of their frigates Alvares Cabral.)

"The UK Government are in contact with Tehran and are warning them to back off. There is clear evidence that the Portuguese tanker did not encroach Iranian waters and were over fifty miles outside their territory. At the present, Tehran are stalling and arguing with our government. This may give us ample time to close the distance and put the two warships within easy range of our missiles. I apologise, but it is going to be a bumpy ride for the foreseeable future while I see how much speed I can get out of this tub."

I had been on the ship for less than a day and the action was beginning already. This was no undercover subterfuge; this was simple straightforward warmongering.

Long heavy swells were building up as we moved west and there were forecasts of storms coming off the East African coast, which meant that this heavy weather would continue throughout the journey. There were short periods of calm, but they lasted only a few minutes.

Lieutenant Wilkins sent a messenger down to the cabin to asked me to meet him at 0830 at the Diving Store.

Sophie had heard my conversation with the young lad and said, "I had better get down to the store and tidy it up before the boss gets there, it's in a bit of a mess."

"That's alright, we can go down there together, I need you to show me the way," I replied.

"No," she said, "you go and get breakfast and I will meet you at the Dining Room at quarter past eight."

I did not argue with her but just nodded my head. She really did not want me to go down there. *Well, it must be bad, and she is feeling embarrassed about it.* About ten minutes later, she was gone.

It was only 0745 and I wandered down past the galley to the dining room. I smiled to myself; the dining room was nearly empty. Nobody seemed to like these heavy seas. I felt fine and ate a big breakfast.

True to her word, Sophie appeared on time, carrying a bacon sandwich in one hand and a hot cup of coffee in the other. She grinned at me and said, "Alright, now at the store, all clean and tidy for the boss, or should I say both bosses."

I just smiled.

She finished her coffee, and we made our way to the Diving Store; the ship was lurching, and we had to hang onto something all the way. As soon as we opened the upper deck door, the wind nearly knocked us off our feet.

Sophie said, "We only have to go about ten feet and we will be out of the wind."

As soon as we rounded the corner of the superstructure of the ship, the wind died down. The Diving Store was set in at the rear of the Superstructure and quite sheltered from the wind. There was nobody on the upper deck that could be seen and the only things flapping around were the tie downs for the chopper.

There was only one clip securing the door and on opening it, we found Lieutenant Wilkins seated at the small desk inside.

He stood up and said, "Welcome, Jenny, so good to meet you. I was due to fly off back to England tomorrow, but I imagine that is on hold now until this emergency trip is over."

I responded, "Good morning, Sir, nice to meet you too."

He knew that I was the same rank as him but with Sophie in the store with us, we had to play the protocol game.

He went on, "I might as well hand everything over to you now so that I can leave as soon as an opportunity arises."

He turned his attention to Sophie. "Sophie, can you keep yourself busy with the safety equipment up in the main passage while I do a hand over to Jenny, it should only take about a couple of hours."

Sophie opened her mouth to speak, but Dave Wilkins cut her short, "Now please, Sophie."

She did not look very happy, but went on her way back inside the ship.

"Sorry about that, Jenny, but most of the stuff I need to talk about is confidential and not for anyone else's ears."

For just over an hour, we went through all the Diving Record cards. Dave also had the private records for each diver kept in their personnel records that the Provost stored in his safe.

The male divers were:

Bryan Root

Steve Sells

John Kidley

Dave Knox

Barrie Willson

The female divers were:

Sue Jones

Brenda Jones

Lula Lewis

"Before you ask, yes, they are sisters. Brenda is the eldest of the two and both are good divers, and they take care of their equipment, probably better than any of the boys. Having said that, they are all great divers, the boys just tend to be a little untidy. I must mention Lula; she is the oldest diver that we have and likes to mother the rest of the team. Of the few times we have done a night necklace, she has always been the lead diver swimming along the keel and is completely fearless. Then there is Sophie who is not a diver, but she services all our equipment as well as the Ship's Safety Equipment. She is good, but at times she appears to be a little vacant. She tends to be overprotective of the Diving Store as if it was her property.

"You now have an overview of the divers and their good and bad points. The team overall work together very well and I have been giving them lots of practice operational dives, I suggest you continue with that practice."

I nodded my agreement.

"Where do you keep the main Diving Log with all the dives you carry out?"

"On the bookshelf in the big hardback blue folder," he answered.

(A Necklace is where the divers are all attached to each other. Starting at one end of the ship they are spread out in a straight line under the ship and complete a thorough search of the ship's bottom, usually from bow to stern)

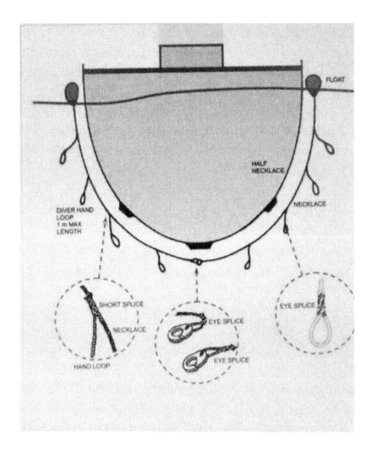

"The Captain also wishes to see it every month and he signs it off; also be aware that he will sometimes initiate an emergency dive without notice. Keep the team on their toes. You will never know what is coming. He is very innovative with every operation being different."

"No pressure then." I smiled at him.

"Now there is something else that I need to tell you about. We believe that someone is leaking intelligence from the ship to unfriendly foreign operators. Chatter out there tells us that they always know our location and training exercises, and even some of our secret operations have been compromised. Jenny, just keep your eyes and ears open. The reason you have been selected for this task is that nobody on board knows of your real status, and being a Clubswinger and a diver gives you free rein all over the ship. That, fortunately, means you appear to be privileged in being able to visit the Wardroom and the Captain without it seeming unusual."

I nodded, listening and absorbing every word.

He continued, "Jenny, your reputation precedes you, and every one of our agents onboard by now knows all about you and is expecting great things from you; you are going to be a huge asset for us."

I felt a little embarrassed at such a great accolade and just nodded humbly.

I spent the rest of the day wandering from mess to mess to introduce myself to the ship's company. There had been no Physical Trainer before me, although they did have an active soccer and rugby team. Lieutenant Dave Lancaster looked after the soccer team and Chief Micky Byrne the rugby team. Quite a few said they would like to have some sort of workout and exercise on the upper deck, weather permitting.

I spoke to Chief Byrne about the team sports kit. He said these were kept in the sports store up near the bows.

I grinned at him and said, "Nobody told me about a sports store."

"I have a key if you would like it. Dave Lancaster has one and I believe the Provost Marshall keeps one. I will show you the store if you like."

"Thank you," I replied.

As we approached the sports store, I began to regret taking him up on his offer. The ship was bouncing around very heavily and with it being so far up in the bows, it felt like being on a roller coaster.

Mick opened the door; inside was quite spacious but it was very untidy with gear strewn all over the place. I put some of it down to the movement of the ship, but I think it was untidy anyway.

"Does anyone look after the store?" I asked Mick.

"Not really, I try to look after it when we have had a game of rugby and I think Dave Lancaster does when his boys are finished, but in between not much is done. When it is tidy in here, there is just enough room for a couple of people to use the weights, but not right now." We locked the store and I thanked Mick for showing me around. I told him to keep his key and I would get one from the Provost Marshall.

Then came an announcement over the Tannoy: "This is the Captain speaking. I apologise for the uncomfortable ride, but we have made extremely good time and we should reach the *Alvares Cabral* Portuguese tanker before daylight tomorrow. The Iranian warships are closing in on them, and we should get there at about the same time. Another message has been sent to them from our government telling them to stand down, but Tehran and the ships are not complying. London has told us to take whatever action is necessary to prevent what amounts to piracy by the Iranians. We will be going to Emergency Stations at five o'clock in the morning and I will keep you informed of anything further."

Mick said, "I must go and organise my people and make sure that they are ready for closing up for Emergency Stations." He left me and ran off up the main passageway.

Over the Tannoy came another announcement: "Physical Trainer to the Bridge."

The Captain was waiting for me on the Bridge.

"Good evening, Jenny, just thought I would catch up on how you are settling in before all this nonsense gets too serious," he explained.

"Quite well, Sir," I replied. "I have seen most of the divers, done a small inspection of the Diving Store, and found out that I also have a sports store. I have visited several of the messes and had a long chat with Chief Byrne."

"Good man, Chief Byrne," he added. "Willing to do anything he can to help with the smooth running of all departments and not only his own. Jenny, do you have any questions or are you happy to continue what you are doing and getting yourself settled in?"

"I am fine right now," I answered.

"Just make sure that you keep your eyes on anything and everything. If you see or hear anything unusual, do not hesitate to come forward immediately; it could be crucial," he said.

"I learned that lesson incredibly early on just after I started my training at MI6," I told him.

"Got a commendation for it too, I understand."

I just smiled coyly.

"If I am not on the Bridge or in the Wardroom, just come and bang on my door. Remember you are allowed access to the Wardroom at any time, and nobody will question you coming in or out," he said.

For a few moments, the Captain stared out of the Bridge windows, but all was dark and there was nothing to see.

"Jenny, we may need to go to Action Stations in the morning depending on the situation. I would like you up here on the Bridge at 0700 tomorrow. I think it would be good for you to see how diplomacy works, or not. Have you been issued with a set of Number 8's and anti-flash gear?"

"Yes, Sir," I replied.

"Wear it tomorrow when you come up here."

He looked thoughtful then carried on talking. "We need to get Dave Wilkins off as soon as possible, so I am hoping this distraction will be over quickly so we can get him away. He has a vitally important task to fulfil at Dartmouth. It may seem as if we have a lot of agents on this ship, but out in the fleet, we are very thin on the ground. You know all too well how long it takes to get someone vetted to join our elite group of watchers."

I smiled at him and replied, "Yes, I do, Sir."

I returned to my cabin; Sophie was lying on her bunk reading when I entered. She looked up and said inquisitively, "What did they want you on the Bridge for?"

Without any hesitation, I answered, "I haven't been allocated a place for Action Stations, so I am required to be up on the Bridge in the morning."

Sophie returned to her reading.

I unpacked my brand-new No 8's ready for the morning and then took a shower and climbed into my bunk. It had been a full day and so many things were on my mind.

✿✿✿

Despite all of that, I slept soundly and woke up at 0600 to the sound of the Tannoy: "Call the hands, call the hands, call the hands."

It was not as loud as I expected, but it was but loud enough to hear clearly. Sophie did not move and so I left her until I was dressed and then woke her up. She just moaned and sat up on the side of her bunk.

"Oh, is it morning already, just give me five minutes and I will be ready. Are you going for breakfast?"

I replied, "Yes, but I have to be on the Bridge at seven."

She rushed around the cabin and was ready in no time at all.

The Dining Hall was packed as everyone was preparing for a long day. There was nowhere to sit, so I grabbed a couple of pieces of toast and a mug of coffee and returned to my cabin, leaving Sophie waiting for a space at one of the tables.

I sat and finished off my toast while sipping my coffee, wondering what the day would bring. I was ready by 0630 and anxious to get up on the Bridge to find out what was happening.

On arriving on the Bridge, I was surprised to see so many people, many of whom I had not yet been introduced to. The Captain was out on one of the Bridge wings with a pair of binoculars, the Commander was standing next to him and they were in deep conversation as the Captain continued to stare through his binoculars.

The ship was almost stationary and was wallowing in a heavy swell. The Captain shouted through the Bridge doors, "Half ahead both engines."

The order was repeated down to the wheelhouse and the ship started to move forward slowly.

It was quite misty and difficult to see very much outside. The sun then came out and, almost by the second, the visibility started to improve. As the ship started its turn, we were almost blinded by the intensity of the early morning sun's glare. Dead ahead of us we could see the Portuguese tanker passing from left to right. Almost immediately, two small warships came into view, almost flanking the stern of the tanker.

The Navigating Officer, who spoke Iranian, was given instructions by the Captain. The Captain then shouted into the Bridge, "Officer of the Watch, switch on the cameras and recorder and pass me the loud hailer."

The two Iranian warships could clearly see us, and it was obvious that they were no match for our firepower, but it did not seem to faze them as they kept their positions on either side but to the rear of the tanker.

"Navigator, tell the Iranians to stand down," ordered the Captain.

In the meantime, the CRS (Chief Radio Supervisor) was in contact with London.

"Sir," shouted the CRS, "London says to warn them that further actions will follow and if they do not comply, fire a shot across their bows."

"Thank you, Chief," the Captain replied, and then said to the Navigator, "Pass the message from London."

The Navigator relayed the message through the hailer.

Several minutes passed and there was no change.

The Captain then shouted into the Bridge, "Starboard thirty."

"Starboard thirty, Sir," came the reply.

The ship made a right turn so that we were now running parallel to the tanker.

The Captain then shouted to the Officer of the Watch, "Hands to Action Stations, Gunnery crews close up."

The Officer of the Watch complied with the order.

The Captain grabbed a microphone that was in front of him and ordered, "Operations Room, this is the Captain, plot a course and speed to keep us half a mile to starboard of the nearest of the Iranian ships."

"Aye, aye, Sir," came the reply.

For the next ten minutes, orders from the Bridge to the Operations room and then relayed to the Wheelhouse continued until the Captain had the ship exactly where he required it to be.

The Gunnery Officer appeared at the Captain's side with a microphone in his hand and he was instructing one of the gun turrets.

He then said, "Stand by for the Captain's order."

"Lined up and ready to fire, Sir," came a voice from the Aimer.

"Navigator, give the Iranians one last warning," ordered the Captain.

The order to stand down was passed one more time and still, nothing happened.

The Captain wasted no time and he said loudly, "Fire one salvo."

There was an exceptionally large bang, followed by a whistling sound as the projectile punched its way out of the barrel and went accurately just several feet above the bows of both Iranian Ships.

The Captain waited for what seemed an age but was, in fact, less than a minute, to see if the Iranian warships had taken any action. There was none and they continued to remain close on the stern of the *Alvares Cabral.*

"Navigator, I think we have been patient long enough. Warn them that the next action will cripple one of their ships if they do not move away," said a very stern-faced Captain.

"In the meantime, Officer of the Watch, tell the Ferris team to man their stations."

The Captain spoke to all that were within earshot of him. "This will be the first time that we have used the Ferris for real, although I have seen it at the Gunnery School in practice. It is impressive and one hundred percent effective and right now we are the only ship in the fleet that has this capability. You will see shortly why it is called the Ferris."

There was complete silence for a couple of minutes as everyone was watching in anticipation of what came next. The Captain looked around, gave a forced smile to those around him and said, "Enjoy the show."

The Captain issued his directive again, "Gunnery Officer, let's do this now."

"Ferris team, the Captain is ready to give the order," barked the Gunnery Officer.

"Captain, the Ferris team is ready."

The Captain lifted the microphone to his face and said very slowly, "Fire Ferris."

There was a slight pause and then an incredible whooshing sound and two exceptionally large wheels catapulted away from the launcher and sped away from the ship towards the furthest of the two Iranian ships. The two wheels had a heavy wire cable linking them.

I was mesmerised standing there on the Bridge witnessing a first of its kind for the Royal Navy or anywhere else in the world. The two wheels accelerated as they travelled, and in the space of just a few seconds, covered the distance to the targeted Iranian ship. The wire separating the huge wheels, which were spinning incredibly fast, hit the ship's radio and radar installations. The wheels were dragged in by the wire and like a huge electric saw, completely decapitated most of the superstructure. Even from this distance, the noise was deafening as tons of metal were torn like twigs from a tree in a hurricane. The debris cascaded onto the deck and over the side into the ocean from the stricken Iranian ship.

Not a single person was injured in the operation, but the ship had been completely incapacitated.

The other Iranian ship veered off to port and departed the area immediately.

Now I knew why it was called the Ferris; the two huge wheels looked incredibly like two horizontal Ferris Wheels but moving at an unbelievable speed. The surgeon-like work that the two wheels did, and the absolute precision and skill, was a credit to the operators who did an incredible job.

The CRS was on the phone to London with a full report of what had transpired. London confirmed to him that due to the cameras and the recorder, they had been able to view and hear the complete event.

A few minutes later, a signal came from Admiralty in London with the simple words, "BZ *Dornik*, you did us proud."

(Bravo Zulu, also referred to as "BZ," is a naval signal, typically conveyed by flag hoist or voice radio, meaning "Well Done" in actions, operations, or performance.)

The Captain sent a signal to the *Alvares Cabral* tanker advising them that we would follow them for twenty-four hours just as a safety precaution and suggested that they returned to their original course. They did this and we tucked in behind them like a shadow.

Two hours later we launched our chopper to scout the area but there was no sign of any further ill intent by the Iranians. The chopper pilot reported that the Iranian ship that had fled from the area had returned to the stricken vessel and it seems they were trying to take it in tow.

While he was in the air, a message came from the Captain of the *Alvares Cabral* asking if the helicopter could fly over and pick up a package from them. The Chopper hovered over the ship and dropped a line down to them; a small container was hooked onto the line and was winched up.

The chopper landed and the pilot carried the small container to the Bridge and handed it to the Captain. Inside was a case of Glenfiddich Malt Whisky with just the words 'Thank you' scribbled on it.

We followed the *Alvares Cabral* until daylight the following morning and the Captain instructed the CRS to send a message to them saying that we were leaving them now. An exchange between the two ships continued for about ten minutes and we then veered off to starboard and back to safe anchorage at Diego Garcia.

✧✧✧

After the excitement of the previous day, I slept well that night, and early the next morning I was once more invited to the Bridge. I was back in my PT clothes and feeling far more comfortable. Dave Wilkins was dressed in his civilian clothes and had a few suitcases with him. He was leaving. He had a flight from Diego Garcia at nine that morning that would take him to Cyprus where he would get a flight back to Brize Norton in England and on to Dartmouth for the start of his new project. All those on the Bridge wished him well and he was whisked off by the Chopper. It would be many years before our paths crossed again and under very different circumstances.

Chapter 6. Real Work Begins

Over the next few weeks, I settled into shipborne life and got to know a lot of people onboard. Some I got to know better than others. Mick Byrne was a huge asset to me and helped me with getting the sports teams enthused and we did a lot of onboard circuit training and sports-specific training. A few diehard enthusiasts formed a small group of dedicated weight trainers.

The work that Sophie did with the Diving Store and the Safety Equipment was a credit to her, although at times she seemed to be absent-minded. She and Lula complemented each other and when we were diving, the two of them had everything ready to go for the whole team. At times when we only needed one or two divers, Lula was always the first to volunteer and she had far more diving minutes than any of the other divers.

Looking after the Diving Team and overseeing the Safety Equipment and being the Physical Trainer was very much a full-time job, and being an agent for the government all at the same time was onerous. I felt I could be doing more, but was hazarded by time constraints. At one of our regular meetings in the Wardroom, I mentioned my concerns to the Commander. I did not want him to think I was whinging, but was concerned I was not doing enough.

"There is an easy solution, I can get you an assistant who can be trained as a Trainee Physical Trainer. We have such a man; he is only just an Able Seaman, but we have already earmarked him for early promotion and later we might find ourselves involving him with other activities."

I smiled at Commander Mike Cheetham and said, "You must mean Dave Gibson; he is already helping me out with managing the sports store and the training."

"I am," said Mike. "Why don't I take him away from what he is currently employed in and give him to you as your full-time assistant."

"Thank you, that sounds great," I replied.

Mike smiled and said, "Good, consider it job done."

"Just one thing more, Jenny," he added. "We have confirmed that someone is sending some sort of signal from the ship, but with a ship this size, it is like looking for a needle in a haystack. The signals are infrequent, and their duration is not long enough for our technical team to focus on their location, so be extra vigilant as you move about the ship."

"I will, Mike, I will."

With the help of Dave Gibson, I was able to spend far more time going from department to department, mess to mess, cabin to cabin, and all the other places that people tend to congregate. I saw nothing unusual at all. At our regular meetings, it appeared that all the members were also doing the things that I was doing, and they too were frustrated at finding nothing.

The *Dornik* stayed at an anchorage close to Diego Garcia for a nearly three weeks while we had some new hardware placed in the Operations Room. This was top secret and gave us the ability to home in on chatter. We could pick up radio chatter signals for up to one hundred miles, and the chatter could be increased to full hearing capacity able to be understood in plain language. We had several linguists onboard which, between us, added up to over twenty languages plus a working knowledge of up to thirty more. Unfortunately, this was not going to help us with the signals that we were emitting from somewhere onboard that gave away our position.

During the time we were at Diego Garcia, we managed to play two games of soccer against the US Airmen's team. The rugby team had more difficulty trying to get a game. Most of the Americans played only American Football. However, with about an hour coaching session, Mick Byrne managed to get the American Servicemen to adapt their game. The referee was asked to be very lenient with the teams with regard to any infringements. It was not exactly rugby, but both sides had a great time, and many tales were told in the bar after the game.

I had also organised and carried out two dives on the bottom of the ship with all but one of the diving team. Bryan Root had twisted an ankle playing rugby against the Americans and the Doc had told him to rest it for a couple of weeks.

It felt good to get back in the water again; I had missed it during the long training in London. Lula went first and we traversed along the port side of the ship from the bows working our way to the stern. The water was warm and was noticeably clear. We could see many fish of different bright colours flirting with us as we passed by. Lula had a large red fish with black spots bumping into her mask; I think she was as curious of the fish as it was of her. It stayed almost attached to her until we reached the A-Bracket housing that gives support to the propeller shafts and protects the rudder.

Lula swam in and around the A-Bracket and gave me a thumbs up. She caught us up as we then traversed back along the starboard side. We spent several minutes clearing seaweed that had attached itself to the Sonar housing.

(Sound navigation and ranging is a technique that uses sound propagation (usually underwater, as in submarine navigation) to navigate, communicate with, or detect objects on or under the surface of the water, such as other vessels.)

After we had completed the full sweep of the ships bottom, we surfaced near the bows. The water under the ship's bottom was less than forty feet deep and I removed my mask and asked the divers if they would like to descend and go and look at the sand and shingle bottom below us.

We descended slowly, taking in the clear views all around. There was white sand and shingle directly beneath us, but as we traversed east, there were protrusions of coral sticking up. We turned and headed towards the south, away from the shore and had only travelled about fifty feet, when a steep drop fell away before us. The steep wall was covered in huge, sharp coral, cascading away like huge mountains down into the deep blue depths. The coral was covered in soft green and brown filigree seaweed that was swaying back and forth in the gentle swell. A plethora of fish of many sizes and a multitude of rainbow colours swam teasingly in and out of the coral columns. It was breath-taking and almost magical as it tried to entice us to venture further into its mysterious depths.

It had been an exhilarating swim and a great opportunity for me to be able to lead and interact with my diving team.

***

The following morning, we were suddenly on the move again. Sophie said that this happened frequently.

She added, "You had better get used to this, Jenny. Being a surveillance ship, we are always flitting from one place to another at the whim of our leaders in London. We rarely know where we are going, and if we are lucky, they tell us after we have been and gone. Sometimes not even that."

I responded the best I could saying, "I imagine with all the problems in the world today, it wouldn't be right for us to know everything. What we do not know, we can't tell."

"I suppose," she replied.

I went onto the upper deck where the sun was shining brightly on our stern and slightly to the starboard side. We were heading towards the northwest, I ascertained, hoping that my geography in relation to the sun was correct. We were returning the way we had gone recently when we went to rescue the *Alvares Cabral*. At the time, I had no idea that we were going much further than that.

Once more I was summoned to the Bridge. The Captain asked that a message be conveyed to the Commander, the Gunnery Officer, and the Chief Radio Supervisor, who were invited to meet us in his cabin in thirty minutes.

Before leaving the Bridge, Captain Crowe asked me to join him on the starboard Bridge wing.

"Jenny, we have a crucial project to do in the Yemen. The Islamic terrorists in that country are a threat to worldwide security and we need to install a listening station and access to the country right under their noses."

Mike Cheetham appeared on the Bridge and went out onto the Bridge wing where the Captain and I were talking. He backed off when he saw that we were in conversation, but the Captain beckoned him over to join us.

"Mike, I am just briefing Jenny on our classified penetration into Yemen. The rest of the senior team will be up soon, perhaps we had better adjourn to my cabin now," he suggested.

We made our way down to the cabin; the CRS was already in there and waiting for us. Although I had seen the CRS on several occasions, we had not formally been introduced; I did not even know his name.

The Captain apologised saying, "Sorry, Jenny, this is William Overton, Bill to anyone who is anyone." He smiled.

I shook hands with this giant of a man who had to be about six feet five inches tall. Although, his handshake contrasted with his size and was very gentle.

We waited several more minutes and the Gunnery Officer, Robin Hills, appeared. He had joined the Royal Navy as a boy seaman at HMS *Ganges* and was on the verge of becoming a Commander. He had been recruited into the Secret Service a little over ten years ago.

We all sat around the Captain's dining table and he started his briefing.

"Our conversation here is classified Top Secret and only a minimum of personnel need to know what we are doing. I have just told Jenny the basics, but we will now discuss it in more detail."

He laughed and said, "Mike here was a clearance diver many years ago and still manages a few dives here and there just to keep his hand in, although his qualifications are not up to date because of an injury sustained in a previous operation. Jenny needs to know that, because, Mike, you will be managing the dive from the ship and, Jenny, you will be leading the team in the water."

Mike and I nodded at each other.

The Captain continued, "Jenny, I want three of your best divers that you believe can be fully discreet to carry out this task and are able to competently complete this type of operation at night. I will get that list from you after the meeting. Bill, you will need to be listening for any chatter that may indicate a problem for our divers. Robin, using your best lookouts, you will need to be scouring all sides of the ship to observe any possible incursions from unfriendly forces. Any questions?"

"Yes, I have a question," said Robin. "Are we going to anchor the ship?"

The Captain replied, "No, we will be underway at all times, patrolling up and down at slow speed and the ship will be completely blacked out. No lights at all to be showing. The Ship's company will be told that we are doing a night exercise with the divers in the event of a real situation. They will not be told that it is a real situation."

He nodded at Robin and Bill and added, "I will brief you separately, but right now I need to speak to Mike and Jenny about the dive."

After they had gone, we discussed how the operation would be conducted. The dive would be carried out using the inflatable Gemini dinghy. The Captain's concern was who could drive the Gemini and remain completely discreet. I suggested that I drive the boat until we were close enough to the shore and then drop an anchor over the side and swim in the rest of the way.

"Jenny, you are going to have a lot on your plate. Are you sure that you can cope with the boat as well as the operation?"

I nodded and said an emphatic, "Yes."

Little did I realise at the time how fast things would deteriorate.

The Captain spoke again. "Jenny, can you tell me which divers you have in mind for this project. No written lists, this is where we have to rely completely on verbal communication so that nobody else can have any inkling of what we are doing."

"Yes, Sir, I thought I would use Lula Lewis, who is the most experienced diver, Steve Sells, and Bryan Root. I have checked all the logs and they have done more hours than the others and have proved themselves extremely professional."

"Good, but not a word until six hours before the dive."

I nodded.

This time when the Captain spoke, he became profoundly serious, "This will be your first operation and I feel like I am throwing you into the deep end. Let me explain the project and then after I have completed your brief, I want you to verbally repeat it back to me."

"Yes, Sir," I replied.

"The task itself is simple, however, it is fraught with danger and I cannot stress enough that your lives are more important than the job. If anything goes awry, get the hell out of there."

"Yes, Sir," I said.

"Your task is this: you will take a completely watertight alloy box that is light and easy to carry and bury it as near to the top of the bank above the waterline as you can. It contains a very high-powered listening device that can pick up chatter for up to half a mile and signals up to twelve miles. You will also have a folding pointed lightweight shovel to dig with. In addition, you will carry two arrow-shaped anchors that have a high-pressure explosive charge that will fire several feet into the bank just below the water and splay out so that they cannot be removed easily. They will have a six-foot long fluorescent polypropylene strop attached to each one. Repeat your instructions back to me."

It was not a difficult task to implement, and I repeated his instructions almost word for word.

"Now here is the underlying threat to its success. There is a known Islamic Terrorist training camp less than four hundred yards from your point of ingress and you must not underestimate the ability of your foe. They are ruthless and brutal, and to them, you are completely expendable. They have frequent searches of the immediate area of the camp, but they feel completely secure in the knowledge that nobody in their right mind would attempt a seaborne attack. Do you understand the risks? How do you feel about the operation?"

"A little apprehensive, but this is what I was trained to do. My only concern is briefing the team at such short notice before the event," I answered.

"Sorry, Jenny, we cannot afford to brief them too far in advance; that is how the cards are stacked, unfortunately. One more thing, you know what I am about to tell you is standard procedure, however, I must give you that warning again. If you or any of your team are captured alive, the British Government will deny all knowledge of your existence."

"I understand, Sir."

"One more thing, we go tomorrow night," he added.

I left the Bridge, and I could feel the butterflies in my stomach. I hoped that the confidence the team was putting in me was well-founded. Someone in my training had once said that if you felt nothing when faced with danger, then you were not human.

I knew that I needed to keep as busy as possible for the rest of the day. Sophie was not in the store and so I checked on all the equipment that I would need for the following night. I checked the flashlights and made sure that the batteries were fully powered. Some of the compasses were old and to be on the safe side, I opened four brand-new ones that were still sealed in their boxes.

The Gunnery Officer was going to supply the fluorescent rope strops and Commander Mike Cheetham would bring the encased radio. I found Steve Sells and told him that we were expecting the Captain to order a night dive soon and asked him to make sure that the Gemini Dinghy was fully inflated and ready to go. I told him it would probably be at extremely short notice and we must be completely prepared should he order it today.

Cheerfully, Steve Sells just grinned and said, "Will do, Boss, I'm on my way now."

The day seemed to drag on; I was both nervous and excited at the same time. I was sure in the fullness of time I would become accustomed to these operations, but the trepidation I felt was indescribable. A mixture of fear, thrill, emotion, suspense, and many other feelings all rolled into one. I felt as if I was on the edge of a precipice about to launch myself into the unknown. In reality, that is exactly what I was going to do.

***

Despite the events of the day, I slept surprisingly well and woke early in the morning, refreshed and ready for whatever the future had to bring. The Captain had set the start time as 2300. I was to ensure that they had eaten a substantial meal by at the latest 1630 and to assemble the team in the Wardroom by 1700. The briefing would take about an hour and then as far as the rest of the divers and the Ship's company were concerned, this was a night dive at the whim of the Captain to test the team's speed and capability. The rest of the divers who were not part of the operation would assist their colleagues in preparation for the night dive.

The day went according to plan and everything was in a state of immediate readiness. Sophie had helped me check all the diving equipment. She had been on the ship for quite some time and knew that the Captain had his whims and would throw exercises just to keep the crew on their toes, so today was not much different.

Sophie reminded me that he always checked the Diver's Main Log and to make sure that we had all the diver's personal diving logs ready for his inspection. I thanked her and made sure all the divers brought their logs with them.

At 1600, the complete diving team was in the Dining Hall having their dinner and wondering what was in store for them this evening. At 1645 there was an announcement over the ship's Tannoy.

"The following divers muster in the Wardroom Flat at 1700: Talbot, Lewis, Sells, and Root."

All the divers looked at each other, and Bryan Root chuckled and said, "I wonder what fun and games the Skipper has come up with now?"

The rest of them just laughed at Bryan but they were all wondering the same. If only they knew, I thought, if only they knew.

At 1700 hours, all four of us were waiting outside the Wardroom in the Wardroom Flat. At exactly 1700, Lieutenant Annette Saunders opened the door to the Wardroom and invited us in. Sitting at the large Wardroom table were the Captain, the Commander, and the Gunnery Officer who were the first of the Secret Service team that I had met initially on arriving on the ship. Also, there was the Chief Radio Supervisor and the Provost Marshall.

We were invited to sit. There were few smiles around the table, and it was a little unnerving. The Captain started his presentation, using an old-fashioned chalkboard to demonstrate the geography and topography of the area we would be working in. There was a hushed silence as he explained what we were required to achieve. He repeated each sentence slowly, making sure that all heads were nodding.

"Now let me make it abundantly clear that no details are to be shared with the other divers or any of the Ship's company. I know I am asking a lot of you all, but for our country's security and safety, it is imperative that you keep this to yourselves. The other divers will be led to believe that you are just carrying out a night operation exercise. We go at 2300, and if all goes according to plan, you should all be back in your bunks by 0300."

The mood was sombre and thoughtful among the team as they dispersed and went to their messes and cabins.

The problems would start soon enough. At 2100 there was a knock on my cabin door. The Provost Marshall asked me to go with him to his office.

"How quickly can you brief another diver?" he asked. "Lewis has been taken sick, she collapsed in the main passageway and she is being examined by the Doc."

"What is wrong with her?" I asked him.

"The Doc thinks it may be kidney stones," he answered.

"I think it is too late to brief someone right now, but I might task John Kidley to come with us and coxswain the Gemini dinghy. I will tell him to put the outboard motor on, we will only use it if we have to make a quick exit from the beach," I told him. "It will also be good to have another pair of hands on the paddles as we go in."

Wiggy said he would go straight up to see the Captain and brief him on what had transpired with Lewis and our slightly adjusted plan.

Although time was running short before our departure, I wanted to check on Lula Lewis and see how serious it was. The Doc said that she was now comfortable, but would be out of action for up to a week. She was the only patient in the sick bay and was awake but looking extremely sick. She had a deathly pallor and her skin felt very cold and yet she was sweating profusely. She smiled feebly and whispered, "I'm so sorry."

"You just get well; we will be back on board in no time," I told her reassuringly.

It was a little over an hour before our departure and I went straight down to the Diving Store. The diving team was already there and busy putting on their diving suits being helped by the rest of the team who were not taking part in this evening's exercise. John Kidley was helping Bryan Root to put on his suit, and I pulled him to one side and briefed him on the change of plan. He seemed quite pleased that he was being involved in tonight's operation.

Then he handed me a small plastic bottle and said, "Is this yours? It was lying on the floor of the store and I picked it up when I got here."

"No, it's not mine and doesn't have a name on it either," I replied.

I opened the bottle and inside were three small white pills. There were no markings on the pills and no indication of what they might be used for. At that moment, Commander Mike Cheetham arrived ready to supervise the night's events from the ship. I handed him the bottle of pills and asked him to hold on to them for me. He looked puzzled and I said, "I'll explain later."

We could see the lights of Yemen on our starboard side as we approached the entrance to the southern end of the Red Sea. As soon as we turned to starboard to enter the Red Sea, the ship would go dark. The only light that we would have on was a small blue, fluorescent light that we had in the Diving Store that could not be seen from any distance.

Steve Sells and Bryan Root hung a Jacobs ladder over the side and John Kidley lowered the dinghy over the side and secured it by ropes to a couple of cleats. Mike lowered the encased radio and two polypropylene strops and their anchors down into the boat.

Time now seemed to stand still as we checked each other's air bottles, gauges, headlamps, and masks. Our compasses were attached to our wrists and we each had a diver's knife. We all gave Mike a thumbs up and I said quietly, "Divers ready, Sir."

"OK, Kidley, off you go," said Mike.

John Kidley went down the Jacob's Ladder, carrying a small kedge anchor and a coil of rope to the boat and then held the boat tight against the ship's side as the rest of us descended into the boat. I was the last to go down.

It was quite bumpy as we sat in the dinghy waiting for our next order. We had barely been in the boat a minute or so and everything went dark. All the lights on board the ship were turned off. The only light we had were the dials of our luminous compasses, but it was enough. We all sat in complete silence as the ship turned sharp to starboard to enter the red sea. We hugged the coast of Yemen for about three miles and the ship's engines went quiet as we drifted slowly to our drop-off point. We heard the engines reverse as the ship came to a standstill.

Mike was leaning over the side, although it was so dark that we could not see him but just heard his low voice.

"Are you ready in the boat, Talbot?" he whispered.

"Yes, Sir," I whispered back.

"Then, you have a go, and good luck," he replied.

Steve Sells and Bryan Root were in the bows with John Kidley and I in the stern. The outboard motor was attached to the stern board but lifted out of the water and tightly secured.

I whispered to John, "As soon as we leave, make sure that the motor is down and ready for running."

"I will," he replied.

It took us about twenty minutes of hard paddling to reach the entry point. We could all see the tree that was our marker on the shore close to the water. We checked our compasses and set them to a course of 080 degrees, our return course to the boat would be 260 degrees. We were ready to go. We slipped over the side of the Dinghy into the tepid water of the Red Sea. It was refreshing after the exertion of paddling from the ship in a full diving suit.

John Kidley attached the long length of rope to the kedge anchor and lowered it over the side. The depth of water was only about twenty-five feet, and the anchor was quickly embedded on the sand and shingle seabed.

Bryan had the encased radio; Steve and I carried a rope strop each. A thumbs up from John in the boat and we submerged until we were swimming just a few feet above the seabed. We knew from the charts that the bottom was quite flat until we neared the shore, and then instead of a gradual beach incline, it was more like a river with a steep bank.

Although it was a dark night, the water was exceedingly clear, and it was easy to follow each other towards the shoreline.

I surfaced first, only about fifteen feet from the beach, and all looked clear and quiet, then Steve and Bryan surfaced. In just a few yards, the beach shelved up and we were standing in merely five feet of water. Keeping our heads just above the waterline, we scrambled in the shallow water towards the bank.

After reaching the bank, Bryan looked over the top and quickly dropped back down again. He whispered to us that there were quite a few lights a couple of hundred feet back from the bank and there appeared to be a gathering of people and the smell of food cooking. He then went back up the bank a little way and, using his diver's knife, started carving a hole in which to house the concealed covert remote listening device.

In the meantime, Steve and I moved to the bottom of the bank with one of the rope strops each. As instructed, we placed them about eight feet apart with the anchor points pressed into the clay and sandbanks. We both fired simultaneously, and apart from a dull thud, there was no other sound as the anchors buried themselves securely into the base of the bank.

I then checked on the radio that Bryan had buried into the bank near the surface of the water. The only tell-tale sign was the black-painted antenna that broke the surface of the water but was barely discernible, and you would have to know it was there to find it.

The hard part was done; it was now time to return to the boat. The journey back was simple enough and I surfaced a couple of times to make sure that the boat was where it should be. The first time I was unable to see it, but the second time I could see that we had drifted quite a way to the north of the boat and so we had to adjust our direction. We had not noticed the current on the journey to the shore, but it was quite strong on the return journey. It was hard making our way against the tide, and by the time we got to the boat, we were exhausted, and John had started to become genuinely concerned.

He was delighted to see us and helped us all into the dinghy. We did not hear it or see the boat coming, but just as we started to paddle back towards the ship, a huge spotlight came on, completely illuminating us. We had no idea what it was until we heard someone speaking in a foreign tongue through a loud hailer. I was the only one who spoke any Arabic, but I was unsure of what they wanted of us.

In the meantime, John had dropped the outboard into its running position and pulled the cord. It did not start first time but on the second pull, the engine burst into life. He turned the boat one hundred and eighty degrees and opened the throttle. There were shouts of anger from the boat which took several minutes to take chase. John zig-zagged the dinghy to take us out of the spotlight.

They could not see us, but it did not stop them from firing in our direction. John continued his zig-zag pattern but also moved to the right in a big arc. It was easy to see where they were, because they kept the big spotlight shining from side to side trying to get sight of us again. Then they suddenly cut their engines to see if they could hear us. John heard their engines sputtering and immediately cut the dinghy engine.

So, there we were playing cat and mouse as they tried to figure out our position. Earlier, the current had hindered us while trying to swim back to the boat, but now it was assisting us and taking us further away from them.

✳✳✳

In the meantime, onboard the Dornik, they had seen the spotlight from the boat and heard the machine gunfire. They were watching both boats on radar and the Captain, although fearful of what was happening to his divers, knew that this was just a small Arab Dhow with a big engine but had no radar capability and if his divers could continue the evasion tactics then the Dhow would not find them.

The Captain moved the ship so that it would end up ahead of the dinghy and, without showing any lights, they would almost run into the *Dornik*. John Kidley was a good seaman, and he knew how to handle a boat. It was most fortunate that he was in the boat and not Lula Lewis; the outcome might have been completely different.

***

It was another three hours before a hungry, weary, traumatised team of divers was finally pulled from the water by their colleagues.

I was the last one to be hauled up to the ship from the dinghy. I stumbled as I landed on the solid deck, saluted Mike, grinned, and said, "Mission successfully completed, Sir."

He answered, "Well done, team. At one stage, we were very fearful of the outcome, but your courage and the expertise of an incredible coxswain resulted in an outstanding, successful operation. Thank you to all of you and especially to you, Kidley, for bringing them home safely. The Captain says he will debrief you in the morning. Go and get a shower, breakfast, and a few hours' sleep. The Chief Chef is in the Galley and he has prepared a hot breakfast for you all personally."

As we all trundled off to get a hot shower, daybreak was just showing in the east. Streaks of red clouds were strewn across the open sky and a scorching red ball hung like an orb to greet the day.

***

The Captain called us to his cabin for a debriefing at midday, thinking that we would have had enough sleep by then. The debriefing did not last long, and he offered his sincere congratulations on our successful mission that could have ended in disaster. He confirmed that the radio was already picking up valuable information.

"It is imperative that you keep the details of your sensitive operation to yourselves and do not share it with any of your shipmates or it could compromise future operations. You all worked exceptionally well, and, Kidley, I believe that you quite probably saved the lives of your team. Well done. If there are no questions you are free to go about your duties. Talbot," he added, "I would like you to remain for a few moments."

After the others had gone back below, he said, "Thank you, Jenny. This was your first real active operation, which you handled very professionally. Unfortunately, our enemies never stop trying to harm us and our allies, which brings me to your next project. Our leaders in London think it is too soon for you to be given a project of this magnitude, but all your trainers, including our ship's team, believe it is within your capabilities. One of the deciding factors is not just your outstanding skills, which you have already shown, but we need an agent who is fluent in both Spanish and French and you fit the bill perfectly. I have recommended that you are the agent for this task. I am not authorised to divulge the details of the operation just yet because there are many other factors, which include the support package that needs to be in place to protect you. Be patient and I will send for you in due course."

He stopped for a moment in thought, then continued, "In the meantime, go and get the crew fit and continue to keep alert to anything you see that doesn't seem right."

"Thank you, Sir," I replied.

"Jenny, I did say that we can be on first-name terms when we are on our own or with the senior team," he added.

"I know you did, but I feel more comfortable calling you, Sir, so that I cannot slip up at the wrong time. Perhaps when I have been part of the team for some time, I will be able to cope with it better," I answered him.

He gave a broad smile and just nodded.

I left the Captain's cabin and went looking for Mike Cheetham. He was at the Diving Store, talking to the complete diving team, telling them that it had been an extremely successful night exercise, and everyone had done their job well. I smiled at his deception and at the members who had been on the operation and were fully aware that it had not been an exercise but something far more menacing.

As soon as Mike had finished talking, I took him to one side.

"Do you still have that bottle of pills?" I asked him.

"I do," he said handing them over to me. "Is something wrong?"

"I am not sure, it may be nothing," I replied. "I will let you know as soon as I make a few enquiries."

I put the pill bottle in my pocket and went to my cabin. Sophie had just come out of the shower and was busy drying her hair.

I pulled the bottle from my pocket and asked her, "Do you know who these belong to?"

For just a fleeting second, I thought that Sophie looked nervous; her eyes did not make contact with mine.

"Yes, I think they are Lula's indigestion pills," she answered.

There was nothing wrong with someone taking indigestion pills, but something did not seem right. My suspicions had been aroused and I knew I needed to find out more. Sophie turned away and continued drying her hair.

I made my way to the sick bay to enquire about Lula's health. She was sleeping and it gave me a good opportunity to chat with the Doc. I did not mention my suspicions about the tablets, but asked him if he was able to determine what they were for and what their make-up was. His reply was not all that helpful and so I pocketed the pills again.

"How important is it?" he queried.

"I found them under suspicious circumstances and need to know what they are," I replied.

He looked thoughtful for a moment and then said, "When we have an opportunity to go ashore, I can get them analysed for you; just leave me one of the tablets and I will do my best." He then smiled at me.

I thanked him and went to see Mike to explain the situation and tell him who I believed the tablets belonged to. We discussed it for several minutes and he said, "Unless we find something to the contrary, you are right. We need to get a medical analysis first. I will mention it to the Captain. Keep a close eye on her and if you get the chance, try to get a look at her mobile phone."

"Will do," I replied.

The rest of the day was spent at the Diving Store with Sophie and the divers who had been on last night's excursion. We checked all the equipment that we used, and John Kidley washed the outboard motor down with fresh water and cleaned the inside of the dinghy, which had a surprising amount of shingle and sand in the bottom.

I took a stroll down to the sick bay to check on Lula. The Doc said that she had taken a little food but was now asleep and preferred me not to wake her. I agreed with him, but he still let me go in and just look. Her mobile phone was sitting on her bedside table. I glanced around, but the Doc had taken the opportunity to slip down to the canteen while I was in there. Lula was lying on her side and I picked up her phone and took mine out of my pocket.

During my training, I was taught how to easily transfer contacts from my mobile phone Android to Android using Bluetooth, Wi-Fi Direct, and via SD card. I could also transfer all her recent messages. It took less than two minutes to get all her contacts and her messages.

I replaced her phone and waited until the Doc returned from the canteen loaded down with washing powder, razor blades, confectionery and cigarettes, and a few other items. I thought it a bit strange that he was a Doctor and a smoker. Most doctors try to convince people that smoking is bad for you.

I found Bill Overton in the Operations Room and explained to him about my investigation of Lula Lewis and that I had copied all her contacts and all recent calls and texts onto my phone.

"Bill, can you investigate these for me and determine if there is anything suspicious on her phone?" I asked him.

"Of course," he replied.

"There are a couple of things that do not seem to be right." I also told him about the tablets.

"I will get onto it straight away," he said. "If I find anything, I will tell the Captain and I am sure he will want to see you immediately."

***

The ship was now traversing through the Red Sea and the Captain used the journey to carry out several operational exercises. We had a few exercises, which included lifeboat, boiler fire, serious injury, with yet another ship's bottom search by the ship's divers. He kept us extremely busy, and finished the week with an oil RAS: Replenishment at Sea. This is when a supply ship comes alongside, and we get replenished with oil for our boilers. This is done whilst both ships run parallel to each other at about twenty knots. This can be quite treacherous and needs a skilful helmsman at the ship's wheel.

We were about to enter the Suez Canal when the Captain asked for me to go and see him immediately.

I found him on the Bridge, and he said, "Did you find anything on your last dive, Jenny, because we believe that we have narrowed our search of the strange signals coming from low down at the rear of the ship."

"No, I didn't," I answered him.

"Well, we are about to enter the Suez Canal. As soon as we exit into the Mediterranean, I will find a suitable place to stop the ship and I would like you to take a dive on your own and check out the area at the stern thoroughly. It might be a good idea to do it after midnight so that nobody else can see what you are doing. I will ask Mike to come and keep watch over you. OK, here is Mike now."

"Jenny and I were just talking about you, Mike," he said.

"Obviously, nothing good," replied Mike with a grin.

The Captain then told him about our discussion and Mike agreed with the plan and said that he would make himself available.

The Captain spoke again. "Once your dive is over, I would like you and Mike to come to my cabin to discuss the mission that I mentioned to you briefly the other day. It is going to take some extensive planning and liaison with the MI6 team, and it might be for an extended period. The intel that we can gather will be priceless, but it will be a dangerous mission. The priority being to keep you as safe as possible."

"Yes, Sir," I replied.

That evening I took a group of about twenty enthusiastic keep-fitters that used to turn out regularly for my daily workouts. Several of them did not play any sports, but they really enjoyed keeping themselves fit. Of the regulars, nearly all of them were over thirty years old. The only two regulars that were under twenty-five were my divers Brian Root and Steve Sells.

At about 1800 we entered the Suez Canal at Port Suez. The Suez Canal connects Port Said on the Mediterranean Sea with the port of Suez on the Red Sea and provides an essentially direct route for the transport of goods between Europe and Asia. The Canal is approximately one hundred miles long, and about a thousand feet wide at its narrowest point. Of course, we were going the other way.

I had heard about the Gully men who were lithe and agile Arabs who would swarm up the ship's side using ropes and netting to try to get aboard every ship. The Captain was kind enough to have a few nets placed over the side of the ship to give the Gully men a sporting chance of earning a few dollars. Cruise liners would allow them to come aboard to perform, sell, or earn money in a thousand different ways.

However, military vessels would not allow them over the guard rails, and so they peddled their wares and stage performances hanging precariously over the ship's side and as close to deck level as possible. One famous Gully man made a living producing baby chicks from everywhere on his person and yours. Many souvenirs and gifts were bought from these men to take home for family and friends. It was a lot of fun to watch all these characters hustling the ship's company to make a sale from their almost impossible position over the ship's side.

It takes about thirteen hours travelling at about eight miles an hour to complete the journey through the canal. Commander Mike Cheetham called me up to the Wardroom to talk to him as we were nearing the end of our Suez Canal journey.

"Jenny, the Captain is going to take the Ship into a bay close to Cyprus and anchor for forty-eight hours. Royal Airforce Base (RAF) Akrotiri is in the south of the island, near the city of Limassol. The plan is to anchor the ship close to Akrotiri and Limassol and grant shore leave to those not required for duty.

"The RAF are going to provide a few launches to transport the ship's company who want recreation shore leave to get to and from the shore. We will also launch all our ship's boats to allow the largest number to have some leave. The Captain has decided to grant shore leave to as many as possible and only keep an absolute minimum onboard. This will give us the opportunity for you and me to carry out a night dive without too many people around."

I smiled at him and said, "That sounds like fun. Mike, the only thing that bothers me is that Sophie likes to spend a lot of time in the Diving Store, and I am concerned that she may not wish to go ashore and might disrupt our plans."

"Leave that to me. I will speak to the Provost Marshall and ask him to get her an invitation to the RAF Sergeants' mess along with a few others so that she will not be suspicious."

I nodded in agreement with him.

"One more thing, can you and Able Seaman Gibson liaise with the helicopter pilot who will fly you to Akrotiri for you to organise sports for as many people as possible. As soon as we exit the canal, make sure that the pilot is ready to fly you to RAF Akrotiri. I will get the CRS to contact them and ask them to be ready to receive you and give all the assistance they can. They are used to this as it is a frequent occurrence from many other ships of the fleet visiting them. You have a busy time ahead of you. You will dive tonight while everyone else is partying ashore. Sorry, Jenny," he added.

I looked at him and said, "This is what I was trained for and I am happy to do all of these things, including the adrenaline rush." I smiled with excitement.

∗∗∗

By 0700 the following morning, Dave Gibson and I were up on the flight deck waiting for the pilot. He arrived and gave us a thumbs up and we climbed into the chopper, but not before he had attached the identity DORI on the front. We heard a message from the Operations Room: *On take-off, make your heading 065 degrees.*

After arriving at RAF Akrotiri, a young Sergeant took us straight to the Gymnasium where we were greeted by two Physical Training Instructors. The first order of the day was coffee and then we sat with them and organised some games for the day. The most important was to see if rugby and football were a possibility. They were very keen to put out a side for both games. One of the Instructors said that there was not a lot of local opposition to play and so they would drop everything to get a game when any ships came in.

They also made available six squash courts and hoped they might have enough to players to make it into a match but if not, we could make use of the courts anyway. They had several competitive tennis players and would have a strong group to make up six or eight pairs by the time the ship arrived. They also had a good indoor and outdoor hockey team. The indoor game was with a puck and basically a free for all, which sounded like a lot of fun, but the outdoor hockey would be a proper hockey game for serious players.

The Akrotiri team were top of the local hockey league and we hoped we could get a team together. I assured them that we had enough players to participate although with being at sea for such a long time, they were not match fit. The older of the two instructors told them that his team liked to win, so playing an unfit team was good for their ego to have yet another win under their belts. Dave Gibson grinned at them and told him that they would not get an easy win because he was the team captain, and the ship would put up a good fight, nevertheless.

By the time we had put together a comprehensive sports programme, including a cross country competition, it was mid-morning and we were invited to the Sergeants' mess for coffee. We then returned to the ship, which by now was a lot closer, and it only took about fifteen minutes and we were back on the flight deck.

I called together all the sports team captains and promulgated the sports programme to them. They were all delighted to be able to get out and get some real activity, having been cooped up on board for many weeks and only my sports fitness to sustain them physically.

It was a hectic but enjoyable day. I met up with Mike Cheetham briefly to update him on the day and that I would be going ashore with the teams and would be back on board early in preparation for the night's dive.

He grinned and said, "Please don't get injured today."

"Don't worry, Mike, I am not taking part in anything likely to get myself injured. Just in the cross country which will give me a good workout," I responded.

At 2230 the ship was like a ghost town; the sports teams had a great day, winning the rugby and the soccer but losing the hockey by one goal – no disgrace at all. I came second in the cross country and it was a free for all in the tennis and squash with arguments over who had won overall. Everyone had a great day and many of them were going back to the camp that evening to partake in a few alcoholic beverages at the Sergeants' bar.

The rest of the crew had disappeared in the direction of Limassol and would be letting their hair down for the evening.

Mike had put a chain across and a sign up on both sides of the upper deck saying: No Entry, Stores Delivered. A couple of tugs had been alongside during the day and delivered food stores for the ship and Mike had intentionally left them on deck to be put away the following day so that nobody was allowed anywhere near the stern of the ship. This would allow me to dive unobserved by curious members of the ship's company.

By the time I was down at the Diving Store, it was 2330 and Mike was already there. Between us, we carried a Jacob's Ladder, secured it to a large cleat on the port side of the ship adjacent to the Diving Store, and dropped it over the side. I quickly put on my diving suit and Mike helped me secure my neck ring. I had a headlamp attached to my head and Mike had also brought a handheld waterproof flashlight which I could easily slip inside my diver's belt.

Fifteen minutes later I started to descend the ladder. It took me several minutes to acclimatise to the dark. I stayed at the bottom of the ladder, half submerged, until I had cleared my mask of condensation and then with a thumbs up from Mike, who was leaning over the side, I slipped underneath the surface of the water. I turned on my headlamp and started swimming towards the stern of the ship, just under the surface.

Despite it being the Mediterranean, the water was quite cold, and I was glad that I had my dry diving suit on. I could have opted for a wet suit but had no idea how long I would be down. I started to descend towards the propeller shaft and had a bit of a scare as I disturbed shoals of small fish that blasted their way past me. They had been feeding off the seaweed and moss growing from the ship's bottom.

Just about everyone who has dived at night has seen little flashing lights in the water. Usually, this comes from small organisms, but several marine creatures can make their own glow. This is produced by a chemical reaction called bioluminescence, like the way that fireflies light up. There was a myriad of them tonight and it was quite a light show.

I sat across the shaft and looked all around for several minutes using just my headlamp. Because of the long period we had spent at sea, and being stationary many times, there was a large build-up below the waterline of shellfish, seaweeds, and other organisms. This causes drag, which slows the affected craft and increases its fuel consumption. It also increases carbon dioxide emissions by ten to fifteen percent.

The divers can clear some of it, but the task is too great to have any real effect, and so whenever the ship docks, antifouling needs to be carried out. Tonight, however, it was quite difficult to see the ship's bottom clearly because of the build-up. I was told that there was a new system that would be fitted the next time the ship had a refit that would carry out the task of antifouling twenty-four hours a day automatically using a system called ultrasonics.

Unfortunately, that was not going to help me now. I had initially thought that it might be quite an easy task to search the stern of the ship, but I spent a lot of time pulling long strands of sticky and sometimes almost unbreakable strands of seaweed from the ship's bottom. It was slow progress, but I methodically searched inch by inch back and forth across the ship. During the first hour, I had found nothing of interest and needed a change of scenery, so I started on the screw area. It was very dark in the recesses of the A-Bracket, and I had to use my flashlight, which slowed down my progress quite a lot.

My air tank was starting to deplete now quite rapidly, and I knew I would have to surface very soon and probably arrange for another dive. I was starting to feel a bit disappointed. I thought I could make a final search around the propeller shaft itself and dropped underneath it. Almost immediately, I spotted an area underneath the shaft and behind a clamp, which was one of the many that supported the shaft. This area was about two inches in diameter and my flashlight picked up the area that appeared to have a lot less growth than the rest of it.

I pulled myself in close to take a better look, and could see something that was about crown-sized. My flashlight made it glint in the dark, gloomy shadows. I took my knife out of its sheath and touched the surface of the circular disk. It was not a jolting shock but just a gentle buzz that sent a tingle up my arm. Initially, it made me jump back, not because it hurt, but it was unexpected. I immediately realised it was extremely low voltage and placed the point of my knife behind this disk and it came off very easily. I ascertained that it was magnetised and with the low level of electricity, it stuck easily to the steel hull of the ship. Although only crown-sized in diameter, it was just over a quarter of an inch thick.

My air gauge read zero and I knew I needed to surface very soon before I found myself in trouble. I carefully secured this coin-sized disk and made my way to the surface. Mike was directly above me and looking quite concerned. He gave a visible sigh of relief as I pulled myself up the ship's side on the Jacob's Ladder.

He had a smile on his face and said, "You worried me, Jenny, what did you use for air?"

"What? Didn't I tell you I was half mermaid?" I smiled back.

After the long dive and almost running out of air, I almost tumbled back onto the deck as I reached Mike. He grabbed my arm to assist me to my feet.

I fumbled in my knife sheath and, looking extremely happy with myself, produced the disk. I could see his delight when he saw it.

"What is that?" he asked excitedly.

"Not sure," I replied, "but it shouldn't be there."

Mike then said, "Jenny, go and get your diving kit off and then have a hot shower and off to bed. It is almost 0300 and you need to get some sleep. Quite a few people have already returned from shore so be careful when you go down below."

I knew that Sophie would be back in her bed by now and so knew I needed to be careful just in case she woke up when I entered our cabin. I made sure that the Diving Store looked the same as it did before my dive. After entering the cabin quietly, I was in the shower in just a few moments. I was in my bed and just about to turn off my bedside light when I heard Sophie say, "Where did you go, and did you have fun?"

"Yes, I did," I lied quickly knowing that I was becoming a lot more proficient at lying since I had become a part of MI6. It was a matter of survival and lying proficiently could make the difference between life or death on some occasions.

"The RAF Sports Officer invited me up to the Officers' mess for a few drinks. Then I was stuck on the jetty for nearly an hour waiting for a boat to collect me."

Sophie just sighed and turned over and went back to sleep.

***

I fell asleep quickly after that and woke up when Sophie gave me a shove at 0815.

"The Commander has just sent a message to ask you to go up to the Bridge with a report of how the sports day went yesterday. I hope you have written something for him. And be quick; he is waiting," she said.

I groaned and jumped out of my bed and dressed quickly.

Mike was pacing up and down on the Bridge and invited me to go out onto the port Bridge wing. I started to talk to him about yesterday's sports, but he brushed it aside.

"We have more important matters right now," he said urgently. "There are a few things that need further investigation. I have spoken with the CRS and the Captain and we have concluded that Lula is either innocent and we have jumped to the wrong conclusions, or she is a provost of deception and exceedingly ruthless and clever. The metal object that you recovered is, without doubt, a transmitter of some sort. However, we are unable to ascertain its origin; all we know is that it is giving off a signal and pinpointing our position all the time. As for her mobile phone, that was also very deceptive. She calls her mother at home about once a week and the number checks out. She only has one other number stored on her phone and we are unable to source its origin. The CRS sent the details on to head office and they have reached a blank. When you try to call that number, a female voice says to *please enter your pin*. Our top people are still trying to crack it. We are stumped, Jenny."

I was as equally confused as he was and was not sure what to say.

"Has the transmitter been disabled?" I asked him.

"No, not yet, we are still trying to find the source," he replied.

"I have an idea. Why don't you disable it and then let me replace it on the bottom of the ship in the same place. If it is someone on board, either Lula or someone else, we need to place an underwater camera somewhere near its location and monitor it every time we stop or organise a few more dives with the team," I suggested.

"That's a great idea, we will do just that."

"I will go down to the sick bay and check on Lula's condition and also see if the Doc has discovered any more details about those tablets we found," I added.

Mike continued, "Alright, Jenny, I will inform the rest of our team about your ideas and the Captain will adjust our itinerary accordingly so that you can get more operations with the diving team."

I took my leave from Mike and left him on the Bridge waiting for the Captain to appear. I suddenly realised that I was very hungry after last night's operation and needed a good breakfast, so made my way down to the Dining Hall. After a hearty cooked breakfast and coffee, I felt much better and headed to the sick bay.

The Doc was out on his rounds tending to any sick bodies onboard, so I walked through into the small ward at the rear. I pulled open the curtain and saw Lula sitting on the bed and looking a lot better.

She looked up and saw me standing there and said, "Hi, Jenny, thank you for looking in on me; hopefully, the Doc will release me later today if my health continues to improve."

"Oh, that is good news," I responded. "I don't suppose you will be well enough to dive for a few days, will you?"

"The Doc says I should be fit to dive in a day or two providing I am still improving," she answered.

"Did he find out what was wrong with you?" I asked, trying to be as casual as possible.

"He thinks it might have been a grumbling gall stone or irritable bowel syndrome; I have a history of both," she responded.

"That's great news that you are improving, because the Captain says that he intends to keep the diving team busy over the next few weeks and I definitely need your valuable input and participation," I enthused.

The ship was already steaming west along the Mediterranean and we should be in the vicinity of Malta within a few days. I went up onto the upper deck to get a breath of fresh air. I was still tired from the activities of the last few days and needed to blow the cobwebs away.

The sea looked so calm and peaceful as I wandered along the upper deck towards the bows. I went to the furthest point possible at the bows and looked over the front of the ship down at the water. What a sight: there were four beautiful silver dolphins, two on either side of the bows diving in and out of the water and keeping pace with the ship. Each time they appeared, a considerable amount of spray burst from them into the beautiful sunshine causing a rainbow effect as the sun shone through the spray.

Just a few yards away to the port side of the ship, there was a small shoal of flying fish jumping parallel to the ship and keeping pace with it. They are fascinating to watch as they use their elongated pectorals to catch updrafts of air and sail above the water for five or six hundred feet before dropping into the water all at a similar time and then propelling themselves back into the air to continue the process again and again. Although they are a spectacular sight, historically they learned this skill to avoid predators such as marlin, tuna, mackerel, and swordfish. It did not matter to me why they did it, it was joyous to see, and along with the dolphins could keep an audience spellbound for long periods.

I stopped and chatted to a few of the Ship's company; some looked the worse for wear having overindulged the night before. Most of them were delighted that they had been given an opportunity to play one game of sport or another. Most of them thanked me for the effort I had gone to organising the games at such short notice.

Lula was released from the sick bay later that afternoon, although I was not aware until that evening at about 2000. I went for a walk on the upper deck after dinner and was surprised to see the lights on in the Diving Store. As I approached, I could see that the door was slightly open and heard the sound of raised voices coming from inside. My first inclination was to barge in and find out what was going on, but instead, I stopped short as I heard Lula shout at whoever else was in the store.

"I can't do this anymore," she said. "You need to let him know that this is becoming very scary now and I want no more of it."

I immediately recognised the other voice when she spoke. It was Sophie, the storekeeper, and the girl with who I shared a cabin with.

"It's not that easy, Lula, you are in far too deep to pull out now," she said threateningly.

Instead of going in, I realised that this was something incredibly crucial to the investigation and it seemed to be bigger than any of us had imagined. I pulled back and listened for as long as I could, standing completely still.

Sophie continued talking in a threatening manner.

"Lula, you have been paid a lot of money, so what do you think will happen to your mother when the money dries up? Who do you think will pay for her treatment? You also know of my involvement and other people are also reliant on your compliance. You cannot stop; they will not let you."

Lula went completely silent and did not seem to know how to respond; she appeared to be in over her head.

I listened for several more minutes and knew I needed to slip away and let someone know what I had heard. This was the first time I had ever gone straight to the Captain's cabin door without invitation. Annette Saunders answered my knock and invited me into the cabin. He was on the phone and turned in his chair and signalled for me to sit down. Annette asked if I would like coffee or a cold drink. I put my thumbs up to her and said, "I would love a cup of coffee, please."

"One cup of coffee coming up," she said and disappeared into the small kitchen.

By the time she came back with my coffee, the Captain had just put the phone down.

"Hello, Jenny, I don't get to talk to you often these days, what can I do for you?"

I looked at Annette Saunders and then back to the Captain.

"It is alright, you can speak freely in here. By the way, you did a great job with the sports team in Cyprus and everyone onboard are chanting your praises. You seemed to have settled in extremely well and made a great impression," he said beaming.

I offered a quiet, "Thank you."

I then proceeded to tell him of the conversation I overheard between Lula Lewis and Sophia Lynch. He looked profoundly serious and then called for Annette Saunders who had gone to the kitchen in the interim.

"Annette, contact the Provost Marshall and tell him I need to see him immediately in my cabin."

"Very well, Sir," she replied.

He picked up a microphone and said, "Bridge, this is the Captain. Is the Commander on the Bridge? Tell him to come to my cabin immediately."

"Yes, Sir, he heard you and is on his way."

Mike Cheetham bustled into the cabin and looked at me and then the Captain inquisitively.

"Mike, we have a situation. Jenny, repeat what you have just told me."

I was about to respond when the Provost Marshall came in.

"Right, Jenny, let's hear your story once more." Captain James John Crowe was on his feet and pacing back and forth as I told the story of what I had heard from outside the Diving Store.

All three of them were looking gravely serious when I had finished; the Captain turned to the Provost Marshall and said, "Wiggy, find out where Lewis is and invite her down to your office; try not to alert her to anything until you have her safely in your custody. Interview her, and when you have finished, bring your report back to me and make sure that she is locked away securely in the cells."

"Will do," he replied gravely, and left the cabin.

The Captain continued, "Well done, Jenny. Fortunately, they did not see you from the Diving Store, so your cover is not blown. Once we have all the information extracted from them, we will then take further action if anyone else is involved."

I returned to my cabin and Sophie was listening to the BBC World Service on the radio and was seemingly unaware that there was an investigation in progress.

"Anything interesting?" I asked light-heartedly.

"Yes," she said. "I was just listening to the News from London; apparently a large network of terrorists has been arrested and charged with acts of terrorism. They were planning a massive bomb threat on churches and clergy in the London area. Over sixty people have already been arrested and they are expecting more arrests soon. They said it was the biggest terrorist plot since World War II to be uncovered in Great Britain."

I did not know how to respond and just said, "Wow."

It was getting late, and I told Sophie that I was going to take a shower and go to bed. I told her it had been a hectic couple of days, and I needed a good sleep. I thought that if anyone needed me, they would send for me.

***

It was about 1100 the following day before I heard anything. It came as dramatically as it always did. The Tannoy announced, "Physical Trainer to the Bridge."

Overall, the ship's company seemed a lot more relaxed and satisfied that many of them had been given the opportunity to participate in some sports. Others were simply happy that they got to go ashore and let their 'hair down'.

I made my way quickly to the Bridge wondering what had transpired since the events of yesterday. Robin Hills, the Gunnery Officer, was just coming down from the bridge and we met as I went up.

"Jenny, come with me to the Captain's cabin."

When we got there, Annette Saunders quickly ushered us inside.

Sat at the Captain's table were the Captain, the Chief Radio Supervisor, Provost Marshall, and the Commander.

The Captain said, "Jenny, Robin, good morning, please take a seat."

He looked profoundly serious as he continued. "What I am about to divulge is extremely serious and may affect our future program and any actions that we take. A lot has happened since yesterday and, to be honest, I have had to deal with many things, but this has shocked me, and I know it will shock all of you."

He looked around the table and sighed heavily and said, "Regrettably, we have been compromised. Yesterday Jenny overheard a disturbing conversation between Lula Lewis and Sophia Lynch that resulted in Wiggy taking two of his Regulation Petty Officers to arrest Lula Lewis and confine her to the cells for further investigation. On completion of his initial investigation, Sophia Lynch was then also arrested and confined to a cell."

He stopped talking for a few moments, and before he resumed, asked Annette Saunders to bring us a pot of hot coffee. She was well prepared and within a few minutes returned with coffee for all of us.

"Let me carry on. Wiggy will continue to interview these two women today and after that, they will be transferred ashore by helicopter and ultimately back to England to be interrogated by someone from MI6. Now, our conversation must not go any further than this room because we do not know how high this corruption may go. I had every reason to believe that all our trained agents were beyond reproach. But here is the most shocking news of all: Lewis and Lynch were recruited as enemy operatives by none other than the previous Diving Officer, Dave Wilkins."

There was total silence in the room as the Captain let his words sink in.

"I have sent a highly confidential signal to our handlers in London advising them of the situation; they will deal with Wilkins and try to find out who else is involved on board. It is good that we have intercepted this traitor before he does any more damage at Britannia Royal Navy College and recruits any more enemy operatives. As of right now, we do not know which country is responsible, however, we could take a good guess."

Everyone in the room was thinking the same thing although Iran was not mentioned.

The Captain spoke again saying, "Jenny, you have only been on the *Dornik* for a very short time and already you have become an invaluable member of our team; thank you from all of us, and well done."

There was a nodding of heads and a warm round of applause from the team at the table.

I responded with a quiet, "Thank you. May I ask a question and also make a suggestion?"

The Captain replied, "Of course, what's on your mind?"

"Can we still return the transmitter/receiver on the ship's bottom with it still in operation mode? Now that you know exactly where it is, could Bill create a triangulation point to assess its exact origin? For example, as soon as the enemy ping us to find our position, we could take a bearing and then say, travel to the north of the Mediterranean somewhere near the south of France and wait for them to ping us again. Then we take a reading and then take the ship south to, for example off the Algerian coast and wait for yet another ping. Yes, they would know where we are, but we would have three bearings to pinpoint them. Then we switch it off."

There seemed to be a nod of approval from around the table and Bill said, "Yes, I think we could do that. Good idea."

The Captain said, "Let us get back to work and be extra vigilant while Bill and I work out a plan of action."

"Jenny, you go and liaise with Mick Byrne and tell him to find you another appropriate Diving Store and Safety equipment operator. By now, the whole ship will be aware that Lewis and Lynch have been incarcerated, but they will not know why, and we must try to make sure that they do not find out. I will come up with a plausible reason for their detention and broadcast it as soon as I can fabricate something believable." He gave a wry smile.

Mick Byrne wasted no time in finding me a replacement, in fact, it was not a difficult task. He promised to take care of the training for the Safety Equipment which would take him just a few days.

He grinned at me and said, "With regards to the Diving Store, I think you will find him already acquainted with the diving equipment."

I looked at him, puzzled. "Alright, Mick who is it?" I asked.

He continued smiling and said, "I think you will be pleased with my choice; would you be happy with John Kidley?"

I could not have agreed more and nodded my assent.

John Kidley was only an Able Seaman, but the job he was being offered was for someone of at least a Leading Seaman or even a Petty Officer status. Of course, he could not jump from AB to PO in a single move, but after speaking to Mike Cheetham, we had him promoted immediately to a Temporary Leading Seaman with the promise of a very quick confirmation to Leading Seaman within three months.

I was sitting in the Diving Store later that evening, checking through everything to make sure that there were no clues or anomalies that Lewis or Lynch had left behind. John Kidley would be very thorough, and I did not want him to come across any clues as to what his predecessor had been up to. I did find a few strange notes that seemed to be the work of Lewis and Lynch but did not understand them. I put them into an envelope and was just about to lock up and go back to my cabin when Mike appeared.

"I thought you might be here; looks like you have had a busy day," he said.

"Sure have," I answered.

"Mike, I have no idea if these are anything incriminating but I have collected everything I could find from Lewis and Lynch lying around the store." I handed him the envelope.

"Thanks, I will give them to Bill to check out," he answered.

"The Captain has decided to head to the Isle of Capri. As soon as we have dropped the anchor, you will go back down and replace the disk on the hull of the ship."

I just nodded.

"After your solo dive on the ship's bottom, he has decided to give the divers a break from exercises and let you all enjoy a few hours diving around the Isle of Capri. This is one of the most gorgeous places in the world to dive and you will enjoy every second of it. The Isle of Capri has attracted the rich and famous for centuries, which includes Emperors Augustus and Tiberius in Roman times to, since the 1930s and 1940s, every well-known Hollywood star. It has almost all year-round sunshine, and has some of the Mediterranean's most sparkling clear blue waters, and the outstanding cliffs are some of the most spectacular anywhere in the world.

"It is a diver's dream, where you can relax and drift in and out of the caverns and caves. There are more than seventeen thousand varieties of fish in the Mediterranean to view and you are spoilt for choice with the many rainbow colours that are overwhelming and astounding. One of the most stunning is the parrotfish; females are coloured a brilliant red and yellow, with a striking saddle of silver across their backs. Males are coloured grey, and their fins are pink. If you have a spare dive set, I would like to come with you. I will see if I can give myself time off if you would be happy for me to tag along."

I smiled at this man's gracious manner who never took anything for granted.

"If you would like to come with us, I would be delighted. It seems that you have dived here before and you would be a valued dive member for our team."

The distance from our current location to the Isle of Capri was about a thousand miles and it would take about three days to get there. It lies almost due south of Naples at the bottom of the Gulf of Naples.

It seemed noticeably quiet in my cabin now that Lynch was no longer there. However, there were advantages. I had a cabin to myself that was the same as an officer's cabin and there were no plans for anyone else to share it with me. In the days to come, Annette Saunders would bring me some fresh coffee or a bowl of fruit. I would also later get the occasional invite up to the Wardroom for dinner, although I had to do it surreptitiously.

***

I had an early breakfast the following morning and was down at the Diving Store by 0800. To my surprise, John Kidley was in there and greeted me with a grin like a Cheshire cat.

"Thanks for my new job, boss."

I just nodded and smiled back.

"Jenny, I have to report to the Provost Marshall at 1100; any idea what for?" he asked.

I looked straight at him and said, "I can't imagine, John, I guess you'll have to go and find out."

I do not know what time he had started that morning, but the store was immaculate. He said that he had to meet with Chief Byrne at 0900 for Safety Equipment training and as that was close to the Provost Marshall's office, he would go straight there from his training.

There was little chance of any sports while we were in Capri, so I started to find out if any of the ship's company would like me to organise any boat trips around the island or go snorkel diving on one of the stunning beaches. I made a list, although many said they would just enjoy going ashore for a walk around and visiting some of the local bars and restaurants. Some of the keep-fit fanatics said that they were going to run up the steep roads and paths on the island. We were going to be there for a few days and so I might do some running myself.

I returned to the Diving Store at about 1600 to find that Kidley had returned. He looked at me and said, "I believe that you are responsible for this," showing me his newly sewn on Leading Seaman's badge. "Can I ask, what happened to Sophie?"

"I don't know, I think it was something that happened before I joined and it has only just come to light," I answered him, which was partly true. He never mentioned it again.

***

Three days later, in the early hours of the morning, the ship anchored off the Isle of Capri. The sound and feel of the anchor hurling into the sea is quite noisy and vibrates as it is released and can be heard and felt around the ship.

I knew that this was my cue to get to the Diving Store and get ready to dive. The water was so clean and warm that I opted for my wetsuit, making it a lot quicker to get ready. Kidley was already at the store and knew that I would be diving. He had been briefed that I was going to check out the Sonar housing that appeared to have an obstruction. I already had the disk on me and would only be submerged for ten to fifteen minutes.

Kidley dropped the Jacob's Ladder over the side for me to climb back aboard on my return. As soon as I was ready, I jumped from the ship's side into the water. The water felt so refreshing and the sun was already quite warm. I swam along the ship's side until I was almost parallel to the Sonar housing and then submerged.

As soon as I reached the housing, I did a sharp right turn and made my way to the prop shaft. The water was clean, and the visibility was incredible, even so far back on the ship's hull. I turned to look forward and could see the complete hull and the anchor chain as it ran through the crystal-clear water to where the anchor was lying on the sandy bottom. There were a plethora of multi-coloured fish and even a couple of small sharks playing in the depths.

Although the homing device disk had only been off the bottom for a few days, a considerable amount of seaweed growth had replaced the spot I had recently removed. It took just a few minutes to remove it again and bond the disk back in place. Almost immediately, I could feel the gentle vibration of the low current electricity.

By the time I had returned to the ship, Kidley had placed the inflatable dinghy close to the ship's side, ready for the divers to make their short trip to caverns, caves, and pillars that were close by on our starboard side.

The Jones sisters were almost ready to go and Root and Sells appeared minutes later. The divers present helped Kidley lower the dinghy into the water. We could not all get into the dinghy at the same time, so Kidley took those that were ready over to a flat rock where they would wait for the rest of us to join them. Knox and Willson appeared just after the dinghy had left with the first divers, and a few minutes later, Commander Cheetham appeared in his wetsuit. He chatted good-humouredly with us while we waited for Kidley to return. Of course, there was no Lynch or Lewis. It was strange, but their names were not mentioned all day.

We all enjoyed a fabulous morning and once the air was expended from the tanks, we just free-swam and -snorkelled round this beautiful area, taking in the breath-taking scenery both above and below the water. The caves and caverns went deep under the island and yet it was still exceptionally light wherever we went. Much of it looked as if it was manmade. It was stunning.

After all the stress and tension of the last few weeks, it was good to see them all unwind and have some fun. Sells and Root even tried chasing an eighteen-inch shark that had come curiously close to look at us. They gave up and came back to join us on the rocks, and to our mirth, the small shark followed them back as if it wanted to play.

Chapter 7. A Terrifying Project

After the Isle of Capri, my life took on a hugely different look. Everything seemed to move very quickly. The ship docked in Gibraltar where two MI6 operatives from London – Thomas and Gerald – came onboard. My time on the ship was effectively at an end, and the project that Captain James John Crowe had outlined, was now about to commence, and would be chillingly life-changing with incredible consequences.

The brief was that I was to infiltrate a terrorist group that had recently come to light, but were moving with breakneck speed and making waves throughout Europe and probably other parts of the world. I was about to embark on a fast-track program to become a member of the group before too many more atrocities were committed.

They had claimed responsibility for slaughtering a group of monks and nuns at a monastery in a sleepy village near Martigny in Switzerland, for no logical reason. They had bombed an orphanage in Madrid and claimed that they were getting rid of unwanted children and thus reducing the weight on society. Then there was the slaughter of another twenty factory workers in a chemical plant in Dusseldorf, Germany. Their reason for this outrage was that the chemical plant was ruining lives and killing people.

Their rhetoric was scary, and it was accelerating at an alarming rate. All the above had happened in the last six months and nobody knew anything about them. They had to get someone on the inside to find out who was funding them and essentially cut off the head of the organisation.

MI6, however, did know that they were recruiting hippies, down and outs, and dropouts from universities and many of them had been recruited in Fuengirola on the Costa del Sol in Spain.

I felt a chill run down my spine; this was something I had never envisaged happening to me. So far everything had been easy. What I had done had been exciting but had not put me in any real danger. I realised in that moment that I was scared, very scared, and I could feel my heart thumping and beating fast.

Did I genuinely think that what I had been doing was going to continue? Swaddled in a safe environment? *Wake up, Jenny*, my head screamed. *This is the real thing that you read about in spy novels and see in the movies.*

One of the agents was talking to me and for a second, I did not hear him. "Are you OK, Jenny? You look ill."

I snapped out of it and said, "Sorry, I have been on the ship for a long time, and it is taking me a while to regain my balance." I lied knowing full well that the impact of my immediate future was terrifying.

I pulled myself together as this was what I had been trained for but had never actually expected it.

"Right, now that you are back with us, here is what is going to happen."

For the next few hours, I was briefed on what had been planned and the immediate changes to my lifestyle. A tattoo! They were getting me tattooed! A body specialist being flown out from Liverpool who did a lot of work for the agency and tattooing was just one of his decorative arts.

Well, at least I knew the hotel that I was staying at. I was driven from the ship round to the Caleta Palace on Catalan Bay where I had stayed during my Spanish language proficiency days.

***

During the next few days, my looks changed dramatically. They gave me a tattoo that was not safe for public view. I had a small Nazi Swastika tattooed just below my armpit on my left breast. The public would not see it, but it could be shown to the right people or perhaps I should say, the wrong people. It would endorse me to others of being an anarchist, and a disruptor.

Then the horrible man pierced my left ear, and I was fitted with a simple gold ring, but high on my ear, and not in a place that I would have expected it. Next was my hair, which was relatively short, but he cut it jaggedly and then put some coloured greasy stuff on it to make it look scruffy; it was also an awful green colour. He gave me a large jar for me to use in future Then he had the audacity to tell me that I looked perfect.

After this I felt as if I was being paraded as the two agents grinned at me like idiots telling me that I was getting close to looking like a hippy dropout junkie.

"Are you ready, Jenny? It's time for your wardrobe," said Thomas.

I found it hard to suppress a giggle at the thought of these respectable, suited men being called Tom and Jerry.

"Yes," I answered. "Sounds like fun, where are we going?"

This time Jerry said, "We are not going anywhere; your tailor has just arrived."

With that, there was a knock at the door and in came an old Spanish-looking gentleman and, I presumed, his assistant who was a young handsome English youth. They both carried two large cases. Over the next two hours, I was prodded and pushed as my wardrobe slowly grew.

Designer jeans, you know the sort with tears and rips, pre-worn cowboy-style boots, and a couple of pairs of gaudily sequinned sandals, several tie-dye shirts, and several deep-coloured T-shirts with the words Gothic Rock and Satanic Bands and a couple more shirts with other slogans daubed on them piled up.

Once more I was paraded around in front of Tom and Jerry as they *oooed* and *aaahd* at my wardrobe. I felt like a cow off to the slaughterhouse and immediately regretted that choice of words.

I felt extremely conspicuous that evening as I had dinner on a private outdoor balcony. My men in black did at least try, ditching their traditional black suits for jeans and scruffy T-shirts; they almost looked human.

***

In the days following this, I was shown dozens of photographs of members of this new terror group called Le Chapeau Rouge (The Red Hat). Several other groups had popped up all over Europe bearing the same name. Many of them were filling the ranks with disenchanted young people from all walks of life. I was shown newspaper cuttings of some of these people rallying in small numbers in Berlin, London, Paris, and Madrid; their numbers were growing.

They portrayed themselves as peaceful protestors against officialdom who were stifling young people and thought that their rights and liberties were being quelled by governments everywhere. They believed that they had rights to more power, more money, and more recognition. On the face of it, the protests had been peaceful, and so many young people were drawn into what looked like an attractive projection of how the future could and should look like.

However, peel away the layers and the controlling forces for the group were dark and secretive, and only spoke to these youngsters in friendly terms, trying to show them a peaceful transfer to a sort of nirvana. It was a total front, and they knew that many of those disheartened souls would be easily manipulated into going much, much further than just peaceful protest. It was rife with corruption, theft, murder, terrorism, and mayhem and someone or some other groups were cultivating these young people.

My task was to infiltrate the group by becoming one of those disenfranchised people. I would become rebellious, angry, outraged, easily provoked, and opinionated and my trainers were confident that I would be noticed.

I would also be scrutinised and investigated by someone in the hierarchy of the group; they were fastidious in making sure they knew exactly who they were recruiting. Even as I was being prepared for my future in Gibraltar with Tom and Jerry, my back story was being created. I would have a new name and new background, which I would need to commit to memory. It would be difficult initially to become that person, but over time it would become second nature. I would be that person. I would become Yvonne Rushton, known as Bonny.

✳✳✳

I continued over the next couple of weeks in Gibraltar to prepare myself for an uncertain and terrifying future. I trained hard daily on keeping myself fit, by swimming, running up the Rock of Gibraltar, and pumping iron in the hotel gymnasium. This part of the training I enjoyed and was not a chore. On the second day of my fitness regimen, I was introduced to a Spanish boxing coach who ran a seedy boxing school in La Linea, Spain, just over the border from Gibraltar. He had been paid well to get me ready for a fictitious upcoming underground boxing tournament back in England. He worked me exceedingly hard, and I fought some good boxers, or maybe I should say fighters, on many occasions over the coming weeks. A number of my opponents in training came from poor families and were enthusiastic, but were brawlers rather than boxers. They just wanted to make a little money to support their families.

It was now approaching the end of November and the temperatures started to fall, even in Gibraltar, and at times it felt wintry. Although the agency needed me to get into Le Chapeau Rouge quickly, they knew it would be suicide for me to go unprepared.

At the end of my first week, I was presented with a small fluorescent green Volkswagen Beetle with a few dents in it, but in perfect working order. On the back seat and floor, there were several magazine and newspaper cuttings which included articles and photographs of various protests in towns around Great Britain. There were also a few front-page magazine photographs of me strewn around the car from various towns that I had allegedly boxed in.

Headings like, 'Bonny Outboxes Boys,' 'Bonny Beats Bolton's Best Boxer,' 'Girl Sensation Will Soon Turn Professional.'

In the glove compartment was a new passport in the name of Yvonne Rushton with a photograph of me in it. Inside were several stamps of places I had allegedly been to since my passport had been produced two years ago. I needed to learn about all the places I had been, including the stamp two days previously of me crossing the border after disembarking from the Cross Chanel Ferry, from Folkestone to Boulogne.

Meticulous care had been taken to build up my back story, including learning how I had grown up in Strathmore House, a Mueller home for orphaned children in Clevedon, Somerset. Mueller homes are no longer operating and closed many years ago.

Over the coming weeks, everything I did was as Bonny Rushton. The cartoon characters, my trainers Tom and Jerry, coached, groomed, intimidated, badgered, and angered me until I did become Yvonne (Bonny) Rushton. I knew my whole story from about six years of age until the present day. My real name faded into the background as I ate, trained, slept, and existed as Bonny Rushton.

My hair, clothes, earring, and tattoo had become familiar, and I had stopped grimacing when I saw myself in the mirror. This was my look and I embraced it.

It was now the week before Christmas and my trainers informed me that I would be relocating to Fuengirola on the Costa Del Sol on the second of January. A small room had already been paid for close to the busy seafront in that town. They informed me that they would be returning to Head Office in London while I would be driving myself to Fuengirola.

They had worked me, what felt like, to death, but in the end, I was quite fond of them and was apprehensive about being on my own.

Tom hugged me and said, "Bonny, you will be contacted soon after your arrival by a friendly face who will be your shadow during this next phase. Please stay safe and be careful."

I packed my one large suitcase in the trunk and watch my trainers drive away. I climbed into the driving seat of my car and, without warning, just burst into tears. The fear and terror of my forthcoming project seemed to envelop me. I was overwhelmed with panic, fear, grief, and uncertainty. My emotions ran completely amok, and I was having difficulty breathing. I must have sat there for nearly half an hour before I calmed down enough to start the engine. I drove slowly along past the bars and restaurants that lined the road of Catalan Bay towards the border to Spain.

There were no planes due to land or take-off so the drive across the runway to the Spanish border took only a few minutes. My heart finally got back to a regular rhythm and I was soon leaving La Linea on my way along the coast to Fuengirola. I did not feel as if I wanted to hurry to my next destination and drove quite slowly, keeping to the coast road.

In less than an hour, I pulled off the road at Estepona for coffee at a little coffee bar on the beachfront. Although it was January, the sun was quite warm and sparkled on the calm Mediterranean Sea and it felt like a comforting salve draining me of some of my anxieties.

From now on I would have little control of my life and would be manipulated by the evil forces of terrorism and anarchy and an intricate tool for the British Government. I felt as if I were utterly alone and wondered if I could carry this off. I did not feel brave at all. I sat for a long time near the peaceful beach with very few holidaymakers at this time of year and sipped at my nearly cold coffee.

I decided to get another cup before continuing my journey up the coast. I motioned to the waitress and ask her if she would get me a second cup. I closed my eyes for a few moments until I heard a man's voice say, "Coffee for Bonny Rushton."

I opened my eyes very quickly to find a tall man with shoulder-length bleach blond hair and beard smiling down at me. Where did I know that face from and more to the point, how did he know my false name? He wore faded scruffy blue jeans and a short-sleeved black shirt with a denim waistcoat with no sleeves. On his feet, he wore scruffy rope sandals.

I looked around; he was on his own and put my coffee on the table next to me.

"Can I join you, Bonny?" he asked with a smile and sat in the vacant chair on my right without waiting for me to answer.

I scrutinised this stranger but was perturbed by his straightforward approach. Was he trying to pick me up? The fact that he knew my name gave me a harrowing feeling.

I did not allow this stranger to get under my skin, smiled broadly, and said, "Why not? But I have to tell you that I am passing through and will be moving on very soon."

The way he moved, the way he spoke, it was all so familiar.

Then suddenly, the penny dropped. I grinned at him and said very quietly, "Good morning, Colonel Wilson, fancy meeting you in a place like this."

He smiled broadly and leaned in awfully close and whispered, "Hello, Jenny, how are you coping?"

"OK, I think, however, this is a far way and a long time since you inducted me into the agency, Dave."

"I know what you are going through, with the fear and the isolation. I thought you might need a friendly face."

The stress lifted slightly, and it was extremely good to see him indeed.

Dave explained that he would be around all the time I was in Fuengirola, but after that, he had no idea who my support would be. He warned me that there would probably be times where there was no apparent support, but someone would always be close by, even if not in view. "But there is no escaping it, you will be in danger and I know you are aware of that. As soon as you are settled into your lodgings in Fuengirola, come down near the Marina where you will find a nightclub called Heaven's Gate. There is a cross-section of humanity in there and they are open from midnight until seven in the morning. Go there for a couple of hours to get a lie of the land. It is one of the many places where there are several disgruntled people, and the recruiters for Le Chapeau Rouge will be there trying to take advantage of it. After the first night, you must become a regular so that you get noticed. Try a couple of the other clubs, but always go back to that one. We will be in the background to ensure that they notice you and they will think they want you on their side."

With hardly another word, Dave slipped away and left me sitting there pondering what my life was going to be like over the coming months. I sat there for about another five minutes and then returned to my car. I drove with more confidence, knowing that Dave would be somewhere in the vicinity, if only for the immediate future.

I arrived in Fuengirola and it only took me a few minutes to locate the address of my accommodation in Calle Moncayo. I had been allocated a small apartment three storeys up, which had a view from the window of the nearby Docks and out across the bay. I knew that the Marina was located somewhere nearby or on the docks and that was where many nightspots were located; including Heaven's Gate the all-night club that I needed to become a frequent visitor to.

I took a shower, changed into my new clothes, and glanced in the mirror before setting off to find the Marina. A stranger with a goth t-shirt with a single gold earring and green hair scowled back at me. *Oh well, best foot forward.*

I was feeling hungry and saw a McDonald's nearby and got stuck into a Big Mac and fries to start my evening.

It was early evening and there were only two other customers in McDonalds, both of whom were dressed in similar clothes to mine, and I wondered if I would see them later. It took only a few minutes to find Heaven's Gate and the nightclub was extremely quiet. I walked around for a few minutes to get my bearings; it was quite big, and I opted to sit right at the end of the bar where I could view the clientele coming and going. I sat there and sipped on a cold beer for nearly an hour before customers started to arrive. They mostly came in groups of four or five and I was surprised at how many girls there were.

One noisy group of girls crowded near to the bar and close to where I was sitting. One of the girls in the group who appeared no more than twenty years of age, talked aggressively and loudly most of the time. Several times she looked my way and scowled. I initially tried to avoid making any eye contact with her. She was dressed all in black, had five earrings in her right ear, and perched on the top of her head was a black cowboy-style hat. She seemed to be the self-appointed leader of the group.

A few more people came in and blocked her from looking at me. The ladies restroom was just behind me and so she had to pass me to get there. As she passed by, she scowled and snarled at me, "Who are you looking at, Green Head?"

I looked away and ignored her.

She came right into my face and started waving her finger at me, shouting, "Do you think you are better than me?"

I tried to ignore her, but she was looking for trouble and poked me in the face with her finger. I raised both of my hands in protection and said quietly but forcefully, "Don't do that."

A couple of her friends grabbed her and pulled her away saying, "Come on, Suzy, she's not worth it."

As she was hustled away, she looked back at me and shouted, "I don't like you; don't come back here again or you will be in trouble."

I moved from where I was sitting over to the far side of the bar, which was out of sight of the group of girls. There were fewer people on this side and there was a small stage where a trio of musicians were setting up their equipment. There appeared to be two guitarists and a female singer.

I glanced around and was surprised to see Dave sitting with two other people at a small table. He saw me but did not attempt to communicate or even show any recognition, so I carried on watching the group prepare for their show.

I decided that I would just listen to the first couple of numbers and then call it a day; it was already nearly two in the morning and I was feeling tired after quite an emotional day and the drive up from Gibraltar. I knew I would probably have to get used to late nights, but for tonight, I needed some sleep.

I walked briskly back to my apartment and maybe I was paranoid, but thought someone was following me. I did not see anyone, but I felt extremely uncomfortable. I felt better once I was inside and had locked the door. Since I joined the Royal Navy, I had never been entirely on my own and it was going to take time to get used to. I would have to adjust to late nights and would need to realign my sleep pattern. Hopefully, I would learn to have a lie in in the mornings.

***

Despite the previous night's excitement, I slept in until about eight-thirty and took a long leisurely shower. I wanted to walk around Fuengirola and look around and find out where the other nightclubs were. Some of them looked a little upmarket and it seemed as if they catered for the well-to-do holidaymakers. I found another nightclub just a few yards away from Heaven's Gate oddly named London Disco, where parties, events, and special offers took place at this London Nightclub in Fuengirola. Entrance with two drinks from Ten Euros. I thought that this place also looked promising for malcontents. I did not see any information about their opening and closing times, but decided I would try this club first this evening before returning to Heaven's Gate.

I also needed to do a little shopping and get some groceries for the small fridge and pantry that I had been afforded. I found a creperie nearby and ventured in to get some breakfast. The coffee was strong and very similar to Arabic coffee, but it woke up all my senses as I tucked into several breakfast crepes. A delicious and simple recipe for the morning, served with butter, sugar, and a choice of jam or chocolate spread. I hungrily devoured a couple of each.

I found two local supermarkets, one of which was a Lidl, and managed to get all the items I needed in there without spending too much money. This made me wonder how long I would be in Fuengirola.

I had been in Fuengirola as a child with my parents, but forgotten much of it, although I did remember an unforgettable small village that nestles in the foothills of the mountains named Pueblo Mijas. It sits over twelve hundred feet above sea level, and I decided to take a slow walk up there and enjoy some long-held memories of this unique historical treasure. I could not remember the name of the church there, but it was pure white, as were many of the buildings in the village.

It took me longer than I expected, and although only about four miles, it was a long hard walk up the very steep slopes to get there. I enjoyed the exhilaration from my effort and was breathing very heavily by the time I reached the Pueblo. All the buildings appeared a lot whiter than I remembered them.

I stopped by the lookout area and gazed down across Fuengirola, the dockside where I was living, and out across the Mediterranean Sea. The sun's reflection off the deep blue waters was intensely strong and I had to shade my eyes so that I could see anything at all. I took a stroll through the Pueblo, which looked as if it had just been scrubbed clean with its crisp white painted buildings everywhere.

I spent about an hour looking around and decided it was time to go back to Fuengirola and prepare for the coming evening and the exciting nightlife. My feelings were mixed with excitement and nervousness at the thought of the days and nights ahead of me. It all seemed so surreal.

My new life was beginning as I made my way from the apartment to the dock, which was just a few minutes' walk away. I arrived at the London Disco just before ten and it was not yet open, although there was a small group of youngsters already milling around outside. Two doormen were already stationed at the entrance so I correctly guessed that it would be opening soon.

As the door opened, the small crowd moved forward towards the door and waited in quite an orderly manner. Many of them appeared to be tourists, but there were several dressed in similar fashion to me, also waiting to go in. I did not feel too conspicuous as I fell in line behind a group of about five or six of the patrons.

The small four-piece group was playing mainstream jazz and already a few people were dancing on the small dance floor in the middle. They looked as if they were holidaymakers, and I could hear that they were talking in English. There was a loud group of young people sitting in a corner furthest from the band who were already getting rambunctious. I saw one of the staff go and talk to them and they quietened down a little for a while.

More people kept spilling in from the street and at one point, I saw Dave Wilson with three others sitting at a table not far from the door. There was no eye contact, and I did not make myself known to him although I knew he had seen me. Whatever and whenever anything was going to happen, was pretty much down to me. Although later in the evening I did not need to put myself out there, someone else was going to do that for me.

A couple of lads came and sat next to me and engaged me in conversation. The usual sort of stuff: what is your name, where are you from, what brings you here. They seemed pleasant enough, but wondered why I was here on my own. I told them the story of my life to date as Bonny Rushton and that I had become disillusioned with life in general and needed a change of scenery. I learned that they were merchant seamen who were trainee engineers from one of the ships in the dock and were in Fuengirola for about three days.

They asked me about the nightlife here, but I told them that I had only arrived yesterday although I had been to the Heaven's Gate nightclub the previous night. I shared that I would probably go along there in a couple of hours.

My two new friends, Allan Jones and Gareth Simpkins, had both served in the Royal Navy, but had only served for about three years each before joining the Merchant Navy where they earned considerably more money. I was unable to tell them about my time in the Royal Navy because of my new identity and life story to date and the fact that I was technically still in the service. Of course, I looked nothing like a military person at all; my looks portrayed a different background altogether.

I slowly sipped on a cold bottle of Holsten Lager until Allan bought me a neat Navy rum. They raised their glasses and said, "Here's to new friends," and drained their glasses in one swallow, expecting me to do the same. I obliged and immediately felt the effects of the warming rum. I declined their further offers to buy me any more rum.

There was nothing sinister about their offer and they laughed when I refused any more rum. Apparently I was a 'lightweight', which I took to mean that I was not a heavy drinker.

As the time approached midnight, I told them that I was going on to the next nightclub. They were game and said they would accompany me if I did not mind.

"Sure," I said, "the more the merrier."

We walked the short distance to Heaven's Gate together.

There was no queue outside and there were about twenty patrons already inside while the band was playing.

What happened next, took me completely off guard. The three of us walked towards an empty table when, without any warning, someone grabbed my hair from behind and threw me to the floor.

"I told you not to come back here again," a female voice screamed at me.

I was very quick to scramble back to my feet and turned to face my attacker with my fists up and ready for a fight. It was the girl, Suzy, who had tried to pick on me the night before. She was riled up and ready, and beckoned for me to respond.

"Come on then, let's see what you are made of," she growled.

As she came at me in a rush, I stepped deftly to one side and caught her a stunning blow to the right temple as she went by. She was tough and went down on one knee but quickly recovered. I kept my balance as she rushed at me again. She was ungainly and managed to get hold of me for just a second before I shook her off. She came in again, swinging wildly at my head, but nothing connected, and this time I caught her with a hefty uppercut as she came at me. She collapsed to the floor, completely dazed. I moved to help her up and she came up with a rush, and to my surprise, she grabbed hold of my head and whispered in my ear.

"Make it look good, Bonny, we have an audience, I'm a friend."

I jumped back from her and landed a number of blows to her shoulders and arms. There were several more assaults from her, and I allowed a couple of them to succeed, but kept her from doing too much damage. The exchange went on for several minutes, and as I finally put her down with a not-so-hard blow to the chin, she sat and snarled at me. "You were lucky, it will not be so easy next time."

I do not know what took them so long, but the doormen pulled us away from each other and threw us out onto the street. I have no idea why, but all they said was, "Come back when you can behave yourselves."

I did not realise at the time, but found out later that the reason we were not barred was that this was a haven for terrorist recruitment, and they did not wish to lose potential clients to their cause. So, of course, we were welcome back.

There was a police car waiting by the roadside, and as soon as the doormen released us, we were pounced on and arrested. They kept asking questions in Spanish, but I pretended not to understand. Suzy did not seem to understand either. We were driven to the Police Station, which was just a few yards away, and locked together in a cell. It seemed odd to me that they would keep us together when we had been arrested for fighting with each other.

I glanced around the cell, and saw a small, barely visible camera nestling in the middle of three lights in the ceiling, and then looked at

Suzy and raised my eyes to the ceiling. She glanced up and saw the camera.

She gave a half-smile and then screamed at me across the cell, "If you had not been saved by the doormen, you would be in the hospital by now."

With that, she sat down on the opposite side of the cell and rested her chin on her chest and seemed to doze off. I leaned back against the wall of the cell and closed my eyes. About half an hour later, a very tall, swarthy-looking officer came to the door of the cell and said in perfect English, "Have you two sobered up now?"

We looked up at him and both answered sheepishly, "Yes."

"I do not want to see you again, now go back to your accommodations and sleep it off." With that, he unlocked the door and let us out.

As I walked briskly away from the police station, Suzy quietly said, "Bonny, be careful and keep safe."

***

The following night, I was back at Heaven's Gate. Once more I saw Dave sitting in a quiet corner of the bar and again, we made no eye contact. Suzy was also there with her bunch of friends but kept far away from me. The two merchant navy engineers were there too and came up and joined me at my table. They were polite and we chatted amiably. Later in the evening, the conversation changed, and they started what I thought was an interrogation. Why was I here and who was I with? I played along with them, not sure exactly what they expected from me.

Gareth asked, "Do you have any particular political leanings?"

"No, I am completely disillusioned with most of the world's policies and politicians," I replied. "And as far as I am concerned, they would be better off getting rid of all of them and start all over again," I added.

Allan chipped in and said, "There are a lot of people who feel like that and would like to see drastic changes in world policies."

"Well, that would be a great idea, but nobody would ever try to implement such radical changes," I quipped light-heartedly.

"You would be surprised," mused Gareth.

The conversation then went back to ordinary, mundane things and nothing more was mentioned about politics that evening, although I had a feeling that I was being checked out.

Towards the end of the evening, or should I say morning, I went to the ladies restroom and was washing my hands when Suzy came in. She looked angry and shouted at me, "Did you steal my watch last night when I fell asleep at the police station? I know you have it." She fumbled in my jacket pocket as if she was looking for it.

My hands were still wet as I pushed her away and said quietly but forcefully, "Didn't you get in enough trouble last night without starting again?"

With that, she ran to the door and opened it, and as a parting word she shouted back, "We are not finished; I am going to get you."

I shook my head in disbelief; I thought we parted, if not friends, at least no longer enemies. Strange girl, I thought.

I was tired and since it was now approaching five in the morning, I decided to return to my apartment. Gareth and Allan were still at the table and I said my goodbyes and left the nightclub. There were no more incidences, and I reached my temporary home safe and sound.

Chapter 8. Recruited by Radicals

As I started to remove my clothes, I put my hands into my jacket pocket and found a screwed-up piece of paper. There was a scribbled note written on it.

You have been contacted. Gareth and Allan are not who you think they are. Be careful and destroy this note after reading it. Dave.

I felt a cold chill run through me, and realised that I had a lot to learn. How could I have been so naive to have fallen for their small talk? They seemed so genuine. It seemed that Suzy was not the enemy, after all. I tore the note up into tiny pieces and put it down the toilet, flushing it several times to make sure that it was completely gone.

I slept restlessly until about eleven o'clock, wondering what the next approach might be.

***

Extraordinarily little happened for the next three days and I was wondering if I had been discarded by whoever had been showing an interest in me.

I exited my apartment to walk to Heaven's Gate as I had been doing every day for the last week or so. As I reached the ground floor, suddenly all the lights went out. Before I had a chance to do anything, someone put a bag over my head, and I was bundled out of the apartment and onto the street. I heard a vehicle door open, and I was thrown onto a hard surface, which I believed to be the back of a truck or van. I tried to struggle and kick, but my efforts were wasted. I had been trussed up well and all I managed to do was hurt myself. The vehicle travelled for less than ten minutes and I was then pushed roughly out of the vehicle onto a hard concrete or stone floor. Up until now, nobody had said a word.

I heard a large door bang shut, which made me think I was in a garage or warehouse. Two strong people, men I think, then half dragged me and pushed me along a passageway, and I could hear a lot of footsteps echoing in the empty space. Then I was virtually carried down a long flight of steps, through a door, and once more dumped on the hard floor.

The bag was pulled off my head and I found myself sitting in a large room with about ten older men staring at me. A tall man with long greasy dark hair addressed me in English with a strong French accent.

"Miss Bonny, may I call you Bonny?"

I answered him angrily and said, "It looks like you just did, what the hell do you want from me?"

He looked around at his band of accomplices and laughed loudly.

"She has a lot of spirit, don't you think?"

They all jeered and guffawed at my predicament.

"You are going to entertain us," he growled gruffly.

I spat at him and shouted in fear more than anything else, "I am not entertaining anyone."

"Bonny, do you know what cage fighting is? You soon will. My dear friends and I have a considerable amount of money resting on the shoulders of our champion who you will fight, and she will win. Even though she will beat you, we just want to have a little insurance. We will pay you a handsome sum of one hundred and fifty Euros and give you a lift back to your accommodation. Apart from the bruises you receive from our champion, you will be unharmed."

"Do I have any choice?" I snarled at this ugly specimen of humanity.

"None, none at all," he snarled.

"Gentlemen, off you go now into the arena and grab your seats while Bonny gets changed into her fighting kit."

He threw me an old Adidas sports bag and pointed at the dirty-looking toilet cubicle in the corner.

"Go and get ready to lose," he sneered.

I had no choice and did as I was told, returning five minutes later in a nice pair of new shorts and a silky top. They had done their homework as the kit all fitted perfectly.

I then went on the defensive telling him that he had made a mistake, and that I had only done a little amateur boxing when I was younger but was not equipped to take on a professional. He chuckled at me and said, "You seemed to handle yourself quite well in the nightclub a few evenings ago; we were looking for potential talent to fill our top of the bill event this evening, and you won. Now get out there and fight."

He pushed me roughly through a side door of the room and down a passageway into a huge underground arena that was packed with both men and women. There were many tables around the side of the ring, with people laughing, smoking, and drinking champagne. The noise quelled slightly as I was brought in and I could feel them all staring at me.

I was pushed up into the ring, and filling the ring was a steel cage, much like a lion's cage that you might see at a zoo or circus. As I climbed into the cage, the crowd went crazy, stamping their feet and shouting out catcalls and a few seeming supporters cheering me.

Then there was a deathly hush as my opponent stepped into the cage. She was about two inches taller than me and had a completely shaved head and a huge set of biceps and massive shoulders. My first thought was that I was going to get slaughtered right from the start. I looked her up and down and noticed that despite her huge upper torso, the lower part of her body was quite skinny. Rightly or wrongly, I guessed that the reason for her upper body bulk was not just from the effort of working with the weights, but also regular use of anabolic steroids. Whichever it was, she looked daunting, and I was preparing myself for the worst. I remembered from my boxing days and my coach Gerry telling me to keep out of reach of my opponent's fists. A lot of good this was going to be; this was not a boxing match and there were no holds barred.

I had seen several cage fights, but they were nothing like this setup. They also had a referee to protect the fighters if things got out of hand. Here there was no such thing. This was almost a fight to the death, although I am sure that once one fighter had been knocked out or injured, the fight would stop; but there was no guarantee.

If my opponent won, would I be let off so easily? And if I happened to win – not much of a chance of that – what would they do to me? Somehow, I needed to survive, but was shaking almost uncontrollably inside. I was sure the spectators and, more importantly, my opponent could see it.

Someone from outside of the cage explained the rules: there weren't any. There were no rounds, and the fight would begin by the bell being rung; it would end when the bell rang again. I began to think that the second bell would be my death knell, and I was having difficulty in keeping myself together. I was terrified.

A voice from somewhere asked, "Fighters ready?" My opponent gave a hard nod and I just grinned helplessly. The bell seemed to explode, and I stood for a fraction of a second, completely immobile. I looked desperately around the crowded auditorium for help. There, in the dark recesses at the back of the place, I saw Dave standing completely still, watching the proceedings. His eyes seemed to pierce into my brain, but he made no motion at all.

I came alive as I saw this gladiator of a woman coming across the ring at high speed. My senses kicked in and I was glad that I had at least kept myself as fit as I could since leaving the friendly confines of HMS *Raleigh* and my trainer Gerry.

I quickly sidestepped as she swung heavily at me and her savage punch whistled over my head. Then she got me in a clinch and was holding on tightly as she pummelled my belly and arms with a plethora of punches. I was a little tense, but they did not have the power that I was expecting. Either that or I was completely numb with the horror of it all.

While she was unavoidably close, she snarled in my ear, "You will leave here in a box tonight, pretty girl."

As she pushed me away, I instinctively threw a flurry of punches at her head. She flinched with a surprised look on her face and staggered back and nearly fell over. I felt a little relieved and I knew that she realised that she had a fight on her hands. The crowd went crazy when they also realised that this was not going to be a completely one-sided massacre.

She came at me again, but was more guarded and did not engage so actively, trying to take me out with solid punches. I began to gauge her ability. She had a knockout punch, but she would have to land it to gain any real advantage. She did not seem as fit as I expected, and I think the huge muscled upper torso was more for effect. I also noticed that even this early, her breathing was becoming laboured.

After a few more approaches and attacks to no real effect, my confidence increased, and although I was still in great peril, I began to loosen up and move around easily. The crowd was warming up to me and right now they were my best ally. I do not know why I did it, but after all my earlier dread I was feeling a lot more confident. I had never done it before, but in the heat of the moment I did a perfect Mohamed Ali shuffle. The crowd erupted, and I could see that even Dave was smiling and was a lot closer to the ring than when I had spotted him earlier.

The fight's action then started to deteriorate, and I could hear a few in the crowd telling their champion that it was time to finish me off. I was not ready to be finished just yet. The big clock at ringside showed a time of thirteen minutes. To me it had seemed an age, but it appeared that time was on my side. I could see and feel that my nemesis was getting slower and even the punches she did land had little or no effect on me. My fitness was beginning to give me an advantage. My biggest worry now was what they would do to me if I did beat her.

I could now see that Dave was a lot closer to the ring and he was glaring intently at me with his eyes almost fixed wide open. At that moment, while I was not concentrating, my opponent landed a substantial hook to my chin; it caught me off balance and I staggered back onto the side ropes. I ducked quickly as I bounced from them and went completely under the straight incoming arm and she missed me entirely.

We were now on opposite sides of the ring and I looked around desperately for Dave. He was standing just a few yards from my corner and I could see his expression. He gave a quick grin and then stared straight at me again and nodded very clearly two or three times. I had never felt so happy in my life. I took his gesticulating as a sign to finish this fight and beat my opponent. I was starting to tire, but my muscle-bound opponent was looking done in. I circled her and made a couple of dummy approaches; she was lethargic and was moving far more slowly. My confidence was increasing, but again this gladiator tried in desperation to finish me off and made a fatal move. She feinted with her left and tried to draw me onto a huge incoming right hand. I neatly sidestepped the blow meant to finish me off and, using her weight and my right hand, landed a huge right hook into her left jaw and she collapsed in a crumpled mess onto the canvas.

The crowd was ecstatic and nearly everyone was on their feet. I looked around and there was no sign of Dave; he had vanished. The crowd was still cheering when the door of the auditorium burst open, and I could see about twenty or more armed police charge into the room. An officer with a bullhorn stood on a chair and demanded that everyone lie on the floor, face down. My opponent, in the meantime, was still on the canvas and I moved to her to see if she was alright. She opened her eyes and blinked hard and then sat up.

To my surprise, she grinned, put out her hand and congratulated me. Incidentally, I never did get my one hundred and fifty Euros.

A uniformed policeman escorted my opponent and me from the cage and ultimately from the underground arena out into the fresh air.

Two cars were waiting outside and I was quickly ushered into one of them and my opponent into the other, and without further ado we were whisked away.

I was taken straight to the address of my apartment, and the driver got out, opened the door, and simply said with a Spanish accent, "Goodnight, Miss Bonny, have a nice evening."

I smiled at his comment as it was about three in the morning and he waited as I entered the ground floor of my apartment.

It had been an eventful evening, but I was somewhat relieved to know that Dave had been there to take care of my safety and I hoped that he would continue to do so. Despite the unbelievable events of that night, I slept remarkably well and woke at about midday that same day.

✳✳✳

I was famished when I awoke and took a shower, dressed, and made my way to the creperie nearby. A man was loitering outside my apartment and he made it no secret that he was following me. It was broad daylight and there were many people around, so I was not bothered too much.

He followed me into the creperie and as soon as I sat down, he approached and said, "I am John Smith, can I join you for breakfast, Miss Bonny?"

I just shrugged my shoulders. *Why did everyone want to call me Miss Bonny, why not just Bonny? And John Smith, surely he could have come up with a better pseudonym than that.*

He sat down opposite me at the table and his opening gambit was, "I saw you fight last night; very impressive." He smiled inquisitively.

"Was that your first cage fight? You looked out of place although a very competent fighter."

I answered, "Yes, it was, although I had done some amateur boxing when I was a kid. I thought it would help if I were going to spend a lot of time on my own. Like an insurance policy in case anyone tried to take advantage of me."

He could see me looking at him intently and knew exactly what I meant.

"Do not worry, I do not intend you any harm, in fact, I have a different type of proposition."

My crepes and coffee arrived. I was ravenously hungry after last night and tucked into them immediately.

"What sort of proposition?" I asked in between mouthfuls of crepes and coffee.

"Well, you appear to be a bit of a loner and not a great lover of politics and the democratic leaders that we seem to have around the world. Would you like to join a group of like-minded people who have banded together to try to make things different?"

I nodded thoughtfully; it had taken some time, but I had finally been approached. I looked at him very carefully: clean-cut with well-spoken English. I wondered what his philosophy on life was and where he fitted into the organisation. Perhaps he was just a recruiter. Nothing about him stood out as being a terrorist. I almost smiled and thought, what on earth does a terrorist look like? If it were that easy, the authorities would be able to spot them a mile off. It made me realise how naive I could be.

I grinned sheepishly and said, "I might be interested; my life doesn't appear to be going anywhere and I am sort of drifting from one place to another."

He did not say anything for several minutes and just sat sipping his black coffee. He waited until I finished my breakfast and drained my coffee cup and then added, "Would you like to come and meet some of my friends? They have regular meetings about half a mile away. Come along and then you can make an educated and knowledgeable decision about joining us, or not."

After last night's chicanery I was very wary and asked him for the address. He gave it to me without further ado. He got up to leave and then added, "Come at about six this evening and you will meet a lot of people who feel about life as you do; I will also be there. I look forward to seeing you later."

I looked up the address on a local map and guessed it was about a ten-minute walk from my apartment. The building had been a hotel at some time in its life and it looked quite cosy as I walked in. The guy who had invited me was standing in the large foyer talking to several other young people; he spotted me and left them to come over and greet me.

"Thank you for coming, I was not sure that you would." He then smiled broadly at me.

I smiled back at him and said, "After last night, I thought I could do with a change of scenery, I didn't take kindly to being kidnapped."

"I understand, I thought you had gone there willingly," he said. "Let me take you in to meet the crowd."

The room must have had about thirty mostly young people and they were all chatting in small groups of five or six. At the far end of the room was a small stage with a microphone front and centre. To the left of the room and against the wall were two long trestle tables covered in pamphlets of varying topics with headlines like:

The British Government has lost its ability to lead the country.

Conservatives need to go.

Roman Catholics in Europe no longer tend to people's faith but are trying to take over governments.

Support the Catalan independence movement.

Set Scotland and Ireland free from Dictatorship.

There were dozens of these pamphlets with similar rhetoric, but at this point no mention of uprisings or terrorism. They were more of a gentle suggestion rather than a call to action. Nothing radical just yet, I thought.

A man of about forty-five climbed onto the stage. He looked like an academic with thick dark-rimmed glasses, a full head of curly hair, and a nervous smile. I guessed he was just under six feet tall. He tapped the microphone a couple of times to make sure that it was working, or maybe it was a nervous habit.

I do not know what I expected, but thought he looked like an Oxford or Cambridge Professor. However, when he began to speak, he was not English. He spoke in English, with a strong East European accent. He told us that he came from what used to be known as Yugoslavia and had left his home country when the Balkans were in turmoil and Yugoslavia was split into the independent countries of North Macedonia, Bosnia and Herzegovina, Croatia, Slovenia, Serbia, and Montenegro.

He explained how his countrymen were worse off now than they had ever been, and he longed for peace to reign in the region. There needed to be a consensus of people willing to stand up for all the basic principles of humanity in so many countries around the world.

So far, he had not said anything militant, but was rather advocating a peaceful approach.

His speech was inspiring, and it is so easy looking back at this friendly interactive evening how many of these gullible young people were sucked into a life of brutality, mayhem, and terrorism. It was a gently, gently approach and it worked so well. Everyone was watching and listening to this quietly spoken man on the stage.

At the end of the speech, we were given several seemingly innocuously worded pamphlets. They were about family, trust, friendships, and learning basic truths. Everyone was also given a compact disc that we were invited to listen to several times. Once more seemingly innocuous, concentrating on fraternity, brotherhood, and bonding with your mentors so that you get to be like them – good honest members of society.

I left the meeting with a feeling of goodwill and felt at peace with my fellow man and all around me. I read through the pamphlets and then listened to the CD. The Academic who had spoken to us that evening spoke to me from the CD and there was soft classical music playing all the time in the background. After listening to this man's words, instead of feeling at peace, I suddenly felt conflicted, but could not fathom why. I listened to it again from start to finish and the gentleness of his voice and the music gave a sense of wellbeing, but again after hearing it a second time, I felt distressed and angry with the world and the way governments were taking advantage of its citizens. I went to bed with angry and disruptive thoughts.

***

When I awoke in the morning, I felt as if I needed a good night's sleep after a very restless night. My training with MI6 had not prepared me for an event like this, and I needed to get a message to Dave and give him the pamphlets and the CD. I had no idea how I would do that unless I managed to see him again at Heaven's Gate. I put everything I had into the smallest envelope possible hoping that I would get the opportunity to pass it to Dave somehow. The day dragged by and I thought the evening would never come. I did some window shopping to pass the time and took a walk down by the docks. The creperie was becoming my favourite place to eat and I spent nearly two hours sipping coffee and enjoying their delicious crepes.

When I arrived back at the apartment, I planned on taking a shower and getting ready for another evening at the nightclub. As soon as I opened my apartment door, I knew instinctively that someone had been in there. I searched everywhere to see if I could find any clues. The clue did not become apparent until I sat down, exhausted, in the armchair. Oh no, where was my envelope for Dave? I searched everywhere I could think of, but no envelope was to be found.

Before taking a shower, I put the safety chain on the door to make sure that I would at least hear someone if they tried to enter. I took my time getting ready, laying out a clean set of clothes ready for the evening out. Finally, all I had to do was take a shower. I waited for the water to heat up coming through the pipes and when it was at the right temperature, I stepped into the cubicle.

The hot water felt so good, and I felt as if it was washing away my worries and fears. I had my eyes closed as the hot water cascaded from my head down onto my shoulders. I reached out and found the bar of soap in the dish in the shower cubicle and felt something crumple in my hand. I opened my eyes quickly and found a piece of paper attached to the soap. I immediately turned off the shower and dried the water from my eyes so that I could read the message written on it.

I have the envelope, Dave.

PS. Destroy the note.

I immediately set fire to it in an ashtray and then flushed the ashes down the toilet and then washed the ashtray. There was a little sense of relief and I made my mind up that tonight's visit to Heaven's Gate would be brief and I would try to get a full night's sleep.

Chapter 9. Arco de Christo

For the next four days, I went along to Heaven's Gate every night, and prior to going there, I went along to various other nightspots and spent less than an hour in each one. Most of them catered for the more upmarket and family-orientated clientele and I could not see that I was likely to be approached by any subversives in these places.

I had already been approached and they had either made up their minds that I was not what they were interested in recruiting, or they were biding their time. During these few days, I did not see Dave at all, and it was a little unnerving not having my guardian angel close by.

I kept to my usual routine during the day and enjoyed going to the creperie for my breakfast and then strolled around the shops, most of which catered for the tourists with many different gift items with Fuengirola or Spain emblazoned on them as mementos of their visit here. Restaurants offering typical Spanish cuisine such as Paella and Tapas, Chorizo, and different fish and seafood dishes were in abundance.

Because of the late nights, it was usually nearly eleven o'clock before I set off for my late breakfast. As I was about to leave, a young lady about my age was standing outside of my apartment block. I did not recognise her, but she must have known me because she greeted me with a broad smile and said, "Good morning, Bonny, I was asked to deliver this to you," and she handed me a small envelope. I looked at it and then hastily put it into my jeans pocket. I looked up to say thank you, but she was already striding away.

It stayed in my pocket until I reached the creperie for my wake-up coffee and crepes. The pale green envelope had my name neatly written on it in full: Bonny Rushton. I was a bit taken aback as I do not recall giving anyone my full name. Someone had done their homework on me.

I was stunned, whoever these people were they certainly did it in style.

Inside was an expensive-looking invitation card with an ornate border around it in the same colour as the envelope and written on it in meticulous and neat script were the words:

Dear Bonny Rushton

You are invited for a weekend of

fun activities at our expense in

our resort from Friday to

Monday this coming weekend.

The coach will be outside at

quarter past eight this Friday

morning to collect you.

Buenos Dias Bonny

This was Wednesday and so I needed to get myself prepared in time for my trip on Friday. I bought some more dye for my hair, only this time I bought some orange as well. By the time I was finished it looked, well not sure what it looked like, but it did look funny. My green was a lot brighter than previously with bright orange at the front. I also bought a couple more pairs of pre-bleached, pre-worn jeans complete with designer holes in them and a matching pair of denim shorts.

I did not go out for the next two nights and tried to prepare myself for the weekend. I had no idea what was in store for me and how safe I would be. I need not have worried because when the time came, it all seemed mostly innocuous.

***

I did not sleep well that night, but I felt more relaxed by Thursday lunchtime. I had still not heard or seen anything from Dave, which worried me more than anything else. I had been warned that I might be on my own at times, but someone would be watching.

I was up, showered, and dressed early on Friday morning with a packed holdall for everything that I needed to take with me. At exactly eight-fifteen and right on time, a large new-looking green coach for fifty-two people pulled up outside my apartment. A large Spanish man got off the bus to open the luggage compartment for me to put my bag inside.

He hurried me along saying, "We need to be quick, there is no parking allowed here."

I just nodded and said, "OK."

Talk about luxury coaches, this was the ultimate in holiday travel. It was immaculate and the interior was stunning and included a pristine-looking hostess who served us with coffee or soft drinks and a few delicious pastries; no expense had been spared.

We stopped about six more times after I had boarded to pick up some more young people. It was interesting to note that none of the people I saw boarding had anyone seeing them off. They all seemed like loners. After the coach picked up the last of the passengers, it was about two-thirds full: about thirty-five people. I recognised some of them from the various nightspots I had visited in Fuengirola and a couple nodded their recognition of me.

After the last stop, the coach started to climb up into the hills behind Fuengirola and I recognised Pueblo Mijas as we passed through it. The stunning whitewashed buildings seemed to sparkle even more in the bright early morning sunshine with dark shadows lining the insides of the narrow Andalusian streets.

The driver of the bus then gave us some information about our trip. He spoke clearly into his body microphone.

"We are going to take the scenic route today to the town of Ronda, which is close to our destination. We thought you would enjoy seeing some of the places of great interest that many of the holidaymakers miss because they stay close to the coast. We will stop for just a few minutes in each place for you to stretch your legs and enjoy some of the beautiful geography and history of the area."

The first stop was the small town of Coin with a population of about twenty-one thousand. It was a very old town and the postcard I bought told me that the town was captured by the Moors back in the 700s and remained in their hands until the late 1400s.

A bustling little town and an agricultural trade centre, Coín deals in various fruits, and sausages too. Also, a popular area for the tourists who stray from the coast, which made it seem much larger than its population portrayed.

There was just enough time to get a cup of coffee and buy a few items of fruit and the bravest among us bought a few sausages, me included, even though we had no idea how we were going to cook them later.

Off to our next destination and the small village of El Burgo with a population of under two thousand. It is located on the Sierra de las Nieves mountain range. We stopped just outside the village to enjoy the stunning views across the mountains and valleys. Our driver told us that many of the peaks are covered in snow in the winter. However, today the visibility was crisp and clear with brilliant sunshine. The classical virgin-white painted buildings could be seen dotted about all over the mountainside and sparkling in the bright sunlight.

Then we all reboarded the bus for the half-hour journey to Ronda and the largest town that we would visit with about thirty-five thousand inhabitants. Our stop at Ronda was the most memorable for many reasons. It is notably one of the oldest cities in Spain and was founded about nine centuries before Christ.

The beauty of this area of Spain was unbelievable, and for a few minutes, I had forgotten why I was here in this part of the world, especially when standing on the Puente Nuevo New Bridge and gazing straight down into the gorge some three hundred feet. It was a stunning sight and gave me a feeling of vertigo. It seems a bit of a misnomer to call it a New Bridge since it was built in 1793. Just a clue as to how little this city has remained unchanged for a couple of hundred years. Another historical fact is that it is also the birthplace of bullfighting.

While I was standing in a crowd of tourists peering over the bridge, a man standing next to me, who I had never seen before, whispered to me, "What an incredible view, Bonny."

I turned as if to speak and he said very quietly, "Do not speak, my name is Robert Penfold, and don't look now but I have slipped a note into your pocket. Read it later and then destroy it."

I just nodded.

We were given about fifty minutes to wander around this historical town before being asked to get back on the bus for the remainder of our journey, which would take about twenty minutes.

On returning to our seats, there was a large black bag on each seat, and as we sat down, our hostess came onto the microphone and said quietly, "Please do not be alarmed. It is just a safety precaution, but as soon as we are out of Ronda, the coach will stop momentarily. I will then ask you all to put the black bag over your head and pull the strings to make sure that you cannot see where we are. We will be stationary for a few moments at that time, and I will come around and check that your bags are correctly positioned."

I wondered if we would be searched on reaching our destination and took the precaution of slipping the note from my pocket to my right shoe and inside my sock. I should not have worried, because all they asked for on arrival were our mobile phones and computer tablets, which they promised to return on departure. I did not have either.

After our black bags had been checked and none of us could see, we set off on the last short leg of the journey. The engine was labouring, and I guessed that we were climbing quite steadily. I was also able to see the sunlight and knew that we were also heading west. The time was just after two in the afternoon, and we seemed to be following the sun, so west was a good estimate.

The hostess made one final announcement, "Please remain in your seats until the vehicle comes to a complete standstill, at which time you will be invited to remove your black security bags. When disembarking, please follow the instructions of the supervisors until you are fully checked into our resort. Thank you all and please enjoy your stay with us."

We could feel the coach slowing down and finally coming to a halt, whereafter there was a whooshing sound as the doors opened. Then a man speaking in perfect English but with a slight European accent told us to remove the bags that were over our heads. It took several minutes for our eyes to adjust to the strong sunlight.

Our host stood at the front of the coach just inside the door, smiled broadly, and said, "Welcome to Arcos Resort. Sorry for the cloak and dagger style of entry, but the black bag event is done for several reasons. Firstly, you can only come to this resort by invitation and we do not want uninvited guests clamouring to enjoy our unique resort. The anonymous entry and the black bags also provide a certain amount of mystique to this very prestigious venue and you could never stumble across it by accident."

He stopped for a few minutes for us to regain our focus and look around the entrance to the resort from the confines of the inside of the coach. The building itself looked like photographs I had seen of a Moorish Castle. The sign across the battlements, although done in keeping with the building, said Arcos, which simply means Arch.

The castle was incredibly stunning, with long winding stairways and huge, rugged battlements to the outward sides. Beneath, on all the pieces of land, stood massive stone boulders. The silos, structures carved into the rocks, maybe encountered both inside and outside the fortification, were used to conserve certain foodstuffs such as cereals.

However, in the centre of this fortification, a huge excavation had been carved out that could not be seen from the outside. Original features had been maintained, but deep inside was a fully up-to-date modern hotel facility, which included tennis and squash courts, swimming pools with sunbathing decks, a gymnasium, sauna and Turkish baths, dining halls, a coffee shop, cinema, theatre (conference room) and delegate rooms for smaller groups as well as eighty individual suites with every facility, queen beds, single beds, bathrooms, and laundry facility. It was truly opulent and luxurious, to say the least, and screamed wealth in abundance. No expense had been spared in creating these extravagant accommodations.

Thirty-five of us arrived on the coach and conveniently there were thirty-five companions already there. Each of us had been allocated a companion who showed us to our rooms. A girl, maybe a couple of years younger than me, was allocated to me.

At first glance, I felt my heart start to beat faster, I knew this girl and I could not remember where from. Was my cover going to be blown immediately? Then she introduced herself: Amelia Lynch. I almost stared at her; this must have been Sophia Lynch's sister, as they looked so much alike. What on earth was she doing here?

She took me on a tour of the hotel and chatted cordially as we visited every part of this plush facility before eventually taking me to my room. Just as she was parting, she said, "Bonny, please be down in the main dining room by seven this evening for dinner, I hope you enjoy your stay here at Arcos."

I walked to the door to let her out and she turned and shook my hand and simply said, "Welcome."

Her handshake had pushed something into my hand and I made no comment but just accepted whatever it was.

It was a letter. Now I had two notes to read, one from Robert Penfold and now one from Amelia Lynch. This really was becoming cloak and dagger stuff.

I went into the bathroom and decided to take a nice hot bath and started to run the water slowly into the bathtub. I removed my shoes and socks and the note that I had discreetly hidden there and went back into my bedroom barefoot, leaving the bath running. I remembered that I had a travel magazine in my case and took it out, slipping both notes into the pages of the magazine. I then lay on the bed and opened the pages so that I could read my notes.

Bonny, Dave has gone on to Corsica to snoop out the area and be prepared for your arrival. For the remainder of your time in Spain, I will be watching out for you. You will meet Amelia at Arcos; she is one of ours and will be your daily contact for the duration of your stay and will bring you up to date with other events.
Stay safe.

Bob Penfold
Read and destroy.

I slipped the second note out from between the pages and slipped it over the one I had just read.

Hi, Bonny, be careful with everything you do and say, there are microphones and cameras all over the place. I have a lot to tell you and the best place is in the Turkish bath because the damp would mess up their surveillance equipment. We may not have a chance to get there today, because after dinner there will be seminars, lectures, and presentations. We could go down for a Turkish bath tomorrow morning before breakfast; be there at about seven o'clock.

All the guests were invited down to the conference hall at seven-thirty, immediately after dinner. On arrival, we were cordially greeted by various members of the staff and shown to a seat.

The first person on the stage was the Yugoslavian gentleman who had spoken at the presentation I had attended a few nights ago with a strong European accent. He advised the audience that there would be three other speakers that evening and they would each give a presentation of well-known orators.

He stepped down from the stage to be replaced by a middle-aged lady with a British accent whose area of expertise was Winston Churchill. She talked about this brilliant world leader and mentioned many aspects of his acclaimed and highly credited career, which included his time in India as an army officer during the time of insurgencies, the Boer War, and finally World War II.

She finished her presentation with his full famous speech **"their finest hour."** It was an inspiring recitation and took a full thirty-six minutes. It ends with the words:

Let us therefore brace ourselves to our duties, and so bear ourselves that, if the British Empire and its Commonwealth last for a thousand years, men will still say, "This was their finest hour."

It was an uplifting moment and there seemed little sinister to recall about any of this or indeed in any of the following two presentations with one about John Fitzgerald Kennedy and the third about the life and tragedy of Socrates. *(Socrates was a Greek philosopher from Athens who is credited as one of the founders of Western philosophy.)*

Everyone was upbeat and talking enthusiastically as they filed out and away from the conference room. Little did they realise that this was the trap that lulled nearly everyone into a feeling that their visit here was of great benefit to all who had attended. This was the hook that pulled the majority into a sinister web of lies and anarchy.

This was not a short-term plan but a much longer one; little by little the narrative would change, not over the period of a few days but in many cases over months and if necessary, years. The seeds were being sown.

***

The following morning, I was down in the Turkish Baths about fifteen minutes before Amelia arrived. I had so many questions to ask her about her sister Sophia, Lula Lewis, and much more. As it happened, she explained much of it without me having to ask.

Amelia told me that her sister Sophia was working quietly behind the scenes for MI6 but only as a listener, and picking up whatever chatter she could. She was given Lula Lewis as her project, who they had reason to believe was compromising the Royal Navy's latest ship HMS *Dornik*.

Lula's mother had been taken sick, and instead of asking for help, she found another way: the wrong way. Her mother needed a heart transplant, but the cost was beyond her capability. She was approached by a foreign agent and was told that she would be paid exceptionally well if she just did an exceedingly small thing for them.

Her mother needed to fly to South Africa and have an operation at the Christiaan Barnard Hospital in the city centre in Cape Town. This foreign agent offered to pay for everything: flights to and from Cape

Town and the full hospital costs, and any rehabilitation costs. They just needed her to volunteer to be considered as a member of the ship's company of HMS *Dornik* and then they would brief her on what she needed to do.

The Royal Navy asked for volunteers to join HMS *Dornik*, a vessel designed specifically for surveillance and other covert operations. Up until then, Lewis had an impeccable service career and was also a talented and experienced diver. She went through a vetting process and was accepted.

As a diver, it took little effort for her to plant a listening device under the ship's hull, which allowed a foreign agent to gain access to not only the ship's whereabouts at any time, but other information such as any exercises it carried out, and the location of any other vessels it had any interaction with. A very precarious situation for a ship like the *Dornik* and fully compromising its capability and capacity as an active surveillance ship.

Lula Lewis had been incarcerated ever since she and Sophia Lynch had been apprehended on board the ship. Much of that time Sophia had spent with her slowly wheedling information from her without Lewis realising that she was divulging damaging information to Sophia and ultimately to the MI6. She had considered Sophia as a confidante. Lewis was now awaiting trial on charges of treason, lying to a Government Agent, and other lesser crimes.

Amelia finished telling me what had happened since I left the ship. Her sister had now been sent on another assignment.

Amelia said to me, "Bonny, be incredibly careful. Only about ten percent of people get selected for their projects and a percentage of that ten are never heard of again. It is an extremely dangerous course to follow, and if they suspect you of anything at all, you will disappear. Think very carefully before you jump in."

I felt extremely nervous and was terrified to imagine the worst. I knew at the beginning that I could be putting my life on the line. I was a willing participant and many others had laid down their lives in the path of preventing terrorism around the world. I was not being brave, but wanted to make a difference for my family and my country. This was something that I needed to follow through.

Amelia and I had been in the Turkish Bath long enough and more guests were arriving to use the facility.

I returned to my room and later I took a walk around the grounds before lunch and enjoyed the splendid views from the battlements.

After eating I decided to go and use the weights and have a workout and then go for a swim. The day was easy and peaceful, and I relaxed on a sun lounger by the pool after my swim.

We were offered afternoon tea with croissants, cakes, and ice cream by the pool at about four o'clock. We had total freedom to do as we wished during the day, but were obliged to attend the presentations in the evening, and were all relaxed by then. All of this was cleverly done to put our minds in a receptive mode, susceptible to suggestions to radical ideas.

Unlike yesterday's presentations, the subjects were chosen because of their friendship with the United States of America and the United Kingdom during the second world war.

The Yugoslavian was back on the stage to present the first of this evening's offerings. This time we saw a far more passionate orator than he had been on previous occasions as he roared into action over his hero Josip Broz Tito, the communist revolutionary and statesman who served in many roles from 1943 to his death in 1980. He was a fearless leader and helped in the defeat of the Nazis, becoming the most powerful partisan in Yugoslav history.

His speech was emotional and his pride in his incredible countryman could not fail to move people. He talked for about forty-five minutes, and said at the end that he did not have the time to extoll the incredible leadership abilities and pride in Tito. On finishing his talk, he quietly said to his audience, "On your way out, please pick up the leaflet that I have compiled about the life and times of Marshall Tito, and if you find it of interest, go to Amazon and buy a copy of *Marshal Josip Broz Tito: The Life and Legacy of Yugoslavia's First*

President. Thank you all for your patience and interest in my talk this evening." He nodded to the audience and left the stage.

The next talk was about Joseph Stalin.

Under Stalin, the Soviet Union was transformed from a peasant society into an industrial and military superpower. Stalin aligned with the United States and Britain in World War II. He was an ally.

In this special setting in the heart of the Spanish countryside, the speaker made no reference to Stalin's brutal regime and his atrocious conduct towards his countrymen. He also neglected to mention how he afterwards engaged in an increasingly tense relationship with the West known as the Cold War. He ruled by terror, and millions of his citizens died during his savage reign. It is estimated that the death toll directly attributable to Stalin's rule amounted to some twenty million lives (on top of the estimated twenty million Soviet troops and civilians who perished in the Second World War), for a total tally of forty million.

Next came a talk about someone who was described up on the stage as the saviour of the Chinese empire; a leader who had all the answers to the world's problems. A certain Mao Tse-Tung created many beneficial cultural changes initially and assisted in the defeat of the Japanese in a coalition with the USA.

Again, here was a leader who brutalised his people, but tonight there was no mention of it, and while most scholars are reluctant to estimate a total number of "unnatural deaths" in China under Mao, evidence shows he was in some way responsible for at least forty million deaths and perhaps eighty million or more. This includes deaths he was solely responsible for, as well as deaths resulting from disastrous policies he implemented and those he refused to change.

His form of communism created inhumane violence and a rift among the Chinese people for which so many paid the ultimate price, and it this leadership that is still running the People's Republic of China.

I felt quite horrified that these presenters were advocating such intensely ruthless leaders and models for us to follow and yet failed to inform us of the so many disgraceful monstrosities that had been brought down on their citizens and countrymen.

I looked around the auditorium at so many bright faces of the young people who seemed flushed with excitement about the things they had heard, and yet I was so saddened that the truth was being held from them. Hopefully, I could be instrumental in eventually bringing this recruiting regimen to an end. I also knew in my heart that no matter how many of these organisations were shut down, many more would spring back up again somewhere else in the world.

✻✻✻

It was soon time to leave this place and I did not get an opportunity to say farewell to Amelia. Although, just as we were mounting the coach to return to Fuengirola, I saw her watching us all board and she nodded and smiled as the coach driver started the engine.

Again, we were instructed to put the black bags over our heads as we left this training centre. We were told to remove them as we entered Ronda. As we travelled back to Fuengirola, it was incredibly quiet on the coach and I wondered what many of them were thinking.

Our return journey did not include the towns and villages that we had encountered on our way there, and consequently, we were soon on the main road and back where we started in a little over forty minutes.

It was good to be back in Fuengirola and I was pleased to get back to my little apartment. I had no idea what was going to happen next and for nearly a week there was no contact from anyone. I continued to visit various nightclubs but did not spend as much time in them as I had previously.

I had begun to think that maybe I had not been selected to continue forward with this group knowing full well that their vetting process was stringent.

✻✻✻

It was at about nine o'clock the following Saturday evening that there was a knock on my door. I was nervous about answering it, but after pondering for a couple of moments, plucked up the courage to see who was out there.

I was surprised to see Allan, one of the sailors who I had befriended not long after arriving in Fuengirola.

"Hello, Bonny, after your visit to our resort last weekend our honourable leaders have found you to be a suitable candidate to come and join us in our fight for equality and justice."

I was completely thrown off balance as I never thought that I would be approached in such a direct manner. Allan's next announcement made the hackles on the back of my neck rise and I suddenly felt a sickening fear.

"Pack your bags immediately; we are going on a trip. Leave nothing behind as you will not be returning."

"Where are we going?" I asked him.

I could feel my legs shaking, and despite having tried to prepare myself for this scenario, I had not been prepared when it came.

"We are going on a short flight for about two hours, is that a problem?"

I tried to smile and said, "Not at all," trying to make light of it and sounding as confident as I could.

"There is a private airfield close to Malaga Airport and we will be taking a short hop to one of the islands out in the Mediterranean."

"Oh, that sounds like fun," I said. "Which one?"

"You will be told as soon as we take off," he replied.

I remembered what Amelia had said to me about the ten percent selected – some are never heard of again, and decided this was not a good time to ask too many questions.

It took me less than ten minutes to pack my belongings and I followed him down the stairs to the waiting car outside. Allan sat in front with the driver who I did not recognise and not a word was spoken throughout the forty-minute journey to the private airstrip.

It was almost pitch black as the car approached the parked jet, which was showing extraordinarily little light. The only light that was visible was over the ramp leading to the door. My bag and other belongings were thrust into my arms and Allan just said, "Hurry, this way," and led me to the ramp.

The cabin lights were very dim, but I could see six other passengers already seated. Allan indicated the overhead locker for me to place all my belonging and then said, "Buckle up; we will be leaving in a couple of minutes."

I heard the engine rev up and almost silently, the jet started to move forward. There appeared to be no lights out on the runway and after a truly short distance, we were airborne.

After complete silence for about ten minutes, the cabin lights grew brighter and Allan said, "I would like to welcome you all. You have been selected from a number of prospective candidates to join many more graduates at our retraining camp on the island of Corsica. You are free to introduce yourselves to each other and please relax for the next couple of hours until we reach our destination."

I looked around the jet and could see several passengers who I had seen at the Heaven's Gate night club. To my biggest surprise, Suzy was one of them. Neither of us spoke but there was a gentle nod of recognition.

Chapter 10. Le Chapeau Rouge

Allan disappeared through a curtain at the front of the cabin and came back carrying a tray with prepacked sandwiches. He then went back through the curtain and returned with a box of assorted cans of soft drinks.

The jet had a superior interior with quality leather seats, and everything looked expensive. However, the refreshments had been bought from a local café and not what one would expect in this setting. Nevertheless, it broke the ice and several of the group started to chat.

Allan had serviced us with refreshments and returned to sit next to me. He was reluctant to talk but I managed to get a few words from him and even a guilty grin when I muttered, "Trainee Engineer indeed."

"Well, it sounded quite plausible when I said it," he replied.

About an hour into the journey, Allan stood up and spoke.

"Can I have your attention for a few minutes?"

He cleared his throat and said, "We will be arriving at a private landing area at Napoleon Bonaparte airport in just over an hour, and a truck will be waiting to take us up to Monte Cinto which will take us about another two hours. The trip is uphill, and will arrive at our destination very close to the highest mountain in Corsica. It will be close to three in the morning when we get there. You will be checked in and given a hot meal and each of you will be issued with a new set of clothing.

"The camp is situated in a very remote area and is a fully walled, adapted fifteenth-century farmhouse sitting on eight acres of land. Your familiarisation training will last about six weeks at which time, depending on your skills, you will all be allocated a new assignment. From a historical point of view, Napoleon Bonaparte was born in Corsica and it is said that he used to spend his summer months at this farmhouse."

A little over an hour later we landed at Napoleon Bonaparte Airport. There was a strong gusty wind as we climbed down from the jet and it was surprisingly warm. As we walked from the jet to the waiting covered truck, Allan explained that the winds were caused by the Sirocco, a hot wind that blows off the coast of Africa during the spring and the autumn and at times can be more than one hundred miles per hour. Higher up on the mountains, it would be considerably colder and on occasions, the wind speed could be a lot higher.

Because of the high winds and the rough terrain, the journey up into the mountains was considerably slower than expected, and it was close to four o'clock in the morning when we finally rumbled through the gates of the ancient farmhouse. Nobody had been able to sleep due to the bumpy and precarious journey, and probably also somewhat to do with the trepidation of our impending new lives.

The truck continued for about half a mile inside the gates and rolled into a compound with what looked like a short row of shops or offices, which had probably originally served as farm outbuildings. In the middle of the row was a building with double doors with a streetlight placed on either side of them. Above the door was a large, lettered sign proclaiming the words, *Le Chapeau Rouge*.

There were mutterings amongst the seven of us until Suzy declared, "The Red Hat, that's what it says, The Red Hat."

That was immediately endorsed by a picture of a red beret emblazoned at about eye level on each of the entrance doors.

As the eight of us, which included Allan, entered through the double doors, we could smell the aromas of cooked food wafting through the passageway. We were ravenously hungry; the only food we had had recently was the single sandwich that Allan had provided as we were leaving Spain many hours before. We were taken straight through to the dining hall, which was a large rectangular room with eight large Formica-topped tables that each seated eight people.

Alan invited us all to sit at one of the tables and promised us a hot meal.

"The leader of our group here will be out to speak to you in a few minutes while you eat your long-awaited meal. After which you will be allowed all day tomorrow to rest and recover from your extremely long journey."

We were all very tired and incredibly pleased to hear that we would be given time to recover.

"Allan, are we allowed to ask questions when he comes to speak to us?" Suzy asked.

"It might be a good idea to leave your questions for a couple of days, by which time you will be settled into camp life and most of your questions by then may well have been answered," Allan replied.

A few minutes later, the door opened and a young guy wearing camouflage trousers and a white t-shirt, complete with a white apron and red beret, came into the dining hall pushing a hot food trolley.

"Bonjour everybody," he said and grinned, and in a French accent declared, "Je suis Pierre, your resident chef welcome to your new home."

He opened the lids to the food and then stepped back and added, pointing at the food with a come and get it gesture, "Bon Appetit."

We all got up, and in a very orderly manner, filled our plates with a selection of food from the trolley, which included French toast, bacon, some sort of sausage, eggs, a selection of seafood, and what looked like English baked beans.

We all tucked in hungrily and had barely started when a tall man fully dressed in camouflage attire, including black military looking boots and red beret, entered the room and stood at one end of the table behind Allan. He was in his late fifties at a guess and sported a handlebar moustache, and looked for all the world like an English Army Officer. When he spoke, it did not dispel that first assessment. He spoke with a very cultured English upper-class accent, and seemed completely out of place for this strange environment.

"Good morning, ladies and gentlemen, welcome to Le Chapeau Rouge. I am the Marshall here and this will be your home for the next few weeks, in which time we will educate you about our group, who the members are, and their reasons for being here, what our goals are and of course some obligatory basic military and fitness training. Enjoy your day off, you will get truly little free time for the foreseeable future after that."

With that, he turned on his heel and marched smartly from the room.

Allan said, "When you have finished your food, you will be shown to your quarters by our night sentry. Your cases etc. have already been sent there."

He looked at everyone in turn, sitting around the table and then said, "Reconvene here at 0600 the day after tomorrow when your new lives will begin. At that time, you will meet the other recruits who arrived here earlier today. There are sixty-four altogether and you are group number eight; each team consists of eight members. Good luck, you are going to need it."

The sleeping accommodation was like a barracks with beds lined up on each side of the room. We realised later when it was light that there were two barrack rooms with a total of thirty-two single beds in each, sixteen down each side of the long rooms; one barrack was for males and one for females. They had the vetting and recruiting process down to a fine art with an equal number of girls and boys all of whom were about twenty-five years and younger. There were a few people already sleeping when we had entered, and we tried to keep as quiet as possible. We were apparently the last group to arrive and had been allocated the beds nearest the entrance.

We were too tired to notice much, and by the time we had put our clothes and personal items in an allocated locker and had made our beds, the red streaks of dawn were starting to appear through the dark clouds. I do not think anyone saw the sun come up, because by then we were all sound asleep. It had been a long day.

I slept fitfully at first, realising how isolated I was from any of my friends and colleagues. However, I must have eventually dropped off because it was about four in the afternoon when I finally roused from a deep sleep.

***

I could see a few people were up and had found the shower rooms and toilets and were now getting dressed in black leather boots, camouflaged trousers, shirts, and red berets.

Each one of us was also issued with dark green puttees (leg wraps), which wrapped around the lower part of the leg from the boots up to about mid-calf. They were for protecting your shoes from taking in debris, and also to protect your legs, keep out the cold and damp, and offer ankle support. Ideal for work over rough territory.

Dinner was at 1800 and we all filed down to the dining hall just a few minutes early. We had all been told to get into our new uniforms so that we would have the rest of the evening to get used to them. We could now also see all the rest of the teams and the full total of sixty-four members.

We were not allowed outside the gates yet, but were invited to wander around the grounds and familiarise ourselves with the compound. Round the back of the kitchens, we found a large, uncovered swimming pool. Although we had enjoyed a good sleep, many were still tired, and having been told that our day would start at 0600, this was going to be the only opportunity to enjoy a good rest before all the activities began the following day.

***

We were rudely awoken by the sound of gunshots from a very animated obnoxious little man firing a dozen or more shots into the air outside our accommodation to rouse us the following morning at 0600. He followed that with loud shouting, ordering us to go and get breakfast, and assemble outside the main doors at 0700 to start the day's activities. His last words to each dormitory were, "Do not dare to be late and make sure you are fully dressed when you fall in outside the main entrance."

When we were fully dressed, we all assembled outside the double doors and stood in small groups looking like a band of untidy ruffians.

That same ridiculously small man with a huge voice appeared out of nowhere and introduced himself.

"I am known as Inch," he bawled at us and without much thought, we began to mutter and smile.

"Keep silent and stand still before I lock any offenders in the cellars." There was a deadly hush. In a loud voice, but no longer shouting, he said, "I am called Inch, not because of my size, but because it means In Charge, and until you deserve my respect, you will all be called Ragga as in Ragamuffins."

He then bestowed on us his revelations of what he expected from us.

"When I am finished with you, you will be able to carry out basic drills such as marching in step, turning while marching, and other manoeuvres, which I will introduce to you in the coming days. For the next hour, you will learn the basics and then we will assess how fit you motley bunch of Raggas are. Do you all understand me? If you don't, then you had better learn English very quickly," he barked.

For the next two hours, we marched together and learned how to stand to attention, and then at ease, and other simple commands.

On completion he said, "I assume that you all know what groups you are in, because now, in your groups, we are going to carry out a fitness exercise up on the mountainside. You will remain in your groups and you will not leave anyone behind. If someone breaks a leg, the rest of the team will carry that person to complete the course. Do you understand so far?" he roared.

In one loud voice, we all answered, "Yes, Inch."

"This first exercise is eight miles long and some of the terrain is harsh and rugged. Remember what I said; this is a team effort, and you will all make it round the course. Let us see which team wins and which teams come in the last three. I have leaders stationed around the course to point you in the right direction."

He then pointed at a very steep incline and said, "You should all have returned in six hours at the most, so by three-thirty this afternoon

I expect to see all of your smiling faces back here and asking for more. What are you waiting for, off you go!"

And as we went on our way, he screamed after us, "Do not forget, march, carry, run, scramble; it's all about teamwork."

I knew that I was fit, and today's rigours would not be too difficult to overcome, but was worried about my teammates. I would need to assess their capabilities under stress and great physical exercise. Two teams took an early lead and I wondered if they were fit or if this was an act of bravado.

The team I was in consisted of three girls and five boys. For the first hour, we kept the pace going quite well, but it was uphill during this part of our journey, and by now all the teams were strung out and we were unable to see any of them. This was hampered by the clouds that clung to the side of the mountain, making visibility difficult; it was also getting colder as the Sirocco winds kept battering us all the way.

None of us knew each other, but we did start to learn each other's names. I knew Suzy and she seemed to be quite fit. Charlie was English and quite a character and still managed to keep talking most of the time. There were three more English team members plus me. Suzy, Charlie, and Kerry.

The rest were all boys: three of them were French, two of them from right here in Corsica and the other from Marseille, and the last one from Malaga in Spain. It seemed strange that the two Corsicans were recruited in Fuengirola, Spain; their names were Larenzu and Petru. Andre from Marseille and Diego from Spain although he preferred the English interpretation which is James.

By now we assessed that we had covered about a quarter of the journey. Andre was over six feet tall, and he was the first one on our team who started to show signs of fatigue. His breathing had become quite laboured, and I wondered if he would be able to keep up the pace.

Through the swirling clouds, just ahead of us, we saw one of the staff gesticulating for us to get a move on. As we passed him, he said in a heavily accented voice, "Just follow the path and in about half a mile you will start to go downhill for a couple of miles. You will also be out of the wind as you put the mountain between you and the Sirocco."

A couple of hundred yards later and out of sight of the staff member, Andre came to a halt and gasped, "I need to stop and get some breath."

I tried to encourage him to keep going until we started on the decline, but he was exhausted. We stopped for about four minutes, during which time one of the teams came running on by seemingly in good spirits. They ignored us as they passed.

We heard one of their members shout, "Just two more to pass, they cannot be too far away."

Andre nodded and said, "I feel better now, let's go."

We could still see the team that had passed us, but we made no impact on the gap between us. In fact, at the next bend, we lost sight of them completely. As soon as we rounded the following bend, we could see the top of the rise, and bright sunshine met us as we started a downhill incline and it instantly felt warmer. Andre's long legs now seemed an advantage to him and he loped into the lead of our group.

The next time we saw a staff member, we were told that we had passed the halfway mark but there were obstacles ahead. The first obstacle became apparent very soon. At some stage, there had been a landfall. A huge round smooth boulder appeared to block our way. It was at least thirty feet high and we had to fathom a way to get past or over it. One side was jammed neatly against the mountainside, blocking our way, and the other was hanging precariously over the side of an immense drop of several hundred feet. We could not see any of the preceding groups so they must have figured something out.

We needed to figure that something out very soon too or we would start to fall further back behind the three groups ahead of us. We noticed a very rough and narrow pathway on an extremely steep incline, almost going back the way we came, but there appeared no other choices. We followed it for about one hundred metres where it suddenly turned sharply on itself, heading back towards the offending boulder. We reached the boulder about two-thirds of the way up it and immediately saw that someone had hammered some steel spikes into its sharp surface. It was a little scary but took only a short time to reach its summit.

Even more alarming was that the only way to get off the boulder and back onto the mountain was a leap of faith. The distance was only about two metres, but the drop below would be instant death if you did not make the distance back onto the mountainside.

Andre went first, and with his long legs, easily traversed the distance. He then stood as close to the precipice as possible and held his hands out to assist each of his team members as they came across. He may have slowed us down, but he was a huge asset to the team when we needed him.

For about five minutes, we kept moving forward at a walking pace until we had recovered from the earlier rigours. We were still traversing downwards and by the time we needed to start an uphill struggle again, we had fully recuperated. We also knew that we were not far from the end and so this was a psychological boost. We had still not seen any more of the groups either behind or in front of us.

Our next challenge made itself apparent long before we reached it. We could hear a continuous noise with it increasing in crescendo long before it became visible. Another alteration in our course took our path round a sharp bend and under a huge rocky overhang; the wind increased as our heading moved back to almost due south. The storm-force Sirocco winds were battering us with considerable force and with it came a painful, icy blast of cold rain.

The winds continued to escalate with every step we took, and the torrential rain made it difficult for us to see or move forward. By now, the noise was deafening, and we were soaked through to the skin. Our group had virtually come to a standstill and at this point, we were unable to communicate verbally.

I moved myself to the front of our group and grabbed their attention. I gesticulated to them to stay where they were, and I would go and see if there was any other way forward. They were reluctant to let me go, but I could not see any other solution.

181

I left them huddled together as close to the rock face as possible. In the meantime, I also kept myself as close to it as possible and inched my way along the narrow path. I had travelled about only twenty metres when the rain ceased, and I found myself inside a wide cavern that was completely dry.

The noise stopped immediately as if someone had switched it off.

It took a few moments for me to realise where I was. I was completely flabbergasted. There was no rain; I was now standing behind a colossal waterfall, and the noise that previously sounded like a locomotive had been muted completely and it was eerily quiet.

I now had the daunting task of making my way back along the storm-ravaged slippery path to lead my teammates to the cavern behind the waterfall. I waited for a few minutes to calm my rapidly beating heart before leaving my relatively calm haven.

Clinging precariously by my raw fingers, I clawed my way back to the waiting team. I tried to shout to them what I had found, but the noise was so horrendous that I could not make them hear me. With a few gesticulations and actions, I made them understand that they needed to follow me. Slowly, we inched our way to the cavern behind the waterfall. I was incredibly relieved when we were all safely behind this gargantuan wall of water.

Once we had passed behind the curtain of water, we emerged safely on the other side. It was only a short distance back to Le Chapeau Rouge, which we could see quite clearly on a plateau below us. We jogged into the courtyard at exactly 1445 and forty-five minutes earlier than the deadline.

The team that overtook us was there and one other, but one team had not arrived yet. I was wondering what happened to it. During the next forty-five minutes, all but one of the remaining teams had arrived. The time dragged on and still no sign of the missing team. We were all getting concerned when dusk started to fall.

Inch did not seem at all bothered about them and said gruffly, "They will get cold out there on the mountain during the night. How can one team so stupidly get lost on this simple exercise?"

By half-past nine it was pitch black when the missing team stumbled into the courtyard moaning and crying.

Inch started shouting at them and all they could do was mumble incoherently. They were cold and shivering and then we suddenly realised that there were only seven of them. Where was the eighth member? One of the girls screamed at Inch.

"She's dead, you pig, ignorant buffoon, she's dead."

Inch got right in her face and bawled at her, "Pull yourself together and don't ever shout at me again."

"Or what?" she sobbed.

With that, he backhanded her across the face and a trickle of blood oozed from the wound he had inflicted.

"That's what," he screamed at her. "This is not a kindergarten; this is war and people get injured or worse, killed. Casualties of war or collateral damage, call it what you like. It happens."

He looked at the sorry, bedraggled group and picked out one of the boys saying, "You come with me, the rest of you go and get cleaned up and then go to the dining hall to get fed."

The other teams waited until they had all showered and changed into warm dry clothes and we all went over to the dining hall together. Nobody had been allowed to eat until all the teams had returned. The boy who had gone with Inch joined us a few minutes later. After interrogating him for details, Inch said that the body would be recovered at daybreak tomorrow.

Little by little, we managed to get all the information from the remaining seven members. Claudia was Italian and only five feet tall. It had been this lack of height that was her downfall. First, they got lost and then tried to speed up. Because of her diminutive size, Claudia just could not get across from the boulder to the solid ground. Finally, she just ran as hard as she could and launched herself into mid-air but did not even reach the mountain. She plummeted without a sound straight down about six hundred feet. She bounced once on the way down and it was all over in seconds.

✿✿✿

As we all filed down to the dining hall the following morning for breakfast, a gurney carrying a coffin was wheeled through the main entrance carrying Claudia's body. It was a very sobering event and I wondered how this might affect the mindset of some of these would-be radicals. These youths, including me, could soon end up in extremely dangerous and hostile conditions and were likely to see a lot more bloodshed and death. Seeing the compassion shown by these teams on the death of a new comrade made me wonder if any of them could or would be able to even take a life themselves.

✿✿✿

The following day we were all issued with a judo kit and led out onto the huge lawn to the rear of the premises. Today there was no sign of Inch, but everyone was now wary of him. He was a brutal instructor.

Instead, this morning the Marshall made an appearance. He spoke to us in calming tones and vastly different from our treatment of two days ago.

"I apologise for the trauma that you have been through with the tragic accident and death of Claudia. We need to put that behind us and get on with the task of getting you all educated and ready to act as operatives of Le Chapeau Rouge."

He looked around the huge lawn and said, "Today will begin your self-defence training. We are fortunate enough to have with us from Japan, the Mixed Martial Arts World Middleweight Champion, Hideaki. He will train you daily for the next two weeks in defence tactics and then for the following two weeks you will learn to exhibit aggression as you grasp how to attack your opponent."

He turned to walk away and then changed his mind and turned back.

"Just one more thing, I need to make something completely clear to you. After the tragic event of yesterday, there were mutterings among some of you that you wished to leave us."

The Marshall then looked profoundly serious and said very forcefully, "Nobody leaves here until your training is complete." With that, he turned and marched smartly back into the building.

It was a scary statement, but what made it worse, was wondering how he knew that several members wanted to leave. It seemed that there was a mole among the members who was reporting back to the management.

I was completely comfortable with the training, but did not allow my expertise to be apparent and purposely made a few mistakes so that I did not give myself away.

In the afternoons we spent most of the time at the range, learning how to use many different types of weapons: rifles, pistols, machine guns, knives, and even a bow and arrow.

Although our training was laid out for us each day, we were all encouraged to continue our individual fitness training, which included swimming, running, and weight training. There was no schedule, and it was left up to us to create our own programme.

After dinner in the evening, we had to listen to lectures, mostly promoted from a screen with various political leaders putting forward their own brand of politics – all completely left-wing socialists bordering on communism. As time went by, the atmosphere at these lectures changed very subtly, and starting at the beginning of the third week, all we were being fed was Marx, Lenin, Stalin, Mao Tse-Tung, Castro, and others. The programmes just continued to move further and further to the left.

✳✳✳

The training was continuous, and at the end of the fourth week, we were all very proficient in martial arts: both defensive and aggressive. I had already been trained in the use of various guns, but listened carefully to the instructor and he took me under his wing thinking that I was an enthusiastic learner. At the end, he told me that I had the potential to be a sniper and asked if I would be interested in further training for this skill. I nodded enthusiastically.

One evening I was out walking in the grounds with Suzy when she broke a bombshell.

"Bonny, keep looking ahead and listen to me; don't show any surprise at what I am about to tell you."

"Of course," I replied.

"In a couple of days, and for your personal safety I cannot tell you exactly when, but I will be leaving here in the dead of night. I am waiting for a message from Dave Wilson who has arranged it all. Just one more thing, the Chef with the French accent is a friend, and he will let you know if we are successful."

My mind was racing, I thought she could easily be recaptured and possibly killed.

"I wish you could have told me more," I said.

"Bonny, stay safe and be on your guard; there are spies among the spies. Chef Pierre is your only friend once I have gone. Dave Wilson will return after I am back home and safe. I look forward to our reunion in London."

We walked back through the gardens to the main building and then on to our barrack room.

✳✳✳

I slept fitfully, worrying about Suzy and the ordeal that was ahead of her. I woke up several times in the night, but all was quiet in the barracks. I rose early and went for a shower with Suzy still very much on my mind. I got dressed and looked around to accompany her to breakfast but she must have gone on ahead because there was no sign of her.

I was only the second trainee to enter the dining hall and Chef Pierre greeted me in his cheerful chatty way.

"Bonjour, Bonny," he beamed.

He slowly lowered his white apron a couple of inches and he had a white sheet of paper with the words 'Gone' written on it. He screwed up the paper and said nonchalantly, "Breakfast will be up in a couple of minutes although the coffee is already made so help yourself."

I suddenly felt a hollow space in my stomach and could feel bile rising in my throat. I started to tremble and had to fight to control my emotions. I was not only terrified for Suzy, but knew that any moment now all hell would break loose when they realised Suzy had absconded.

It was incredibly quiet until mid-afternoon when the vile and wretched Inch appeared back on campus. We understood that he was going to be away for most of the week, but here he was scowling at everyone.

Shouting menacingly, with spittle flying out of his mouth, he told all the groups except number eight to go and get seated in the dining hall.

"Keep quiet, no talking, and I will be there in a few moments."

He waited until they had left and then he addressed group eight.

"Where is she?" he bellowed loudly, beating the top of one of the lockers with a bamboo cane.

"If any of you know where she is, then speak up now and that will be the end of it."

Andre was the bravest to speak up and asked gently, "Who are we looking for, Sir?"

"You stupid fool, look around and you will see that one of your team is missing. I want to know where she is, NOW," he screamed at the top of his voice, smacking the cane on top of the locker so hard that it split into tiny shards and flew in all directions.

Andre became very submissive and said, "Oh dear, is it Suzy?"

"You damn fool, of course it's Suzy," he growled. "Someone is going to suffer for this; one of you must know where she has gone." He threw what was left of his cane towards Andre who ducked away from the projectile heading his way.

"When she is caught, not if, but when, she will be flogged with a rope's end until she begs for it all to end and the end will come quickly. Let this be a lesson; do not try to get away from here. You are ours now and there is no going home." "Each one of you from team eight will go and meet with the Marshall. Andre, seeing that you are the class idiot, you can go first. Get to his office immediately, GO," he barked. "Don't you dare walk down there; sprint as fast as you can."

He then reeled off our names and the order in which we would meet the Marshall, I would be last but one.

I waited nervously for my turn to go and meet with the Marshall. Each of my team members had been grilled for about half an hour each. Finally, it was my turn and I knocked on the Marshall's office door. He smiled sweetly as I entered and invited me to sit down.

"Well, Bonny, it is Bonny, isn't it?"

I just nodded my head.

The Marshall looked long and hard at me and finally said, "Tell me about your friend Suzy."

"What is it you need to know, Sir?" I asked.

"Why do not we start with, let me see. How long were you both friends?"

"We weren't friends," I answered him. "We didn't meet in the best of circumstances. When I arrived in Spain a couple of months ago, she started a fight with me in the night club and we spent the night in a police cell."

"Yes, yes I heard about your altercation," he replied. "Tell me about your fight in the underground venue?"

I pulled a face and explained how I had been abducted against my will and forcefully made to fight another girl.

"So, you like fighting?" he probed.

"I didn't have much choice, did I? How would you have dealt with it?" My voice had risen so that I sounded angry.

He glared at me and it felt as if his eyes were probing into my brain. "You need to control your anger, Bonny Russworth, it is likely to get you into trouble," he said impatiently.

"Rushton," I replied. He looked confused.

"What are you talking about?"

I shrugged my shoulders and took a deep breath and answered him indignantly.

"You called me Russworth and my name is Rushton."

I could see that he was furious that I had backchatted him and he did not like it at all.

"Enough of this crap, where is she?"

I looked him in the eye and said as convincingly as I could, "I have no idea, Marshall," and before he could say anything else to try to get me tongue-tied, I added, "she told me that she didn't like it here and wanted to go home. I told her, 'Well, that's your problem, not mine, I am enjoying my training, go and tell someone who is interested.' I also said to her, 'What happened to the arrogant girl who picked a fight with me in front of her friends just for bravado. I think you do everything for show, and you have nothing to back it up.'"

The Marshall shook his head and said less angrily now, "You show a lot of potential. I like people with backbone; I think you will go a long way in our organisation. Get out and send the last one in to see me."

I nearly stumbled outside his door and I could feel the butterflies in my stomach. That had been a close call and I knew from now on I would have to be extra vigilant. He and Inch would be watching me with greater scrutiny to see if I slipped up.

☆☆☆

The training continued and there were no more notable events for about a week. It was a Monday morning and the Marshall advised that Inch wished to speak to us all. I knew that something was coming when Inch made us line up with the girls in the front line and boys behind them. Almost unashamedly he made sure that I was placed right in the middle.

The Marshal stood on a small wooden dais in front of us all and directly in line with me.

It could not have been more obvious that they were going to try to intimidate me, and I started to prepare myself for whatever was to come.

The Marshall began, "Good morning, everyone, I haven't spoken to you for a while, and I just wanted to update you on your progress here and what happens next."

He looked at the line of boys and then passed his eyes over the girls and his eyes stopped when he reached me.

"Before we talk about your future, I have some good news for you."

I could feel his eyes glaring towards me and there was a wicked half-grin on his face as he watched for any betrayal from me.

"It has been reported that Suzy has been spotted in a café down in Ajaccio, and as we speak, some of our operatives are about to apprehend her, isn't that great?"

Instead of looking shocked, I had a smug smile on my face and nodded my head gently. The Marshall looked astonished, obviously thinking that I would be upset. I had weathered the storm but remained very wary.

✳✳✳

Life continued as normal at camp Le Chapeau Rouge for the next few weeks and there were no more sightings or comments about Suzy. I continued with my sniper training as well as becoming familiar with other weapons.

Then without any warning, our numbers began to shrink. Inch informed us that the missing members had now been allocated positions in various parts of the world, but there were no specific details. I needed to find out more information so that I could share my intelligence with MI6.

That opportunity came from a very unexpected source when the Marshall asked me to report to his office. I felt a little uneasy as I walked over there. He greeted me with a broad smile and shook my hand warmly.

"Please sit down," he offered.

I was taken aback by his frankness, but it did not dispel the apprehension I felt.

"Bonny, you and I have had our differences and I make no apology for that, except to say that here at Le Chapeau Rouge we have a lot to be proud of, but are also aware that there are many organisations who would like to bring us down. I created this training academy from the ground up and have to be thoroughly scrupulous in vetting every member who comes here."

"I see," I commented.

"Many of your comrades have been allocated positions around the world, and as we speak, there will be another five leaving us today to begin their new lives."

"Sir, I have no wish to be rude, but how does this affect me?" I queried.

"Bonny, you are an extremely competent trainee, and I think I can say with confidence you are one of the best snipers to pass through these gates. You also ask great questions and, although mostly respectful, you have spirit and are not frightened to speak up."

I smiled when he said mostly. He knew his comment was not wasted on me and smiled back.

"I would like to make you an offer. Our regular training here is usually about three months for each course; some leave earlier and some later depending on their progress."

"What do you have in mind?" I asked.

"Well, we have a new group arriving in about two weeks and some of our mountain leaders will be moving on to new pastures. Perhaps you would like to stay on here for the duration of the next course and assist in the running of the place? You will add another segment to our curriculum. Help on the mountain where needed, as we do not want any more sad incidents like Claudia. You could assist with the martial arts activities alongside Hideaki and continue with your individual advancement at the range."

"If I choose to move on, where would I go?" I put in. I could see a cloud cross his brow, but he answered candidly.

"There is an opening for a weapons expert in Venezuela that needs to be filled with some urgency and that could be an option. However, Yemen needs a professional top-class sniper who is also fully rounded in many other skill sets. The operation in Yemen is currently expanding their activities in the region. When they have enlarged their new camp, they will need specialists for covert operations in many adjacent localities in pursuit of their Islamic jihad."

I did not wish to seem too enthusiastic with my answer, but wanted him to think that I was genuinely weighing up my options. After several moments' silence, I could see his agitation levels increase.

"If I decide to stay, could I ask for an addition to the programme that I believe would be beneficial to the students?"

I could see his hesitation as he pondered my request and then he said, "I like your style; you are a great leader and now you seem to be negotiating deals. What do you propose?"

"Purchase a map and compass for each of the teams and I will give them a half day's training and then take them out on the lower slopes and put the theory into practice. Then a few days later, send them to complete the full course. Map reading is a skill that could benefit every organisation they go to work for. Also, allow me to put together several different courses to follow on the mountain which will increase their confidence and fitness on unfamiliar terrain."

"That is a great idea, but I need some time to assess your suggestions. Let me think about it for twenty-four hours and we will discuss it at length." He seemed to be nodding thoughtfully as he dismissed me.

***

Two days later, Inch approached me and handed me a carrier bag. He was almost pleasant and said, "This is a gift from the Marshall; he says he looks forward to seeing your new ideas on paper and presented to him before giving you his final approval." With that, he marched away across the courtyard.

I took my carrier bag back to the accommodation and emptied the contents on my bed. There were ten compasses with a nylon string so that they could be worn around the neck, a stopwatch, and ten laminated local area maps plus ten chinagraph pencils.

Now I needed to find out if they were going to allow me to go outside the compound and spend a few days planning the training, or if they expected me to produce it from the maps only.

I spent all that evening poring over the maps to find about three potential courses for the new students. By the end of the evening, I had identified three possible routes and wanted to propose that the teams carry these out first before setting them off completely blind on the eight-mile course that had led to Claudia's death. It would let me educate the new teams in useful skills that would help them be prepared for the final mountain ordeal.

***

I asked to see the Marshall the following morning, and he sent for me about mid-way through the afternoon. I showed him my plans, and much to my surprise, he suggested that I go up onto the mountain for the next few days but insisted that I report to him at 2100 every day with my results.

He also informed me that I had been allocated a new private residence in the main building and I could move in the next day. I would have more pleasant surroundings with a small suite of my own in the main building.

I was even more delighted that he was going to allow me a greater amount of freedom. This was a huge breakthrough for me, but I was not naive enough to think that I would not be watched by some of his close cohorts.

I also had some great news that evening when I went for my evening meal.

Pierre leaned over and whispered, "Suzy is home and Dave is back."

I felt very relieved on both counts, knowing full well that Suzy was safe and could not be used to try to intimidate me, although I think that my relationship with the Marshall and Inch were on a more even keel now.

***

I woke up the following morning, feeling the best I had for many weeks. I knew that this was only a hiatus and things were going to get a lot worse before this nightmare was over. I got dressed in a red tracksuit and, clasping my map and compass, made my way across the courtyard to the main entrance.

A guard appeared from out of the shadows but when he saw me, he said, "Good morning, Miss Bonny, enjoy your day," and he then opened one of the two large doors and let me out.

I was free, if only for a few hours, but it felt good. I broke into a run, and for about ten minutes, enjoyed my new moment of freedom, and then jogged the rest of the way up as far as the boulder.

I scrutinised every inch of it once more to see if I had missed any other solutions, but I could not see any. I thought the plans that I had made would be sufficient to keep everyone safe. I passed over to the other side with ease, having now done it many times. I assessed that if at least one of the team was over five feet and eight inches, then they should all overcome the hurdle. If the tallest member got over first, a rope could be hurled to him, and from then on, by securing each member one at a time, a safe crossing would be achieved. Because of the tragic accident with Claudia, the Marshall had modified the schedule to allow me more time to give them adequate instruction.

Satisfied with my plan, I continued towards the waterfall. Some movement caught my eye and I immediately and wrongly guessed that the Marshall had sent someone to follow me to make sure that I was doing what I was supposed to and not trying to escape. Then I realised as they got closer, that it was two men out taking their dogs for a walk. I watched as they came closer and then they walked on by. The closest they came was about two hundred yards and I saw them disappear behind the mountain.

Every few hundred yards, I stopped to take notes and put some basic plans into place for the new recruits to accomplish.

The wind was less strong today, and it seemed that the Sirocco winds had died down as the season matured. I was looking forward to about five or ten minutes under the waterfall, where I really would get away from everything. It was quite cloudy today and behind the waterfall it seemed very dark.

Without warning, I heard a voice that I recognised from behind a pillar of rock just ahead. I had never been so pleased to see Dave Wilson step out in front of me, and immediately after him, Bob Penfold appeared with two dogs. Dave gave me a hug and Bob said, "Hi, Bonny, we did not have much time to speak last time we met, but I am pleased to see that you are safe and well."

I explained as quickly as I could everything that had happened and that I was likely to be here for a while if I was still required to go to Yemen. Dave responded, "Yes, that is the plan."

"I think I am getting closer to gaining the leader's trust and hopefully acquire some good intelligence from him soon, but I still have to be very careful. He has a nasty little jerk working for him I do not trust at all, who would think nothing of killing anyone he didn't like or got in his way."

Bob Penfold smiled and shook his head. "You must be talking about the nice Mr Inch. We have had our eyes on him for quite some time. If you had not come to take on this mission, we would have taken him out a long time ago. We still can, but the more information we can get, the better it will be for all of us. If he seriously becomes a threat, then advise Pierre and he will get a message to us. Inch enjoys a drink, and we have a young lady under our purview who chats to him most nights in a local drinking hole in Ajaccio. She brings us good intelligence after he has had a few drinks, but to be honest, he knows little."

"We know little about the Marshall's history so it would be useful if you can try to investigate his background. Bob has been here on and off for nearly two years, ever since the Marshall bought the estate. He is a very private and discreet landowner," Dave explained.

Bob looked around and said, "It might be a good idea if you made your way back to the compound. Do not want anybody getting suspicious. There are a couple of the Marshall's goons prowling around, but they are unlikely to see us. I have been here long enough to know every nook and cranny on this mountainside and know how to keep out of sight."

At 2130 that evening, I went to the Marshall's office to show him the plans that I had drawn up. He liked everything I had done, so my freedom to come and go as I pleased continued from then on.

***

A new group of sixty-four people arrived in due course and we had no incidents on the mountain or anywhere else. From time to time the Marshall disappeared for a few days, leaving Inch completely in charge. I noticed that his attitude changed a lot whenever the Marshall was away. He became more brutal and sadistic at these times as if he were not bad enough anyway.

***

We were about halfway through the training of the second course when the Marshall invited me to dinner in his private cottage that coming Saturday evening at 1900. The cottage was situated behind a large privet hedge about two hundred yards beyond the swimming pool. I had no idea that there even was a building back there. I was a little wary, as I had no idea what might be in store for me but there was no nefarious intent.

I knew nothing about this man, and it came as quite a shock that he was married and had a wife living right there in the cottage. Saturday evening arrived and I made my way across the grounds to the privet hedge and found an entrance gap down the left side of the hedge. Behind it, my breath was taken away; this was some cottage. It was large and built in Georgian style with black beams and beautiful pristine white panels in between the beams.

The décor inside was elegant. An entrance hall with black leather armchairs that continued into a huge, magnificent dining room. The walls were covered with antique and priceless framed works of art. It was ironic that at the far end of the dining room, and facing towards me as I entered, was a very large picture of the Fighting Temeraire painted by J.M.W. Turner.

His wife was a diminutive lady dressed immaculately with an impeccable bun hairstyle of pure silver.

"Hello, Bonny, I am Rupert's wife Maud." She spoke very quietly with a genteel aristocratic voice.

Despite the way I looked, she was extremely gracious and invited me to sit at the top right-hand side of the long, highly polished dining table. This was the first time I heard the Marshall's name.

A young lady dressed like a silver service waitress brought in a drinks cabinet and I asked for a Perrier Water. The Marshall invited me to try something stronger. I told him that as a marksman I needed to keep a steady hand and declined as gracefully as I could.

He nodded in acquiescence.

I had never eaten pheasant before, and found it to be extraordinarily rich but not unpleasant. After we had eaten, I was invited into the parlour. This room was as tastefully decorated as the dining room. The couch, chaise longue, and two armchairs were sumptuously covered in deep dark red velvet. I was offered an armchair.

The Marshall sat on the chaise longue and lit a large cigar, which he held in his left hand, and in the right, he held a large crystal glass brandy bowl full of expensive cognac. His wife sat in the other armchair.

"My dear," she said, "tell me about yourself and where you are from."

I knew now that I would need to be incredibly careful and wondered if she had been encouraged to ask probing questions by her husband. After briefly telling her about myself and being raised in an orphanage, I then started to ask questions of my own.

"What part of England are you from?" I asked her.

"A place called Corley, not far from Coventry but out in the countryside. Rupert comes from Keresley, just a few miles away from my home, although he was born in Simonstown, South Africa, not far from Cape Town."

She carried on talking and so I had no need to ask any more questions of her.

"Rupert was in the Army and we lived for many years in Aldershot. He had several short postings to various parts of the world, including Singapore, Australia, Gibraltar, and a few others, and later he was an officer's trainer at Sandhurst. We had visited Corsica on a holiday many years ago and it became our home just four years ago, although we did not buy this place until about two years ago."

By now, the Marshall was on about his fourth large cognac and was beginning to look quite mellow. He smiled benevolently as his wife continued talking to me. A little while later, the maid came in and spoke quietly to Maud and she stood up and said, "Sorry, Bonny, I have to attend to something so if you will excuse me."

She got up and left the room leaving me with Rupert.

"What was it like growing up in South Africa?" I ventured.

"Much of the time it was good, but we had many problems in the country. Apartheid was the major thing; there was much brutality on both sides, and growing up there had a lasting impression on me."

He was opening up to me and I wondered if he would continue to give me valuable information.

"I was just a young teenager when I moved to England; my family had money and I was lucky enough to go to a good school. I went on to Cambridge University and from there gained entrance to Sandhurst

Military Academy. I left the Academy after graduating with flying colours as a Second Lieutenant and had a very bright-looking future. I went from one promotion to the other and was made a colonel in record time."

He went to the drinks cabinet to refresh his drink and find another Cuban cigar. The phone rang and I sat patiently waiting for him to finish.

"Sorry about that," he said.

"One of the other camps is experiencing some problems and I may have to visit them tomorrow and quell the small insurrection. A couple of troublemakers getting out of hand; just a minor problem."

I tried to sound upbeat as I said, "Do you ever get a chance to rest? You always seem to be coming and going."

He yawned and smiled, saying, "I am busier now than when I was in the British Army."

I did not want to arouse his suspicions by asking too many questions, but thought I would take a chance with one simple question.

"Do you have many camps to control?" I asked.

His answer took me completely off guard.

"Let me see now; nine currently, with another three near completion."

"Goodness, no wonder you are so busy," I quipped.

It was far too soon in our improved relationship for me to ask any more questions, but I believe the relaxed atmosphere and the number of Cognacs he had consumed had mellowed him considerably.

He went on, "I think that you might be a greater asset to me than I had previously thought. How would you feel about writing some programmes that I can use at the other venues?"

My heart was starting to beat fast and I knew this sort of information would be of inestimable value to MI6.

I answered him very softly and without any excitement in my voice said, "Do you wish for me to visit any of the other camps or would you like me to prepare something here?"

He rubbed his chin and mumbled something I could not hear and then he perked up and said, "Yes, yes that would be a grand idea. Why don't we discuss it tomorrow after your day out on the mountain?"

He nodded enthusiastically and continued, saying, "Right now I need to concentrate on the problem we have just outside Marseille. I will be gone all day tomorrow and we will meet again here at the house at nine in the evening. That is, of course, if you are happy to come for dinner. Oh, and I promise it will be either pork or lamb and nothing as rich as pheasant."

He guffawed loudly and said, "Goodnight, Bonny, until tomorrow evening."

***

The following morning I was up early so I could get up onto the mountain to finalise all my plans for our current recruits. I had just crossed the boulder when I heard an aircraft overhead. It looked like a Lear jet, but it was climbing rapidly so I was unable to be completely sure of what it was. I watched as it very quickly disappeared.

I soon forgot about the jet. Today there was extraordinarily little wind and I sat down on a small grassed covered plateau and gazed out into the distance. The sun was just coming up and the vista was stunning. I wondered if I would get the chance to explore it more fully. Maybe when this was all over, I could holiday here for a couple of weeks; it was breath-taking, and I knew that I wanted to spend more time here.

Enough of the dreaming, I need to complete my team plans. Here I was doing my best to train would-be terrorists to be the best they could be. At times it was very conflicting, but I knew the result would be worth it once this organisation was closed.

I was able to take more time today; the Marshall was away, and Inch was somewhere down in Ajaccio. The recruits were with Hideaki for hand-to-hand combat training and self-defence.

I made my way down off the plateau and along to the cavern behind the waterfall just in case Dave and Bob were out this way. It had been a couple of weeks since I had spoken to them. The area was empty and I decided to make my way back to camp. I had gone less than two hundred yards when I spotted a man with a dog. He waited until I had seen him and then made his way towards the waterfall.

Bob was in the cavern, waiting for me. He explained that Dave was in Ajaccio watching Inch visiting various stores and businesses. They wanted to know who his business contacts were in case they were in some way involved with the operation or were simply suppliers.

We skipped polite conversation as I brought Bob up to date with my visit to the Marshall's house, his domestic arrangements, his and his wife's first names, and as much detail as I could share about other camps, including the one in Marseille.

Bob was delighted at the huge amount of information I was able to share with him.

"Bonny, this is a huge breakthrough, we have been trying to find out more about this man for about two years. Now we will be able to completely profile him and get a full picture of who he is."

I nodded and said, "Thanks."

Bob continued. "No, Bonny, thank you. Micky Shone was spot on when he originally told us about you. Whatever happens, just know that you are an incredibly brave agent, and we are extremely proud of what you do. We threw you in at the deep end, and your intelligence is going to save countless lives and put a lot of evil people behind bars. HQ is delighted with the work that you continue to do."

He grinned. "They are also going to chip in and make sure that you will never have to purchase green or orange hair dye again."

I smiled and felt very humble after his remarks. I gave Bob a brief wave farewell and made my way back to the camp.

Knowing that I would be going to the Marshall's house for dinner, I decided to take a walk around the grounds to clear my head before once more entering the lion's den.

It was now completely dark, but it was a crystal-clear evening, and the stars were out in full brilliance. I spotted one that I thought was moving, and then realised it was an aircraft directly above me. I watched as it traversed towards the south and then did a right-hand arc and returned towards where I was standing. I was almost mesmerised as I watched its trajectory. It was also losing height rapidly and I wondered if it was in trouble. It was close now and I could hear the deep throb of its engines and see the lights on the fuselage as it disappeared out of sight beyond some trees.

I stood for a while, listening for any further noises, but heard nothing and slowly made my way back to my accommodation.

That evening at dinner with the Marshall and his wife, he seemed less talkative as if he had something on his mind.

"How was your day, Sir?" I asked him.

A deep frown crossed his brow and he answered, "Very troubling; I had to remove a couple of bad apples from the group in Marseille. I love going there – it is an idyllic area and a few miles from the city in a small village called Collobrières. It is up in the hills not far from some stunning little fishermen's villages, although now the coast is filled with tourists. So much more tranquil away from the tourists. We have a small compound hidden away from prying eyes, but only about a quarter of the size of this place. At most we only cater for about sixteen to twenty trainees."

Then he was suddenly deep in his private thoughts and his eyes seemed to have misted over.

His wife looked lovingly at him and said, "Rupert, are you alright, you don't look well?"

"Yes, my dear," he replied. "Very unfortunate, so very unfortunate."

He was noticeably quiet for the rest of the evening and I did not want to push him. He asked about my plans for training the groups and just nodded enthusiastically.

"Good stuff, Bonny, you will be a great asset here."

I noticed that he had not taken a drink all evening and we finished our day with him exclaiming that he wanted an early night. I had not gleaned much from him this evening, but what I did get was valuable.

***

In the morning, there were no signs of either Bob or Dave and I was a little disappointed because I wanted to tell them a bit more about the camp near Marseille. It was considerably colder as I passed behind the waterfall and I ran quickly back to the compound to keep myself warm.

I was unsure of how much value I was providing MI6, but knew that they needed me to move on to my goal in Yemen. However, I could not move it forward any faster.

***

I was in for a surprise a few days later when the Marshall asked me at incredibly short notice to meet him at his office as soon as possible. Confused and apprehensive, I rushed along to his office as soon as I could.

Inch was there and did not look at all happy when I arrived.

"The Marshall wants to see you now," he growled. "What took you so long to get here?"

I was quite used to his foul temper and smiled sweetly at him. Then I replied in a way I knew would irritate him and said, "I had things to attend to that you men could never understand."

He looked totally confused and barked, "The Marshall demands your attendance right now."

I grinned at him and replied, "Did anyone ever tell you what an insignificant and useless little man you are?"

He almost exploded and ran at me threateningly.

I stepped deftly to one side and watched him crash to the floor. He was surprisingly agile and was instantly back on his feet. I had to admit I was terrified of what might happen next, so I took the initiative and as he came at me again, I sidestepped his attack once more and caught him with a right hook to the point of his jaw. He dropped, and this time he was not so quick to get up but looked completely shocked.

With a raised voice I shouted at him, "I have finally learned that bullies like you have no power, no control, and try to rule by fear. You are just a jumped-up nobody who has been given a little authority and tries to use it to intimidate weaker people. Do not ever attempt to threaten me again. Do we understand each other?"

His gaze was on fire and he looked as if he were about to explode, but backed off, looking humiliated and defeated.

I raised my hands in reconciliation and spoke. "Inch, you continue what you do but I will soon be gone, and your power will be restored. However, you do not control me, are we clear? Also, I do not wish to humiliate you any further, so if you do not mention this incident, then neither will I."

He just glared and opened the Marshall's office door to let me in. He remained outside.

Inside the office, two Middle Eastern men were seated at the Marshall's desk.

"Bonny, let me introduce you to Colonel Asraf from Yemen and General Lankarani from Tehran. I have been telling them what a fine marksman and a great asset to this camp you have been ever since you got here."

I nodded politely at them both.

Both men spoke perfect English, and the Iranian said proudly that he had attended Oxford University in England.

The General continued, "Bonny, do you understand you will have to wear a scarf over your head at all times when you are in Yemen?"

I responded to his statement. "Sirs, with respect, I am a marksman. I need to feel the wind on my face, have an unimpeded view, and hearing to enable me to be as good as I am. If I am working with explosives, then I need to be able to hear any clicks or sounds coming from any devices that I am either setting or disarming."

They then continued speaking in Arabic, much of which I understood. They had never had this type of situation before and were in a complete quandary as to what they should do.

"Marshall," the General said, "we will need to discuss this further and look at her full training results during her time with you. Perhaps you can give us all your info about her, and we will return a week today if we decide to take her. If not, then we will need to look elsewhere for our marksman."

"Of course, General," the Marshall replied, nodding politely. The two Arabs then stood up and swiftly exited the room.

Before I had time to speak, the Marshall said to me, "It is a power play, they do it all the time. They need you and will be back. They will accede to your requests, but they may ask you to wear a shawl at mealtimes or whenever you are meeting with someone just to save face, but most of the time you will be free to leave it off. We frequently have this little dance, so I am used to their game."

***

I tried to get out on the mountain as often as I could and although I was no longer in the planning stages of any of the mountain exercises, no one challenged me. I came and went pretty much as I pleased when not required to assist Hideaki. Inch stayed completely away from me.

I had not seen either Dave or Bob for several days and needed to let them know about my impending move to the Yemen. I used the mountain to keep myself as fit as possible, running both up the side of the mountain and jogging back down again after passing behind the waterfall. In the last two weeks alone, I had knocked about ten minutes off my initial time. That, combined with some weight training and swimming, saw me in really good shape, and knowing that where I was going, I would need to keep myself in top form.

My flight had been arranged for this coming Saturday and I would be flying from Ajaccio to Paris and then on to Aden International Airport in Yemen. Thereafter, a couple of hours in a Land Rover to the new training camp, which would be my home for the foreseeable future. Of course, I was acquainted with the camp, having visited it from underwater when the diving team and I had placed a radio receiver and other equipment when I was on HMS *Dornik*. That seemed like a lifetime ago.

Saturday came all too quickly and there had been no contact from Dave or Bob. I was feeling nervous about the move and not being able to speak to them had made this move even more nerve-wracking.

The Marshall sent for me a couple of hours before I departed Le Chapeau Rouge and wished me well for the future. I plucked up the courage to ask him at the last minute why he did this job.

"Bonny, I was badly let down by the British Army and I was accused of something I had not done. I was a good officer and gave them many years of faithful service, but when I left, I was angry. I am still angry. But my new career pays me well. As you know, I live well, and it is my task to find people for many different clients around the world in over twenty different countries. I get paid an incredible finders' and trainers' fee for getting them the right people. I do not mind telling you now that you are leaving, but I made half a million American dollars just for you alone. Thank you, Bonny, I wish you well, and try not to get killed."

I had nothing to say and just nodded as I left his office.

I had the unfortunate pleasure of Inch's company as he had been instructed to take me to the airport; not a word was spoken during the journey and he did not even utter a word as I got out of the vehicle.

※※※

I was completely amazed that I was being allowed to fly halfway across the world unaccompanied. I believe I could have walked away at any time if I had any doubts. The Marshall thought I was committed, and he was quite correct, but not for his reasons. I arrived at Napoleon Bonaparte

Airport at nearly midnight; my departure time was two in the morning with a flight time of two hours to Charles de Gaulle Airport in Paris.

On arrival in Paris, I had about a three-hour stopover which gave me a lot of time to find the Air France departure lounge for Dubai. I wandered around the Duty-Free shops and restaurants and finally settled for a coffee in Starbucks. I think there is a Starbucks in nearly every major airport in the world. Although it was early in the morning, the airport was packed with people. I thought about making a phone call and then wondered if I was being watched and decided against it.

I was feeling a little lost and had no idea if there was any help nearby. I had not realised when I began this project, how isolated and yes, scared I was going to be at times. I could hold my own under most circumstances, but right now I was on my way into the lion's mouth. It was not as if anyone could have briefed me on what to expect, because no agent had ever been so deeply embroiled with an enemy terrorist group. I was going as a marksman and maybe also a bomber, but I didn't know how many people I would have to kill who were enemies of the group and could well be friends of my own government. Did they also know the risks that they could be killed by one of their own agents? Would I hesitate, which could cost me my own life and maybe also give away my reason for being there? Right now, I could do with some answers to my concerns. I remember during my training in the early days, that Miss Morgan said, no matter what happens, 'Stiff upper lip, and all that.' Just for a second, I thought, stiff drink more like.

I made my way to the gate and it was just opening when I got there. They checked my ticket and passport, and I boarded the plane. My seat was right at the back of the plane, the last seat on the right-hand side. The plane quickly filled and at the last minute, an Arab cleric in black robes and a dark beard sat next to me. I smiled and nodded at him as we waited for the call from the pilot telling us that we were about to take off. We were in a line of several planes waiting for take-off instructions and finally the engine's sound increased and suddenly we were rushing down the runway. We continued to ascend for about ten minutes before the engine roar eased and the pilot addressed the passengers.

"We will be flying at 35,000 feet and our journey will take six hours and forty minutes. Enjoy your flight."

The Arab cleric next to me asked, "Is this your first flight to Dubai?"

Where had I heard that voice before?

"Yes," I replied.

"Bonny, you can relax. Bob Penfold at your service."

I felt a sudden sense of relief; someone was looking after me.

I smiled and said very quietly, "Am I glad to see you!"

We were away from anyone who could eavesdrop our conversation, but nevertheless, we kept our volume to a minimum.

I voiced my concerns to him about killing someone. He pondered for a moment and replied, "Bonny, sadly there will be many more casualties in this war on terror if good people didn't die for the better good. I know it is difficult to justify killing someone, but imagine you have a gun to your head and if you do not shoot then you are likely to be killed. We do everything we can to protect our agents and troops, but remember many of them will not know that you are on their side and you become a legal target to them. Each one of us is responsible for our personal safety, even though we will interfere wherever it is possible to do so."

It was a very sobering thought and I nodded in agreement.

Over the next few hours, I learned that the agency now had a full picture of the Marshall and his plans and venues; each one of his camps had been located and were being monitored. He had a pilot's licence and owned a Lear Jet. That, of course, made sense.

"You will learn more about him in the debrief stage when your project is over. Your concern right now will be to concentrate on the camp in Yemen and what other assets they have in the Middle East. Does that make sense?" Bob asked me.

"Yes, of course," I replied

I told him about the two Arab men that I had met in the Marshall's office and explained that Tehran was not only augmenting the terror camp, but also fully funding it. Which included the fee paid to the Marshall for me.

We were quiet for about an hour as a meal and drinks were brought around, but as soon as the coming and going of the air hostess ended, we carried on with our conversation.

"Bonny, there will be help at hand if for any reason you need to be extracted. Your lifeline to the outside world is by the radio receiver that you helped place in the nearby bank of the camp. HMS *Dornik* will be nearby and will be able to listen to your verbal reports. On completion of anything that you relay, it will be acknowledged by a combination of three red flashing lights from the unit followed by a long green flash. If they do not understand your transmission, you will see a continuous yellow light for about five seconds. If this happens just repeat your message."

"OK, understood," I replied.

He continued, "If you need to be extracted, use the word EXFIL three times. The helicopter can be close to your location in less than fifteen minutes and two divers will be in the water seconds later with a spare diving apparatus for your escape. From the minute you say EXFIL to your rescue should take less than thirty minutes. Kidley and one other diver will be your team for the exfil. They are on permanent standby on onboard the ship."

"That's good to know," I said to Bob.

He went on, "Should the situation be the other way round and friendly forces make an attack on your camp, you will then know that we are making the main push on numerous targets, which will be targeted simultaneously. In this event, there will be a starburst of light over the camp and, in fact, over every one of the enemy camps where there are friendly agents. Also, if you are near your receiver, you will hear a siren blast out every thirty seconds. Your recovery will be the same as the previous EXFIL details. Do you have any questions?"

"None that I can think of," I answered him.

"Bonny, don't be heroic, just get as much intelligence as possible but don't put yourself in any danger. We need to know the names and ranks of anyone you meet and locations of all camps that you are able to discern; always listen to every conversation."

"Where do you go from here, Bob?"

"I will be returning to Heathrow Airport and then onto the operations room in London to monitor all movements of our operatives to ensure they have support wherever and whenever they need it. However, Dave is being flown by helicopter to join HMS *Dornik*; he will be always close by."

I think he was waiting for me to respond but I was feeling somewhat subdued at the prospect of what was going to happen to me in the extremely near future and just nodded when he finished talking.

He continued, "We will be arriving in Dubai in a little over four hours and I will be flying straight back to London from there. Because of the Covid-19 virus, no travellers can enter Yemen and therefore you will be flown by private charter. From our understanding, you will be tested and vaccinated if required during your flight from Dubai to Yemen. For now, try to get some sleep; I am sure you are going to need it."

✻✻✻

There was so much going on in my mind that I doubted that I would sleep, but funnily enough, I drifted off almost immediately. The next thing I knew was the cabin lights were coming on and the Captain made an announcement that we would be landing in Dubai in about one hour and a light breakfast was already being distributed.

Bob and I said little over breakfast and I knew he was concerned for my safety in the coming weeks or months. I was just finishing my coffee as the plane started to descend. The hostesses quickly removed all our plates and cups, and we were ready to land.

The wheels hit the runway and Bob whispered to me, "Good luck, Bonny, do not try to overreach. Just do what you can do as safely as possible. In a few moments, I will disappear, and I will see you back in London when this is finished."

The plane was still taxiing down the runway and had not come to a complete stop when Bob stood up, grabbed his briefcase from the overhead locker, gave me a wry smile, and walked briskly down to the front of the plane. None of the staff tried to stop him even though the plane had not fully stopped. I was guessing there was an air marshal on board and the flight staff had been briefed.

Chapter II. Camp Barji

As I left the plane, I was feeling extremely nervous, wondering how this was all going to end. My next concern was how was I going to get to my connection as I had no idea which gate I was supposed to be at. The time had also gone forward two hours and it was four in the afternoon here in Dubai.

I stopped at one of the enquiry booths and asked where I needed to go for a connection to Aden International Airport.

She looked a little shocked and replied, "There are no flights to Aden at this time due to Covid-19. I don't know how to advise you; I am so sorry."

As I walked away, she called after me, "Try asking at airport security, it is on the left after you leave this concourse."

I gave her a little wave and smiled.

I continued walking for several minutes when I was approached by a young Arab wearing a light-coloured kaftan. He looked as if he was just a young teenager and he gave me a wide grin and said, "Miss Bonny, I am guessing?"

"Yes," I replied.

"Tariq, at your service, Miss, please come with me."

I was bewildered, but also pleased that I was not going to be wandering around trying to find out where I was supposed to be. I followed him for a long time through various passageways and eventually down some stairs with a small door at the bottom. He opened the door and held it for me to pass through. I found myself in what seemed to be a large carpark, which was oblong shaped, between the buildings. Several cars were parked on either side of this area.

He beckoned me to follow him, and he led me to the far side of this open space and through another door into the building. He asked to help with my luggage, but I refused, and smiling I said, almost foolishly, "It's OK, I need the exercise."

After almost five minutes of walking, we emerged into another wide-open space between buildings, only this time, there was a small aircraft parked.

Tariq led me to the plane and waited for someone to emerge before nodding at him and pronouncing: "Bonny."

With that, he turned around and ran off back the way we had come.

In broken English, a tall man in swirling robes and wearing a bright red spotted hijab scarf said, "Ah, Miss Bonny, please this way come."

I followed him into the plane and seated at a small table was what appeared to be a medic. He looked up at me and simply said, "Sit."

He produced an injection syringe and filled it with liquid from a small phial.

"Remove shirt," he demanded.

I was reluctant as I was only wearing a bra beneath my shirt. I hesitated for just a moment and slipped it over my head.

He brought the point of the needle close to my shoulder and suddenly stopped, looked at me and pointed at the inside of my arm where the swastika was tattooed and declared, "You Nazi, very good, very good. We need fearless people."

He said no more after that, but just administered the injection and then indicated that I should get dressed.

He disappeared through a curtain and I did not see him again.

The tall man who had brought me to the medic reappeared through the same curtain and handed me a white card which had the words Johnson and Johnson written at the top. Underneath was some Arabic, which I did not understand, and below that was a date and time stamp predated by exactly three weeks. I had been fully vaccinated against covid and only required the one.

Very clever.

I was kept in this makeshift vaccine room for about fifteen minutes and then led into the main body of the plane, which could accommodate up to twenty passengers. It was extremely quiet, and I could see that there were about eleven other young people from various countries and several other older people in standard Arab garb. Most of the young people were asleep. I was handed two bottles of water and a sharp word: drink.

I sat in my seat and tried to doze, along with the rest of the passengers. Without any preamble, a man dressed in what appeared to be combat clothes appeared in the cabin and loudly woke everyone up.

He opened a large box of clothes and, one at a time, called out people's names. He handed each of the passengers a carrier bag from the box and said loudly, "Dress."

Each of us in turn and by name were all given clothes to wear. They had done their homework extremely well; our sizes were all correct.

There was only one other girl in the group, and we were given no special treatment and had to put on our new clothes along with the young men. There were no protocols here. We were all issued with two pairs of socks, one pair of boots, two dark-coloured pairs of combat trousers and jackets. Underneath our combat clothes was our personal and private concern.

The other girl moved down to stand next to me as she dressed and introduced herself to me as Desine from Paris. Her English was quite good, but I told her in perfect French that she could speak in whichever language she preferred. At times, if she did not know the correct word, in English she broke into Franglais, a simple mix of both languages.

We had barely put on our new clothes when the plane started to move forward, and we scrambled to our seats and fastened our safety belts. It was about six in the evening as we took off from Dubai en route for Aden. With a three-hour flight and adding one hour for the time difference, we would not arrive in Aden until about ten at night and then we still had a three-hour ride to the camp. Another late night.

Desine was a likeable girl who was not sure what she was doing here. She was just eighteen years old and had run away from home about a year ago. She had been living rough on the streets of Paris. A group of other young people encouraged her to join them in this group called Le Chapeau Rouge.

"I didn't know that it was a terrorist group and now I am scared to leave."

"What made you leave home in the first place?" I asked her.

"My Père et Mère got divorced and Mère met this younger man and is now married to him. He kept touching me and even tried to force me into bed. I told her but she did not believe me and kept insisting that I was jealous. It was too much so I left home. And here I am."

I felt deeply sorry for her, but I was unable to help.

We both dozed off to sleep for most of the journey to Yemen and only woke as the wheels touched the ground. It was a bumpy landing and went on for several long moments. As well as being quite scary, it was obvious that we were not on a runway. There were hardly any lights visible, making it very dark outside. I guessed that this was an illegal landing in the dead of night and no officials in sight.

We were herded at gunpoint towards an incredibly old beaten-up minibus, which backfired loudly several times before finally starting. There was just a driver on the bus and an armed guard who had a toothless grin on his face. Several people tried to engage the driver and the guard in conversation, but it became very apparent that neither spoke anything other than Arabic. I was not about to divulge to anyone that I understood quite a lot of Arabic. It was better that way.

The ride to our destination was very bumpy and from time to time we could hear sporadic gunfire. There was no chance of anyone sleeping while we were riding over such conditions. Occasionally there were patches of made-up road, but most of it was across baron, sandy territory and occasionally over very rocky terrain. Twice we were stopped by rebels shouting and cheering who had all appeared as if they had been drinking heavily, and the sight of them waving their rifles around was quite unnerving. After several minutes of shouting and screaming, we were waved through. We could see as we drove by their encampment that there were several young girls in their early teens in various states of undress being chased by one or more of these drunken rebels. The driver and the toothless guard were jeering and grinning lasciviously at these hapless youngsters.

Desine was very subdued, her eyes were dancing around nervously, and she looked close to tears at what she had just seen.

I was almost shocked to see Colonel Asraf and suddenly remembered that he oversaw the camps in this area. There was a half-smile on his face as we got out of the minibus and he came to greet us and welcomed us to Barji Camp.

"Hello, Miss Bonny, I hope you had a good flight over here?"

"Yes, thank you," I replied.

"I am afraid we do not have bathrooms and all the modern conveniences that you are used to. However, you and Desine are the only two girls in the camp and I will allow you to share your own tent. I will not allow any, how do you say in English, shenanigans. If any of these half-breeds try to molest either of you, they will be executed. Also, if either of you makes any advance towards any of the males here then both of you will be executed. People think that we are savages, but we have rules here and we need to have discipline."

We were escorted to the far side of the compound to a tent that had been isolated from the other twenty tents. Inside, we could barely see anything at all, so we just dropped the small amount of luggage each of us had and fell on top of an old scruffy, dirty blanket that we had been given. There was no time for luxuries like pyjamas, so we removed our boots and settled down for the night.

✵✵✵

The following morning it was barely light when gunfire erupted close by. This was the camp leader's way of waking up the rebels; it also had a secondary purpose and that was to get everyone used to gunfire so that they would not shy away from the sound of hostility. It worked, because the sound eventually became second nature to us.

Close to the edge of the compound was a small cluster of rusted, corrugated-tin-roofed buildings, which was where the leaders of this scruffy bunch of rebels were housed. Unquestionably, no luxury here, even for the leaders. Looking around at this ramshackle group of ill-dressed rebels, this may well have been the best that they were used to. The rest of us at least looked the part; about fifty of us all dressed in matching uniform but no hats. I thought that this might be a problem because during the day there would be constant blistering sun and no protection from its lethal rays. Fortunately, in my luggage I had a headscarf which may come in handy.

An old raggedy Arab who wore clothes that looked nearly as old as he was, cooked breakfast. The cooker was an old oil-stained fifty-gallon barrel that had been roughly ripped apart and had very sharp protrusions.

He cooked some hard, tough, chewy meat and bread. The meat was burnt, but the bread was surprisingly quite good. Not that we had any choice, and everyone wolfed it down hungrily. The water had been decanted into old plastic Coca-Cola bottles from an ancient well with crumbling sides and was dragged up by rope in a large wooden bucket. The water was warm, salty, and brackish.

After breakfast was over, we were all split into different groups and I was allocated to what was known in English as the 'sharpshooters' team. There was just me and four young men. They all spoke English quite well, although a young Serb struggled to make himself understood. We were walked across to the range that was at the far end of the compound behind the leader's tin huts.

The Serb was an excellent shot with a handgun, although he complained that the gun he was given to use was far too heavy and had a bent firing pin. Nevertheless, he scored way ahead of us on the range.

I chatted to the Serb who said everyone referred to him as Serb and he used that as his name. He had learned to shoot initially when he signed up for the Serbian Army as an artilleryman and although he was a good shot with the rifle, he far preferred the handgun.

"How did you get involved with the group?" I asked him.

In broken English, stopping sometimes to correct himself he said, "I joined a youth group called, **Црвени шешир**."

I looked puzzled, not understanding the words he was trying to convey, shook my head and said, "Sorry, I don't understand."

"Ah, wait, wait, in French, it is called Chapeau Rouge", he struggled to get out, but I understood him.

I smiled at him and spoke, "I too joined Le Chapeau Rouge, in Corsica."

He grinned broadly and said, "Ah, the Marshall at HQ."

I nodded and smiled again.

I did not want to startle him with too many questions but waited until I had taken my turn on the range with the pistol. I came third out of the five of us.

I walked alongside him as we went and collected our rifles for the next round of the training and evaluation.

"Where were you based in Serbia?" I asked as casually as I could.

"It is an exceedingly small town called Golubac and close to the Romanian border. Golubac Fortress is a tourist venue, but behind a certain derelict building about half a mile away is a private wooded area that also has derelict buildings. These have been renovated on the inside but appear untouched as though for hundreds of years on the outside. This was our camp. Each training course was for about twenty-five people and the instructor was a former British Royal Marines Sergeant."

I was the last to go on the rifle range, which I think was intentional. They wanted to test out the others before comparing a woman among the group.

One of the young men scored eighty-eight percent on the static target, seventy-two percent on the moving target and seventy-six percent on the pop-up targets. He looked incredibly pleased with himself for scoring far higher than the other three young men. He was very arrogant and came from Germany and gave a Nazi salute when he had finished and clicked his heels for good measure. He then pointed at me and sneered pompously, saying, "Beat that then, pretty girl."

It took me a few minutes to sight my rifle; I gauged the wind with my scarf and settled into a comfortable position. There was just a gentle breeze but nothing significant even though the static target was about a quarter of a mile away. I scored ninety-four percent for the static and I glimpsed my arrogant opponent start to shift uncomfortably as I got up and walked around for a few moments before settling in for the second round of the moving target. The German started making obscene gestures and screamed abusive language at me, but I could barely hear him; I just concentrated on the target. I gently squeezed off the rounds, scoring an off-centre bullseye for the first six shots and then after a slight adjustment, gaining the last four dead centre. According to their calculations, I had scored ninety-seven percent on the moving target.

I glanced over towards the German, but was unable to see his face; he was shouting at the two Arab officials sent to oversee the exercise. I was preparing for my final test: the pop-up targets. One of the official's rifle-butted the German in the side of the temple, he dropped limply to the ground, and they left him where he lay.

Somewhat disturbed at what I saw, forced me to concentrate even harder on my final targets. The pop ups were only visible for a couple of seconds and the temperature was soaring in the blistering Yemen sunshine. There was no time to wipe my eyes between shots but I found that blinking hard was quite effective. Eighty-nine percent; great score but I knew I could have done better. I knew that I could not affect the conditions on any set day, so I was extremely happy with my scores.

The two scruffy overseers were grinning from ear to ear when they showed me my scores. One of them kept looking at me saying, "Best, best, girl shoot."

Someone found a bucket of water and threw it at the German who was still lying motionless on the ground. He moaned and opened his eyes, holding his head with both hands.

More cold meat and some sort of root vegetables for lunch and some bread. I pointed at the bread and one of the instructors muttered, "Malawah."

"Good," I told him.

He just grinned as if I had given him a medal.

After we had eaten, much to our surprise, a small number of nomadic pastoral Arabs wandered into the compound with several camels on long tethers. The camels all had saddles place behind the hump.

It soon became apparent that we were expected to try to ride these ungainly creatures. I think that they were looking for volunteers to go first and I decided that this was a good time to volunteer and get it done because the tension was only going to get worse as the day wore on.

I felt most ungainly as one of these pastoral Arabs tried to push me up into the saddle, but with a lot of pushing and pulling, I found myself facing the undaunting sight of the camel's hump in front of me. This was not too bad, as my guide held onto the tether and lead me round in a large circle. After a couple of circuits, I was beginning to feel a lot braver. Then the camel stopped, and my guide showed me how to grip the pommel.

After that, he passed me the tether and grinned up at me.

"Go," he said and slapped the camel on its rump. It was like a bullet from a gun, and I shot forward. It was only the pommel that saved me from a huge tumble over the rear of the camel. Barely hanging on, the camel bolted in a straight line out into the desert with me hanging on for dear life. I knew that somehow, I would have to take control of this frisky animal. Slowly, I reined in the tether until it was quite tight and managed to loop it around the pommel. The camel's head started to turn the tighter I pulled, and he was eventually heading back the way we came. It was not easy, but I seemed to be able to slow him down if I kept the rein tight. I have no idea how I managed to stay on this beast's back; it was certainly not skill that kept me up, just sheer desperation.

Several others passed me as I completed my first camel ride. One or two of the others had ridden one before and did quite well, but some were complete disasters from start to finish. I was hoping the arrogant German would fall off, but it turned out that he was quite an accomplished rider.

After the triumphs and disasters of the riding lessons we received, they wanted us to try an ancient game that was played with camels. They would lay a camel down on his side and invite us to jump over him, then they would add another and then another and so on. One by one, our numbers decreased and finally, there was just me and a young man from Somalia. I knew he would have an advantage over me – he was tall, lithe and athletic and he had played this game before.

Apparently in the Yemeni form of the game, the camels are placed side by side standing up, but for our benefit, they lay the camels down. I managed to clear three camels, but the young Somalian jumped an incredible five camels.

Then it was back to the shooting: pistol shooting until it got dark. This exercise had us all running through the scrubland and at certain intervals, a picture of a notable inspirational western character would pop up; without stopping we would have to aim our pistol and fire. They used Margaret Thatcher, General de Gaulle, Marshall Tito, Ronald Reagan, Paul McCartney, Elvis Presley, Gerard Depardieu, Winston Churchill and Michael Jackson. This was to test our resolve and see if we would fire at someone who was an inspiration to many.

By the time we arrived back at Camp Barji we were exhausted. I wondered if the idea was to confuse us or check on our physical abilities. Probably both.

✻✻✻

Over the next ten days, we went out every day, learning about various countries that we could be visiting soon. Also details about security arrangements of prominent political figures and leaders throughout Europe. Painting dark pictures about these people so that they all looked like very evil leaders that needed to be removed from power. It was a great brainwashing exercise. I too had a very productive ten days learning more and more about the characters of the team I had become a daily part of. I passed on intelligence of about fifteen of them, the training camps they had passed through, the names of leaders, and how many of them were controlled or run by the now infamous Marshall of the complete Le Chapeau Rouge organisation.

During these early days at Barji Camp I saw truly little of Desine and often she was fast asleep when I returned to our tent. I had seen her a few times from a distance during the day, but she always looked incredibly sad.

I also learned about the terror camps in Eritrea where they were escaping one form of terror to join another. Also in Somalia, Northern Iraq, another in the North of Yemen, Kuwait, and state-sponsored groups in Turkey, Pakistan, and Iran. My daily evening walks down to the waterside were becoming a regular sojourn and nobody at the camp paid me any attention. I was very much a loner when we were not out in the field training for war.

I did not comprehend until this was all over just how much detailed intelligence I had managed to convey to the *Dornik* and ultimately MI6.

So far, I had not been called to commit anything radical or revolutionary, but that was all going to change. I listened to every word the leaders told us and continued passing on information. Then I had a message that Colonel Asraf wanted to see me. I smiled as sweetly as I could when he entered the room. There were two other men in the room with the Colonel and I knew them both. They were two of the leaders involved directly with my training.

"Young warrior, I have a task for you, and I do not wish any failure on your part. I have seen the results of your training and I am incredibly pleased with your ability and dedication. Fairly close nearby there is a local band of rebels who are trying to stall our long-term aim, and we know that they are planning an attack on this facility. I plan to execute a pre-emptive strike on their facility. You will take out their leader, Asman, and the German will take out their second in command called Basri. The plans of these amateurs are like our own, but if they fumble it, then the chances are it will put back our agenda by many months."

I nodded seriously and simply said, "When?"

The Colonel continued, "Three nights from now will be the darkest night for about two months, so we must go at this earliest possibility. If we leave it until later, they will most definitely have attacked us by then. So, it will be on Wednesday at thirty minutes past midnight. We know from our scouts that they change their guard at midnight and those going off will be eating in their tents and preparing to sleep. The others will be contemplating another non-productive long night. We are going to disappoint them. You and the German do your business, and the rest of the team will take out all of those eating and some of those who will be currently on guard."

"Colonel," I ventured, "how will we recognise our targets?"

"You will both be given a photograph of your man and we know approximately where they will be. The rest will be up to you to observe and eliminate. The backup eliminations will commence after the first shot is fired by either you or the German. It makes it a little harder if you are not the one who fires first."

"Is it alright if I discuss this with the German?" "But of course, it could be fatal not to."

I already had a plan in mind for getting closer to the German that I believed may be fool proof. Up until now, I had not been able to get any details of where his initial camp was so I could pass it on.

The German had not spoken to me since the incident when he was knocked out. He scowled at me and cursed me in German. I tried to be conciliatory and, at first, he just ignored me.

"Look, I am sorry about the other day, but I didn't hit you, it was the Arab."

"What do you want?" he muttered.

"Well, you and I have been selected for a special operation against a rival group; why don't we plan and do this together," I replied.

I continued, "I don't even know your name, I am Bonny."

He growled back at me, "I know your name, everybody does."

He sounded less aggressive, so I continued the approach and said to him, "We might have more in common than you think."

"Like what?" he said.

"Don't be offended and do not think this is a sexual approach; it is not, but I would like to show you something."

His anger seemed to have subsided, and he now looked extremely interested.

I leaned towards him so that nobody else nearby could see anything and pulled back my shirt top revealing my back, near my armpit. I waited for a response.

"What is it I am supposed to be looking at?" he retorted.

I smiled at him and pulled back my bra strap, and there he could very clearly see my small Swastika tattoo nestling almost in my armpit.

"Fraulein, was ist das?"

I grinned at his total bewilderment. I teased him a little, "I thought you might know, it's a swastika."

"I know it's a swastika, but how? Why?"

"I think he was a great man," I said lying to him.

He suddenly relaxed and said, "Das ist gut, mein gott. My name is Maximilian, just call me Max, it means—"

I cut him short, "I know, I know it means the best of the best, but sometimes just give a girl a break."

He guffawed loudly.

He shook my hand and said, "Truce."

We talked well into the evening as he told me about his grandfather who was a high-ranking Gestapo officer and then his own father who always aspired to be like his grandfather but never really came up to his father's expectations. Max was disappointed that he had never met his grandfather who had been one of Adolf Hitler's closest confidantes. Max went on to say that the European countries of today were weak and ineffectual, and he aimed to do something about it.

Long before midnight, Max and I were dropped off at the outskirts of the rebel stronghold. We discussed the approach and I believed that the best position for a kill would be in the camouflage of an old oak tree overlooking the ten-foot barrier. The tree was far from any light, and the heavy foliage in the upper branches would render us almost invisible. The only downfall would be if the other rebels could get to us; we had truly little chance of escape, but hopefully, the rest of our backup would have done their jobs and eliminated any threat. He agreed with me and suggested that I take the higher position as my target would be more likely to be in an upper floor room of the three-tier complex.

I climbed about ten feet above Max and got myself into a comfortable position. And then prepared for my first real live target. I was feeling incredibly nervous and had to keep myself busy until it was time. I had zoomed in with the telescopic sights several times before I was comfortable with my sightings. There was no wind at all, so that made the process far simpler.

My heart was thumping so loud I am surprised Max did not hear it from his perch just below me. We sat in complete silence for about five minutes, which felt more like an hour. The adrenaline had kicked in, and each second had slowed down to almost a standstill.

A few seconds later, Max whispered, "The lights are on upstairs."

I could see a passageway light through the rear of the room I was watching. Then the room light flickered on and it was like an explosion in my head. I glanced down at the picture of my target, Asman, and there he was, silhouetted in the door frame. I whispered two words to Max below, "Target sighted."

From that second on, all sounds and distractions were eliminated from my consciousness. It took just a few fractions of a second to sight my target and I gently squeezed the trigger. It all seemed to move in complete slow motion; I could see my bullet closing the gap to my target, and then it was all over as he crumpled without ever moving past the threshold of the door.

Below, I could hear Max going through the same motions and heard the gentle pop as his bullet left the barrel. This time I heard the crash as broken glass exploded and the room lights seem to make the shards twinkle as they cascaded into the room. I was quick enough to catch a glimpse of the single hole that appeared in his temple as Basri toppled over onto his desk.

At that moment, all mayhem broke out, with shouts and screams filling the quiet night as the rest of the team annihilated the remaining members of this group. When it was all over, Max and I shinned down the gnarled old oak and made our way back to our transport.

The two rebel leaders and all the other rebels had been killed apart from two; they had been back in the kitchen preparing a drink for the rest of their associates. A successful mission and two prisoners taken – the Colonel must have been delighted.

I thanked Max and wished him goodnight, and then wandered through the camp and down to the waterside. I needed to clear my head before sending my report. I felt sad that I had just taken a life, but reconciled it with the thought that if it had not been done, it could have been me lying out there somewhere.

I finally got down to the waterfront and passed my message back to HMS *Dornik*. I knew that they would be pleased about the outcome of tonight's operation, but all I wanted to do was lie down and sob.

I thought that being in a terrorist camp there would be continuous activity, but for days on end, it was sheer boredom with nothing happening. I was not able to keep myself as fit as I would have liked. I had always taken it for granted that I would have a gym to train at and a swimming pool. The Red Sea was warm to swim in, but the current was extraordinarily strong at times and nobody else wanted to swim. I kept close to the shore, but was always wary of the tides and whatever may be lurking in the water.

We had access to the range whenever we wanted to practice, but there were no regular training sessions for anything. It was a very shambolic way of life. The only time that I saw any real discipline was when fresh recruits arrived, and then it was only busy for them as they went through the sort of induction that I had undertaken.

⁕

I had been there for about a month when intelligence was received that the SAS would be making a raid on one of the terrorist camps about two hundred miles east of our location towards the Oman border. I was not aware of the camp, so this was useful information. Knowing that the SAS was an extremely covert branch of the British Armed Forces, I began to wonder where the leak was coming from.

Colonel Asraf sent for me and Max and we discussed this raid by the SAS on our East Yemen group. He told us he did not wish to send a full force but just two snipers. If we sent in a full team, it could well end up as a blood bath and at this crucial time, we wanted to keep it low-key. We would be flown in under cover of darkness and flown back here on completion of the kill.

I tried to be as delicate as I could and asked the Colonel, "What is so crucial about this particular project?"

"I will give you all of the details closer to the time, but we are mobilising a big operation in about six weeks. The General in Tehran is organising a massive hit on British, American, and European Forces based in Europe. This is to soften them up for several follow-up attacks in ten major cities in Europe. Our organisation is not capable at this time of attacking the United States of America, but we have teams over there being mobilised to cause riots and unrest in a dozen of their cities. Overall, it will be one of the biggest operations that have ever been mounted. It will be a great day for us all."

"What part will we play in all of this?" I asked him.

"I must get this SAS situation quelled first before concentrating on our biggest plan to date. Suffice it to say that Iran has coordinated and funded the complete operation with the assistance of Al Qaeda and Boko Haram who also want to establish a state ruled by traditional Islamic law in West Africa and ultimately worldwide, plus the Islamic State who are now on the rise again. The US Administration nearly destroyed them, but after a change of leadership, they seemed to have backed off."

***

I desperately needed to get this information back to the *Dornik* as soon as possible, but did not want to raise any suspicions, so waited until late the following day to take a stroll down to the waterside.

I was getting more and more paranoid about being down there in case I was being monitored. This time I had a great deal to pass on and I was relieved when I had completed it. I then asked for some guidance, although I had no idea how they could give me any. I wanted to know if I had any options with regards to executing one or more of the SAS operatives.

***

Early the following morning was a Tuesday and I received written instructions from the Colonel that he was going to be away for a few days but the attack on the SAS was to go ahead this coming Saturday night. A small Cessna 5 aircraft would fly us there and then return us to the camp when the task was complete. I was handed a large brown envelope with the full details of where the hit on the SAS was to take place. Inside the envelope was a mobile phone and the Colonel asked me to call him when the task was completed.

I passed the details of the above directive on to the *Dornik* that night. Just as I ended my call to them, I noticed a flashing light coming from about two feet along the bank. I nervously reached down under the surface and retrieved a waterproof plastic bag. Inside was a note with the words: *SAS informed: do not make a head shot, hit arms or legs only. We will transmit to the radio and press of a fatality caused by terrorist activity. Good Job and Good Luck.*
MC.
Destroy note after reading, extinguish the light.

I was feeling quite sick and shaking after receiving my instructions, and wondered to myself whether it would eventually get easier. It was a question I was going to ask, providing I survived.

***

Instead of dragging by, the time until Saturday's rendezvous with the SAS came remarkably quickly. The Cessna 5 aircraft rolled into the compound at about ten in the evening to pick up two passengers. Max and I were ready and waiting. It was dark and noisy inside the small aircraft which made things a lot simpler as I was not in the mood for idle talk.

The written instructions included a photo of the building in which the terrorists were housed. There was only one door into the building and just two front windows. There was also a photo of the two buildings opposite that were derelict and had bullet holes and small explosive damage to them both. One more building further down the road was the home of a single survivor of a mortar attack that had killed his wife and two daughters; he would not leave.

I found out much later that his two- and five-year-old children had died immediately, but his wife had received a head wound and lost the lower half of her left arm completely. She had writhed in pain for nearly three weeks without any medical care before dying in her husband's arms.

The Colonel continued, suggesting that we concentrate our guns on the guards that the SAS would surely leave outside the building, while the rest of their team would try to enter and destroy. He said that rebels would know they are coming and be ready for them, and concluded the message with 'Alhamdulillah' (which means Praise be to Allah).

Our pilot had been briefed and knew exactly where to land. At the top end of the small village where we would find our quarry, there was an enclosure behind a factory building, long deserted. He flew the plane in exceptionally low, and before we hit the ground, he killed the plane's engine and we glided for the last quarter of a mile and landed remarkably gently on a sand and grass area.

He killed the lights almost immediately and said, "When you are done, I will be right here waiting for you."

We slipped quietly around the side of the building and as we approached the front, two high-power flashlights were beamed straight into our eyes. We were then surrounded by four men dressed entirely in black clothing. Max was ready to fight, but the odds did not give us an iota of a chance. I raised my hands and clasped them behind my head. By now, Max was completely under their control and they slipped a black bag over his head and dragged him away.

Waiting until Max had gone, one of the men dressed in black removed his neoprene mask and said quietly, "Go ahead, Ma'am, just go easy on our boys."

Panic swept through my mind and I blurted out, "Have you breached yet?"

He answered, "Not yet. We were just about to signal the go now that we have you in our custody."

"Thank God, it is a trap, they know you are coming."

"How on earth could they know that? Everything we do is top secret." He spoke into his wrist communicator and said, "Hold, hold, hold."

On the far side of the road leading down to the rebel-held building were six more men dressed in black awaiting further instructions.

After a brief discussion with the team, their leader said, "Jenny."

It took a moment for the name to sink in, I had not been called Jenny for a long time.

"Yes," I replied.

"Would you go ahead as if nothing was wrong and set yourself up in the closest of the two buildings and we will wait it out and see what happens?"

"Of course," I answered.

He carried on talking to me and his men.

"This could go very terribly wrong if we are not prepared. If the rebels are still in the building, they may just be hiding and waiting for us to breach, or they could have moved outside or into the building down the road and booby-trapped this one; any questions?"

"I think I agree with you, let Jenny go to her sniper spot and we wait."

At exactly two in the morning, I slipped away from them and crossed the road, approaching the first house in the shadows. It was very dark anyway and I doubted that I could be seen. I climbed the rickety broken stairs to the first floor, side-stepping the holes in the wood and heard the creaking of those I managed to stand on. Nobody up here could take me by surprise unless they had wings.

I went through the full procedure: found a good spot to rest the barrel of my rifle, set up my sights for the building opposite, and tested for any wind. There was no wind, so I made myself as comfortable as possible. Being a sniper was so often a waiting game; tonight, it was no different.

At about three-thirty I got up and walked around so I could stretch my legs. I went carefully to the glassless window and took a long look in all directions to see if anything was moving. It was completely silent, and the night was as black as coal. I reluctantly sat down again, wondering how long the wait was going to be. Another hour went by and I thought I could just see some clouds starting to light up in the few minutes before dawn.

There was absolutely no warning, but somewhere beyond the building allegedly being occupied by the rebels, all hell broke loose. I could see the flashes and hear heavy gunfire. Then all went silent for about five minutes and then one shot and then another and after that complete silence.

I made my way to the bottom of the stairs and looked out onto the street. I could now hear people talking and what sounded like things being dragged. A few moments more and a dark shadowy figure jogged across the road towards me.

"It's all over, Jenny, fourteen rebels are dead, and one is badly injured," said the voice, as he pulled off his mask.

"So sorry it took us so long. Do you want to go and get your plane, or do you wish to hang around for a while?"

"The first thing I need to do is discharge my weapon a couple of times, so it appears that I have been working." I grinned at him.

"And secondly, I need to get our narratives the same so that I can remain safe in this hostile environment."

"OK, you tell me what you require."

"I need you to return to your base and send out a press release saying that sadly an enemy sniper executed two of your finest operatives, but in return, one radicalised European sniper was killed, and fifteen radical Muslim fighters died in the skirmish. Say too that one survived and is under armed guard in hospital and will undergo interrogation when he recovers sufficiently to answer questions. The body of the radicalised European sniper will be sent back to Germany for a family funeral."

"It will be done," he replied.

"Can you make sure that the press release is sent to all the major world press outlets?"

He gave a little nod and said, "Johnny Bryant, Warrant Officer, always at your service, Ma'am."

I collected my equipment from the upper room and made my way back to the plane; it was now almost full daylight. The pilot did not seem at all concerned and told me that he had enjoyed a good night's sleep in the cockpit. He looked around and asked, "Where is your partner?"

"Dead, shot by one of the SAS," I replied.

"What is SAS?" he added.

"Special Air Service."

Life is so cheap in this part of the world that the pilot showed no concern for the loss of life. I found the envelope that the Colonel had sent to me and pulled out the phone that he had given me to use. Reluctantly, I dialled his number. I had almost given up on him answering my call when a gruff voice barked into the phone.

"Yes."

"It's Bonny, I have bad news."

"What bad news?" he barked.

I took a big deep breath and answered him, "Max is dead, the rebel group is all dead and I have just managed to reach the plane and heading back to Barji."

"You are an incompetent fool," he screamed. "You are useless; I send you to do a man's job and what do you do?"

"Just wait a minute, Colonel. I shot and killed two members of the SAS, injured two others, and escaped with my life; that is not incompetence, that is professional. There is nobody better at this job than me. What other single marksman could have done that and survived? I am the best that you have."

His tone dropped considerably, and he just said quietly, "I will see you back at camp. One other thing, destroy and dump the mobile phone."

I was shaking like a leaf after my altercation with the bully Colonel, but he had taken his anger out on me and I had returned the rhetoric in full measure.

On returning to the camp, I found out that the Colonel had not yet returned. I was pleased; I was too exhausted to joust with him right now and needed at least a good eight hours' sleep. I slept the whole day through and most of the following night before I was summoned to meet the Colonel in his office at seven that morning.

***

I entered his dirty, untidy ramshackle office awaiting yet another tirade from this bully but was surprised when he said in a gentle voice, "Sit."

He handed me about eight newspapers; some of them were in English but the rest were in Arabic, nevertheless I got the idea of what they were saying.

Jihadist sniper executes two soldiers of the respected British SAS. Their names are being withheld from the public out of respect for the soldiers and to keep their identities confidential for the benefit of their beloved families. Press release from the Ministry of Defence UK.

He looked up and made no apology for his angry outburst and I likewise made no apology to him for mine.

"Good work, Bonny, you have managed to highlight our fight on the world stage; they will start to have some respect for our ability now. I was with General Lankarani all day yesterday and he was exceedingly pleased with your accomplishments in the field. He would like you to go and see him and meet with the Ayatollah in Tehran so that they can both offer their congratulations on your successes, and discuss where you can be of most value in this war against the decadence of the West."

"When will I have the honour of accepting this privilege?" I asked him.

"I have to go to Tehran again next Monday; perhaps you could accompany me on that trip."

"But of course, I would be very happy to do so," I replied. "What about our upcoming attacks on the West, when will that crusade begin?"

"I think we may have to reschedule that for a slightly later time, but we will know more after we meet with the General and the Ayatollah."

I just nodded.

"Oh, just one more thing," he added without any sign of compassion or emotion. "Bad news about Max; just collateral damage in an ongoing war against the infidel."

He stood up and turned his back on me and went to an old rusty filing cabinet and began shuffling papers. I took it that I had been dismissed and went back to my tent.

Desine was sitting on the dirty old blanket and she looked as if she had been crying.

"Bonny, what am I supposed to be doing here? I am not required to do anything, and it goes on for days and days."

I felt so sorry for her and suggested that one of the things she might like to do was to find a way to wash our filthy blanket. I also promised to make enquiries about books or magazines to read to help her pass a few hours a little more pleasantly.

She perked up a little and said, "That would be nice. I really enjoy reading and it would help to lift my spirits a little. Merci, Bonny, merci."

I was not being arrogant, but at times, I was almost treated like a folk hero as exaggerated tales of my exploits started to do the rounds among all the Westerners here in the camp. It was this faux fame that allowed me to talk to virtually anyone. I was able to beg and borrow about ten magazines and six books that Desine and I could read. She was overcome that I had managed to get all this reading material in such a short time.

I grinned at her and said, "Perhaps I will write a story about our exploits once this is all over and we regain our freedom."

"It all sounded so exciting at the beginning, and here we are wishing we were a million miles from this location."

"I will give you a copy and you can have it translated into French," I said with a chuckle. Desine's spirits seemed to lift immediately, and I felt a bit relieved to see her in a better frame of mind.

I still had the phone that the Colonel had told me to destroy, but I thought that it may be useful at some time. It was a burner phone so could not be traced to anyone. The problem was trying to use it here on the camp. For the time being, I needed to find somewhere to hide it safely. I knew that it would soon run out of charge and thought it might be the best thing if I destroyed it.

***

I wondered how we would get to Tehran with the Covid 19 boycott still in place in many Middle East countries. The question was answered very quickly, when early on Monday morning, a car came to collect the Colonel and me from Camp Barji. We were whisked to a local airport, which was completely unknown to me, but it took less than an hour to get there. The car took us straight onto the runway and, standing to one side, was a white aircraft with the words Ayatollah etched in large black print along the fuselage. I guess the Ayatollah had privileges all over the Middle East.

Four hours later I was sitting at the dining table inside the Ayatollah's simple home. I was expecting something palatial, but this was far short of palatial. His wife attended on us and produced a simple but tasty meal of cooked meat and simple locally grown vegetables and home-baked bread, which was delicious. A strange anomaly seeing as the Ayatollah's worth was estimated in the billions.

He was attentive and polite and thanked me for my dedication to the Islamic cause. We had all but completed our meal when we could

236

hear some noise coming from the front door. General Lankarani had arrived, and he apologised for his late appearance. He sat down and the Ayatollah's wife brought him a platter of food. He ate a little food and then began to give some details of the forthcoming attacks planned for next month.

He detailed the attacks, which were terrifying in their scale and enormity.

With a cruel smile on his face and with acid venom, he said, "The following bases will be hit simultaneously: Ansbach, Germany; Bavaria, Germany; Rhineland-Pfalz Kaiserslautern, Germany; Benelux, Belgium; Vicenza, Italy; Aviano, Italy; Lakenheath, UK, and Souda Bay, Greece."

He stopped for a few seconds to let his words sink in.

"Then we have organised riots, burning of buildings and total civil unrest in ten major cities in Europe. They are Berlin, Paris, London, Amsterdam, Brussels, Madrid, Rome, Oslo, Vienna and our 'coup d'etat', The United Bank of Switzerland. This is their largest bank and based in Zurich, which includes over two thousand employees. The bank will be destroyed and, along with it, all the staff and the records going back over one hundred and fifty years. We are having a large consignment of C4 explosives being delivered into the bank vault. One of their most trusted and oldest customers wishes to deposit in a Safe Haven vault several bars of gold. What the customer does not know, is that we have found a way of taking a billion dollars' worth of his gold and replacing it with a substitute shipment of explosives."

He paused for a moment to allow his words to sink in, and then continued.

"To finish our programme, we are unable to hit the United States of America on their soil in a big way, so we have made use of their members of Congress and other major retail operators to start civil unrest in a dozen major cities. New York, Los Angeles, Chicago, Philadelphia, Houston, Phoenix, San Antonio, San Diego, Dallas, San Jose, Austin, and Jacksonville."

I asked the Ayatollah's wife if I could use the bathroom and she showed me to a small but clean and neat one. I had a pencil and paper in my pocket and quickly pulled them out to write down as much information as I could from the frighteningly large list of locations for so many vicious attacks on both the military and civilians. The casualty list would be colossal if nothing was done to mitigate these planned atrocities. I tried to write as quickly as possible so that I would not arouse suspicion. On completion, I tucked the paper down the back of my briefs.

As I returned to the table, Colonel Asraf stood up, bowed his head to the Ayatollah and the General and said, "Very gracious of you to invite us for lunch. I know you are very busy so we must return to Camp Barji and prepare for this final victory which is ours for the taking." I also nodded to the two leaders and followed the Colonel to the door.

***

I was feeling anxious and knew that I needed to contact the *Dornik* as soon as possible; time was not on our side and I was shocked that plans for the attacks on the West were so far advanced. I must have dozed off on the flight back because it seemed in no time at all that we were landing back in Yemen. The car to return us to Camp Barji was waiting for us as we climbed down from the plane. The Colonel was remarkably quiet during the hour's journey back to camp.

I returned to my tent, to find Desine propped up on her pillow reading one of the books I had acquired for her. It was ironic that she was reading a paperback with the title, *Escape to Freedom* by Allan Zullo. The story was nothing like the situation that we were in, but the title must have aroused something in her mind.

She gave me a little wave as I entered and carried on with her reading. It was only about five-thirty but was completely dark outside. I pushed back the flap of the tent and casually said to Desine, "Just going for a breath of fresh air, back in a little while."

I wanted to run down to the waterside to pass on the information that I had, but knew that to do so would bring attention to myself. Instead, I walked in the opposite direction and glanced around to make sure that nobody was watching me. I was becoming more and more paranoid as time went by and the pressure of relaying intelligence back to the *Dornik* was almost suffocating at times.

I had a small torch with me, which was sufficient for me to read my crumpled piece of paper as I settled down on the bank to relay my message. For the first time, on completing my message, instead of the three flashing lights followed by a long green flash, there was no response for about twenty seconds and that felt like a lifetime. Then there was a continuous yellow light for several seconds. My hands were sticky, and I could feel the sweat running down my back and my heart was trying to break out of my chest. My hands were shaking uncontrollably as I took a big breath and repeated the extremely long message. I sighed with relief when I finally received the accept signal.

About ten minutes later, I was feeling far more relaxed and standing in the shower block washing away the dirt and sweat from a long day in my fatigues. Mind you, it was not what you might imagine a shower to be. It was little more than a room about four feet by four feet. A water hose was attached to the bottom of an old aluminium bucket that had holes punched in it.

I had no idea when our pre-empted attack might occur, but if MI6 had done their work, I imagined it might come within about two weeks. I had no idea that it would come so soon.

***

It was only three days later, and I had gone to the range to practice my pistol shooting. The lights were better in there than anywhere else on the camp and I continued to practice as the sun went down. I was trying to improve my skill with my left hand and would take a shot with my right and then swap hands and take one with the left hand. I had two targets pulled up so that I could gauge the accuracy with both hands. I was pleased with the results that I had achieved this evening; my left-hand pattern was getting a much closer grouping than previously.

Suddenly a single shot rang out from somewhere across the courtyard. Instead of discarding my pistol, I shoved it down the waistband of my trousers. I was still wearing my jacket as I would be if I were in action. Outside it was quiet and nothing was moving. I looked across and saw that the Colonel's light was on and I walked across to his office.

As I approached, I heard loud sobbing coming from inside. I did not knock, but just pushed the door open gently. The Colonel was standing behind his desk with a gun in his right hand; lying in front of him on the floor was Desine, clutching her heavily bleeding right leg that had a large bullet hole in it.

I just looked at him in disbelief and said, "Why?"

The Colonel spat back at me, "Not that it is any of your business, she says that she wants to go home, and nobody goes home from here. You die or you live but you stay here."

I pulled out my scarf, which I kept in my pocket, and ran over to Desine and tried to apply a tourniquet to stem the bleeding.

The Colonel, pointing his gun at me, boomed, "Get away from her, let her bleed."

At that precise moment, gunfire broke out in the compound. The Colonel ran to the door and wrenched it open.

"Drones, drones, we are under attack," he screamed.

He slammed the door and turned round to face me, and his jaw dropped when he realised that he was facing right into the barrel of my pistol.

He sneered at me and said, "Look here, girl, put the gun down before you hurt yourself; you wouldn't dare fire it at me and you don't have the courage to—"

He did not finish his sentence as I placed a hole dead centre in his forehead. Eyes wide open, he was dead before his body fell to the floor.

I ran over to Desine, who was sobbing. I did not know whether it was the pain or from what she had just witnessed.

I shouted at her, "We must get out of here, let me help you get to safety."

Desine did not help very much, but I managed to get her up, and half limping and dragging, I managed to get her almost to the edge of the water when I felt an incredible searing pain in my back.

At that very moment, John Kidley just appeared in front of me and right behind him came Bryan Root. As John got to me, another shot embedded itself in my right buttock and I went down. I could see that Bryan had lifted Desine and carried her to the Gemini inflatable that was being held by Brenda Jones.

Chapter 12. Rescued

At that moment, I had not realised that apart from being a diver, Brenda was a qualified nurse. John got me into the Gemini and Brenda let go of the boat and climbed in. John started the engine and raced away from the bank. I could make out a small flotilla of Marine landing craft heading for Camp Barji, ready for an assault.

I could not take it all in, and with all the pain and relief at being rescued, I lost consciousness.

***

I remember nothing for nearly forty-eight hours and when I slowly came to, I could see the friendly face of the Doc smiling down at me.

I was in the ship's sick bay and he simply said, "Welcome back, Jenny."

I smiled and drifted back into oblivion.

The next time I came to, Mike Cheetham was sitting on a chair next to my bed. He said, "Hello, sleepyhead, how are you feeling?"

"Hi, Mike, what a sight for sore eyes." I smiled at him.

I looked around the ward and I could see Desine propped up in her bed, eating breakfast with Brenda Jones fussing around her.

She realised I was awake and came over to my bed.

She put her hand on my shoulder and grinned at me and said, "Thank you, Jenny, you helped me overcome my phobia. Until a few days ago I had never flown in anything, but now I have been winched up carrying a patient: you, and of all things had a flight in the ship's helicopter to bring you and Desine back here."

I smiled at her and said, "Glad to be of service, Brenda, and thank you."

***

I spent the next couple of days drifting in and out of sleep, and when I finally woke up for an extended period, I realised that the ship was not moving.

Desine waved to me from her bed and whispered, "Thank you."

The Doc came to do his rounds and declared that I was out of the woods now, but it would take several months to fully heal. He told me that I may have a permanent limp and he then said gently, "I imagine you will always be a pain in someone's the ass. Talking of pain, do you remember a couple of years ago you asked me to check on the make-up of some tablets? Well, you did not come back so I gave the results to Commander Cheetham. They were simply concentrated tablets of pure fat, which would have exacerbated Lewis's stomach problems instantly."

He left me for a moment and went over to see Desine.

"Bonjour, Mademoiselle Desine, how are you today?"

"I am much better, thank you, and if it hadn't been for my friend, I would have been a lot worse or even dead," she answered him.

"Indeed yes, our Jenny is a real hero," he added.

At that moment, Captain James John Crowe entered the sick bay.

The Doc said to him, "Good morning, Sir, is this a sick call or are you here to see our guests?"

"Your guests, Doc. Now if you have finished prodding and poking them and administering your potions, I would like a moment of privacy with them please."

The Doc replied, "Of course, Sir," and left the sick bay.

The Captain spoke to Desine first.

"First of all, you are not in any trouble and no terrorist charges will be brought against you. We have been in contact with your mother, and she wants you home. She is very sorry that she did not believe you about her husband's attempted sexual assaults and he has now been kicked out and she says that if you can forgive her, she would like to see you very soon."

Desine began to cry and through her sobs said, "All I wanted to do was to go home."

The Captain replied, "Well, that's a good thing then. We docked in Gibraltar this morning and your mother will be here by about two this afternoon. Both of you will be transported back to Paris in a Royal Navy air ambulance where you will receive the best of care from our medics until you are handed over to your family doctor."

Now there were tears of joy and she thanked the Captain for his kind hospitality.

He responded with, "Well, we can't have the French thinking that we are barbarians now, can we?"

The Captain walked over to my bed and said, "From the moment I met you I knew you were going to be trouble, and I was right; the trouble you have caused all those terrorists is inestimable. As your friends, we cannot thank you enough for the incredible service you have done for us, the United Kingdom, and the rest of the civilised world. You really are a true hero. Thank you, Jenny. Everyone on board HMS *Dornik* is incredibly proud of their adopted daughter." He bent down and kissed me on the cheek.

As he got to the door of the sick bay he turned and said, "Don't go back to sleep again just yet, the Naval tailor is coming on board this afternoon to measure you up for new uniforms and Lieutenant Saunders is going to visit you and find out what personal items of clothing you require."

Annette Saunders was waiting outside the sick bay door as the Captain left. We spent the next hour or more chatting about what the *Dornik* had been up to and then some of the things that I had been involved with since leaving them.

She grinned and said, "This is going to be fun; spending the ship's money with no restrictions on what I spend on you. Is there anything you want apart from the things I have listed?"

"Yes, I need you to find out who the tattooist was that worked on me before I went undercover."

She frowned and said, "Anything in particular?"

I fumbled my arm out of the pyjamas I was wearing and showed her my swastika. She looked horrified.

"Yes, it paid dividends but now I need it covered up."

"Of course, I will find out who did it." She winced and pulled a face. Then she went off to do my personal shopping.

The tailor came in the early afternoon and took all my measurements for two new uniforms, including caps. It was the first time I had managed to stand up straight since being shot. He worked quickly and after he had gone, I asked the Doc for a chair rather than get straight back into bed. He advised that I rest it for a few more days but I insisted on a chair.

"Doc, I desperately need to start getting myself moving again."

I had the sick bay to myself now that Desine had gone, and it was quite large. I thought I would try to take a few steps, but after taking just two small ones, I realised that the Doc was right; the pain was sheer agony. I sat back on the chair and just raised my feet off the deck slowly a few times.

✳✳✳

I lost track of time as I recovered a little more each day. The tattooist had put a pretty, but small, and discreet rose over the tattoo, the Doc had removed my gold nose pin and at last, my hair was nearly back to normal.

The days went by and after a couple more weeks, the Doc was pleased with my progress, and I managed to walk across the sick bay and back again without too much pain. I had many visitors from around the ship and never had a moment to dwell on what had happened over the last couple of years. Mike and the Provost Marshall were frequent visitors and, of course, all the divers.

The Captain came down one day and said, "Your new uniforms have arrived, perhaps you would like me to get them out of the bags for you?"

He slowly took them out of the bags and lay them on a nearby bed. I looked at them longingly, looking forward to being able to put them on again. It was then that I realised that something was wrong.

"Sir," I gasped, "they have brought the wrong uniforms, these are for a Lieutenant Commander."

"Oh sorry," he replied. "Did I omit to tell you that you have been promoted to Lieutenant Commander Jennifer Talbot?"

I was dumbfounded.

"Congratulations, Jenny, you deserve it," he added.

The Captain looked serious again for a few moments.

"The ship will be leaving Gibraltar tomorrow afternoon and heading back to Portsmouth, arriving early afternoon on Saturday. Your parents and your sister Jane will be there to meet you and you will all be taken by car to London for two nights at the London Hilton Hotel in separate suites, all expenses paid. Your brother could not attend, owing to Royal Air Force commitments. Then, on Monday morning at 1100, you are to report back to MI6 for a debrief. Please wear your uniform.

"However, in the meantime, we need to show you the courtesy of introducing the real you to the ship's company who all think of you as the Clubswinger."

I looked at him in total shock and said simply, "I was only doing my job, Sir."

"Yes, but it was a job very few people could have carried out so successfully; enjoy your fame, and soak it all in because before long it will be back to business."

✧✧✧

It took a long time to fall asleep that night after the excitement of the day. I eventually drifted off to sleep and slept soundly until 0800. I opened my eyes to see Annette Saunders smiling down at me.

"Good morning, Jenny, I have come to assist you in getting up to the Wardroom where all the officers are waiting to greet you, and then you will have to get dressed in your new uniform because at 1100 there will be full divisions on the jetty for you to inspect the ship's company."

Annette had brought me a pair of jeans and a blouse and some underwear from her shopping trip for me to wear so I could get up to the Wardroom without giving the game away.

As I limped into the Wardroom, there was a huge round of applause from every single officer on board; there was standing room only. Captain James John Crowe stood on a small stool and gave a ten-minute talk about my exploits since I had left the ship such a long time ago.

"I cannot begin to tell you how brave she is, and I am sure you will all welcome her back in your midst. Just to let you know that when she has fully convalesced, she will be spending a few months with us again, just to get her sea legs back. In the meantime, however, we have a small surprise for everyone at 1100 when the full ship's company are required to appear on divisions which will be held on the jetty. Yes, and that includes you, Provost Marshall, even you are not excused."

Neil just grinned at the Captain and said, "Aye, Aye, Sir."

For the next hour or so I was the toast of the Wardroom as all of them clamoured round to congratulate me; it was a very generous and warm welcome back.

It was going to be a huge surprise, not only to the ship's company but also to many of the officers who still did not know that I was a Lieutenant Commander.

It was soon time to get ready, and Annette assisted me wherever necessary to get fully attired in my new dress uniform. My leg and back were still quite painful and I hoped that I would be able to walk down to the jetty without making a fool of myself. A Royal Navy Staff car had been parked close to where the divisions would take place and I was escorted by Annette and Mike down to the car and placed comfortably inside.

Mike then said, "Jenny, enjoy every minute of this show, you deserve it. Everyone will be coming down to the jetty in a few minutes. Don't worry about protocols, this is your moment, and however you do it will be right."

"Thanks, Mike," I replied.

I sat and watched from the back seat of the car as I saw the ship slowly emptying of the crew. All were in their best dress uniforms. Finally, the Chief Gunnery Instructor called the ship's company to attention and everyone, including the officers, all came smartly to attention. A few seconds later, the Captain, Commander, and the Provost Marshall walked across the jetty towards the Chief GI, who marched up to the Captain, saluted, and said, "Ship's company and Officers ready for inspection, Sir."

With that, the Captain walked the few yards to the parked staff car and opened the front passenger door. By now, everyone was craning their heads to see who this dignitary was.

Before the Captain assisted me from the car, he made sure that he was standing right in front of me blocking everyone's view for a few seconds and whispered to me, "Are you ready, Jenny? Give a huge smile and I will help you out."

With that, he put his hand on my arm and gently assisted me to get out of the vehicle.

There was a huge gasp from everyone when they recognised who I was.

Everyone was talking at once.

I heard comments like:

"Isn't that the Clubswinger?"

"Do you see who that is?"

"Did you know she was an officer?"

"She's a Lieutenant Commander."

The voices went on for several minutes as the Captain brought me out in front of Divisions.

Then he looked at me, smiled, and nodded.

I smiled back.

A dais had been placed in front of the ship's company and the Captain stepped onto it. The Chief GI called them all to attention once more and the talking stopped immediately.

"Stand them at ease, Chief," said the Captain.

For the next twenty minutes, the Captain gave the crew a comprehensive cover of my training and then the dangerous undercover operation that I had been carrying out for the last couple of years since leaving the ship. On completion of his speech, the Captain raised his hat and shouted out, "Three cheers for Jenny Talbot, "Hip, hip hooray."

The cheer was repeated twice more and each time everyone raised their caps.

On completion of the cheers, the Chief GI once more brought the crew to attention and marched smartly up to me and said, "Divisions ready for your inspection, Ma'am."

The Captain was now standing behind me and as we started to move, he said, "Inspect the Officers first."

I had never seen so many smiling faces, which continued as I moved on to inspect the rest of the crew. I stopped and chatted to several of the ship's company, but especially John Kidley who I thanked for rescuing me, and then to Brenda Jones who kept me alive until the Doc was able to remove the bullets and stitch me up, and of course, the Doc himself.

It was an incredible morning and we all traipsed back on board and this time officially into the Wardroom. By the time that lunch was over, we were at sea and heading for Portsmouth and I needed to rest my wounds for a few hours.

The ship berthed at a part of the dockyard that I was not familiar with and was a long way from any of the other warships. The *Dornik* still had to keep a low profile because nobody knew what the ship did. As I walked down to the jetty, I spotted Mum, Dad, and Jane and to my real surprise, Graham had managed to get home after all.

After Mum had burst into tears several times and Dad had his usual grumpy attitude, we were soon in the car and heading for the London Hilton Hotel.

***

We all had a great weekend and even Dad lightened up by the time he saw the hotel rooms we were given. No expense had been spared and we took full advantage of the room service. To be honest, I was looking forward to going back to MI6 and getting on with my life.

Chapter 13. MI6 London

My family packed their bags early to leave on Monday morning, and at precisely nine o'clock, my faithful protector Dave Wilson appeared at my hotel room in his Colonel's uniform. I was so pleased to see him again. I introduced him to the family, and they were soon on their way back to Clevedon, although they had to stop off at Royal Airforce Lyneham to drop Graham off for his flight back to Cyprus.

I put on my uniform as I was told, Dave put my case in the car, and we sped off to MI6 headquarters in Vauxhall.

I was ushered in through the front doors at MI6 and Jack Rawcliffe, with a huge smile on his face and looking resplendent in uniform, whisked me through into his office. It was only ten-thirty, and so for the next half an hour, Jack filled out forms for me to sign and at the same time asked me many, many questions about my trip since leaving them. He also advised me that I would be joining the Britannia Royal Naval College at Dartmouth in a couple of weeks to learn all the nitty-gritty of being a Naval Officer before re-joining HMS *Dornik*.

It was finally eleven o'clock and Dave, came to take me through to the main conference hall. I gasped as I walked through the door. I had never seen so many faces. Virtually all the Senior team from the *Dornik* were there, all the officers who had recruited me into MI6 from HMS *Raleigh* and all the many people who had been there to take care of me along the way.

I spotted Lieutenant Commander Bob Penfold standing next to Annette Saunders, then I saw the two sisters Sophie and Amelia Lynch, and my sparring partner in Spain, Suzy Eldridge.

251

The room suddenly went quiet as Commander Jack Rawcliffe took the stage. He coughed a couple of times into the microphone and with a broad smile said, "Can you all hear me?"

"Yes, of course, everyone can hear you, Jack."

He grinned at their animated response.

"Well, that's good because I have nothing to say except to bring our distinguished speaker onto the stage, Captain Micky Shone."

There was very warm applause.

Micky spoke for nearly an hour talking about my introduction into the Royal Navy and thanking all the officers from HMS *Raleigh* for their huge contribution in getting a 'remarkable young lady into our very shady world'.

He then went on to give an accolade to all the officers and ship's company of HMS *Dornik* for their work in developing me for the task ahead, and then praised Dave Wilson, Bob Penfold, and Chef Pierre, Suzy, Amelia and Sophie, and many others.

"I apologise if I have left anyone out."

At the end of his speech, he asked for a rousing round of applause to the guest of honour: Jenny Talbot.

Once the noise of shouting and cheering finally died down, Micky Shone spoke again, "Your full debriefing of this hugely successful operation will begin next week and you are going to enjoy the huge defeat it has wrought on our enemies. Because of your invaluable input, it has made the world a much safer place."

Micky continued, "I have another important announcement. Dave Wilkins sends his best wishes and had wanted to be here. For those of you who do not know, Dave is working as a double agent and is living a covert life in Iraq, working for the terrorist regime who believe he is a traitor from the United Kingdom. His reports are invaluable to us and he is yet one more agent who is willing to put his life on the line for our safety and democracy."

There was a subdued round of applause and nodding of heads.

Micky added finally, "Jenny, make sure you are here tomorrow by ten o'clock at which time I will be taking you down to Buckingham Palace for a private audience with Her Majesty the Queen, who will be presenting you with the MBE. (Member of the British Empire Medal). This will then be placed in our vaults for safekeeping."

Printed in Great Britain
by Amazon